Devil's Afters

(A Devil's Novel)

Dave Page

This book includes corruption and incompetence in the Government, the Met, MI5 and MI6 and also about a secret prison in Kensington but it is a novel and therefore has no direct connection with reality and nor did Devil's Lunch.

This was written in its initial stage some 16 years ago.

DUA is a nickname but stands for Devil's Unlimited Angel.

It is fiction and parts of it may upset sensitive people!

Devil's Lunch was the first book and was initially aimed at bringing the characters together and is based on an operation that would move from London to West Africa on a complete idiot's plan.

Devil's Afters is the book written here and explores the fall and rise of DUA and extends various relationships plus hunting for moles(human ones).

Devil's Teatime explores more of the operation around the countries near Russia but also explores DUA's hidden life and his leftovers.

Devil's Midnight moves to another dimension with Black Magic and is mainly based in the South of France.

Characters

Albert: Cookie's husband and General Handyman.

Alith, Ailsa: Prilloch's mother. Killed by Alec Docherty.

Angerad, Perris: Agent in Russia.

Askew, Simon: Defence Minister's Security Aide. Killed by Prilloch.

Ashworth, John: Lloyds Broker for the Middlesex Street Company.

Benny: A crooked lorry driver. Womaniser. Liar. Has various criminal connections but has blown them by failing to deliver goods. Now looks after the engines on the Lady Joon. Considered a decent guy who just likes women and drink and could not give a damn otherwise.

Bishop: Also called 'The Bishop'. Worked with 'Boy' and pressurised him into accepting the contract for the West Africa role. Works very closely with DUA.

Black, Stephen: Station Sergeant at Wandsworth police Station. Friend of Neville Jones.

Blemmings, Janock: Brussels News Story Blogger linked to Peter Darcy.

Bocek, Agripina: Ex Security Service Russian Specialist.

Bolshoi Dom: 'The Big House', St Petersburg police headquarters.

Bottomley, Cecil: Metropolitan police Inspector. Now relocated to Wandsworth Police Station which he then left.

Boy: IT Specialist. Forced by Bishop to go to West Africa. See Ralf Johnstone.

Brooker, Eunice: Security Service Librarian and Records Supervisor.

Bullifont, Martin: Editor of Peter Darcy's Tabloid.

Chistle: Hotel cum Pub in Hartland.

Christie, Jacob: EU and Africa Minister.

Ciborowski, Larita: Former Eastern Europe to the Russian Borders as an analyst.

Cookie: Roger and Antona Turner's Cook. Married to Albert.

Cozzens, Jeffry: Ex Security Logistics.

Cuddles: Pub in Hartland.

DA: See Scooter.

Darcy, Peter: Tabloid Journalist.

Datri, Marcel: CIA operative attached to Coombe Lane.

Davies, John: Crown Prosecution Service.

Derval, Godfrey: EU and Africa Minister's Aide.

Dimitriadis, Deadra: Junior Agent in the Security Russian team.

Docherty, Alec: Father of Meik. Killed Ailsa Alith and Ahleen Ogilvy. Killed by DUA.

DUA: Government Fixer. Ex Detention Quarters Guard. Organiser. Headed a MOD killing squad.

Gomez, Sasha: Roger Turner Associate—Oil.

Gris: Agent for DUA.

Highshaw, Valene: Cook for the Coombe Lane house. Ex Security Service Coder.

Huron: Old friend of Mr Hoo and the US contact in Abidjan. Now involved in Coombe Lane.

Innocenti, Darius: Handyman for the Coombe Lane house. Ex Security Service Special Tools operative.

Irish: Irish is a weapons and explosives expert who is still mentally scarred from his previous activities and despite his weapons loving tries not to hurt if he can.

Joran, Lorel: Agent in Russia.

Jagodzinski, Lance: Security Service Director.

Jacobs, Nat: Detective Sergeant. Drug dealer.

Johnstone, Ralf: See Boy.

Jones, Ivor: Independent Police Complaints Commission.

Jones, Neville: Detective Inspector, Met Police. A drunk.

Joran, Lorel: Agent in Russia.

Kovalik, Cliff: Ex Security Service Russian Specialist.

Major: The Major is an ex-cashiered Office who had links to DUA and the Security Service. He is alcoholic and usually under control but likely to just start drinking and not stop. He was the main UK Defence Department contact for the Group before the change in plan by London and Mr Hoo arriving and then taking over.

Matthews, Algenald: Defence Minister, Gambler, Conspiring with Arms Dealers and Oil hijackers. Corrupt.

Matthews, Suzanne: Wife of Algenald Matthews.

Matthews, Zeta: Daughter of Algenald Matthews.

Mackintosh, Jimmy: Roger Turner Associate—Banking.

Macguire, Thomas: Security Service General Factotum.

Nantucket, Gloria: Security Service Forensics Doctor.

Norris, Phillip: Temporary Head of Security after Lance's resignation.

Nescott, Silvia: Detective Sergeant replacement for Nat Jacobs.

Mr Hoo: He worked for the CIA. He designed the Lady Joon and has worked on the boat with US Special Forces and CIA because of his knowledge. He has taken over control after the UK cut off all support to the team sent to West Africa. He felt he'd been wronged to had a death wish.

Ogilvy, Ahleen: Meik's mother and Sister of Rosanna Ogilvy. Killed by Alec Docherty. Loved by DUA.

Ogilvy, Meik: Son of a former lover of DUA in Scotland. Carries his father's temper and killing attributes,

Ogilvy, Rosana: The bitch of the family and an Irish connection who hated the Scottish relatives. She egged on Alec Docherty against Ahleen Ogilvy and Ailsa Alith.

Owl, Jonathan: Detective Chief Superintendent – Homicide and Serious Crime Command.

Peres, Nicholas, Sir: Government Security Adviser to the Prime Minister. Israeli spy and Politician. Major backer of Liberal Party.

Perkins, Julia: Temporary Deputy Head of Security Service after Carmella's resignation.

Prilloch: Part of DUA's Team recruited from a School in Scotland at an early age. Has a personal connection with DUA in some way.

Pattee, Ortner: British Agent in Russia.

Pollart, Ewa: HR Director of Security Service.

Rentley, Dirk: Owner of the 'Cuddles' pub.

Salters, Carmella: Deputy Security Service Director.

Scooter: Former Batman to the Major. Thrown out of the Army after helping the Major defraud Army Funds. Rejoined the Major after the Major came out of Prison and has stayed with him since. Gopher and team message boy. Later, under his true self – Sniper.

Sebastian, Romel: De facto Administration Director in the Security Service ... considered to be a major leak of information. Romel is from Latgalia in Latvia and is Roman Catholic.

Simpkins, Cynthia: PA to Algenald Matthews after his separation from his wife.

Sotram, John: Ex Metropolitan Police Officer now Private Investigator.

Smyth, Basil: Owner of 'Chistle' Hotel.

Stapleton, Charles: Assistant police Commissioner for Territorial Policing. Hates Neville Jones and clashes with him deliberately.

Stephens, Albert: Father of Mark. Ex UN Ambassador, confident of African Leaders, extremely well connected in West Africa, Also corrupt, aggressive and overbearing.

Stephens, Mark: Roger Turner Associate—Pirates. Also, a drunk who cannot be relied upon.

Stieff, Marlin: Ex Security Service Finland Specialist.

Talbot, Sidney, Sir: Metropolitan police Commissioner.

Tanning, Jessica: Bishop's early girl-friend.

Tufnell, John: Second Station Sergeant, Wandsworth Police Station.

Turner, Alisea: Daughter of Roger Turner. Now into drugs.

Turner, Amand: Son of Roger Turner.

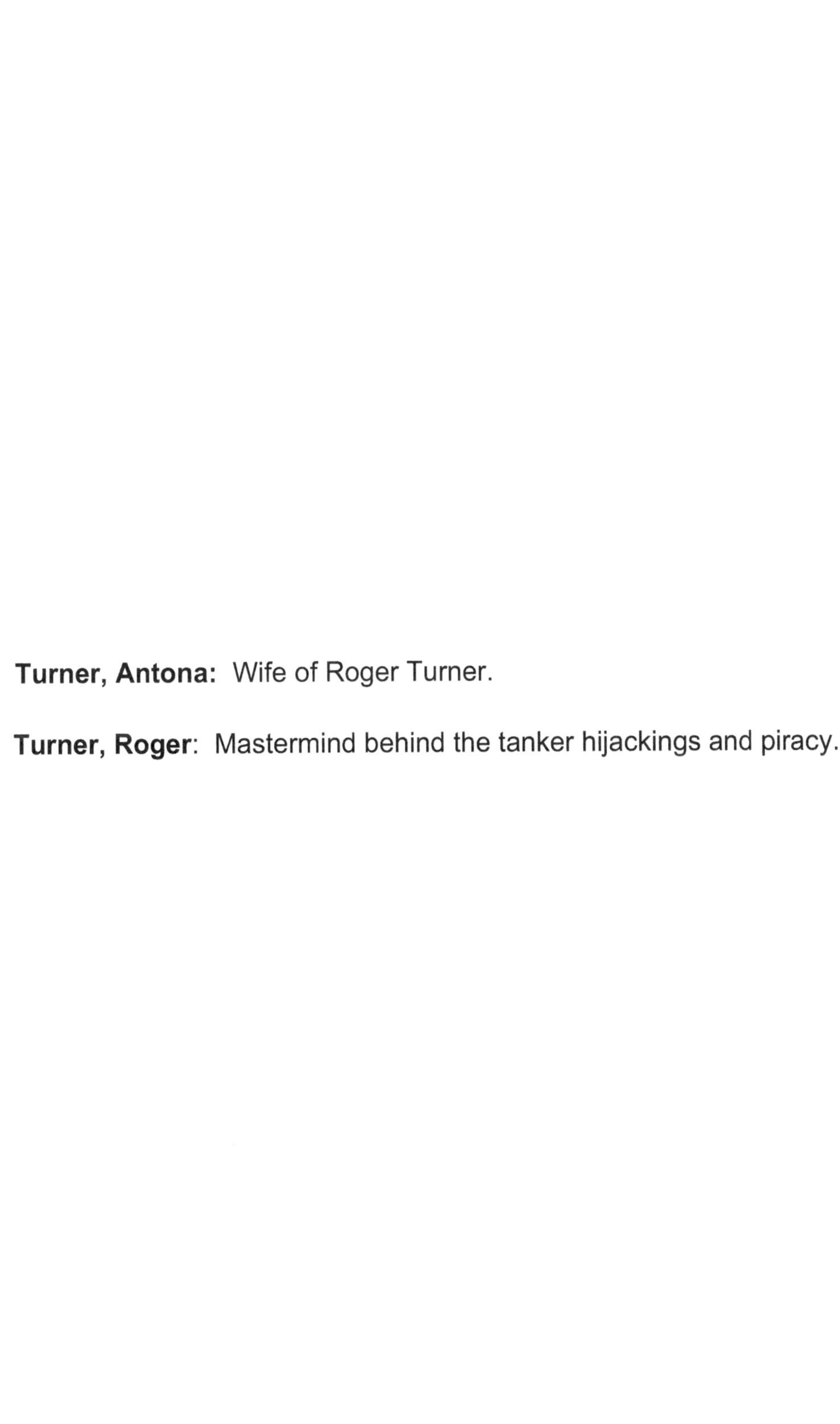

Turner, Antona: Wife of Roger Turner.

Turner, Roger: Mastermind behind the tanker hijackings and piracy.

I

DUA sat thinking about the operation in West Africa…? It was a bigger mess than he had ever dreamt of, and his thumbprints erupting like a neighbour's firework party over the entire show.

Boy and Huron were the only survivors and in the US—supposedly safe…?

Safe from what was his next thought.

No one else survived the final fiery inferno according to his information, perhaps unsurprising as they were already '*Lunch*' before they left the UK with several of them *hunted and hiding*… but… how… reliable is information these days?

Everyone, including the Minister of Defence, the EU Minister, an Insurance guru, Bankers, et al., were all trying to kill them for their own reasons and in everyone's parlance—Lunch had moved into Afters.

Now DUA had to fix the a*fters and tip the servers so as to speak*, but where did he *tip* them, and how long before the *bodies stank*. Still, that was another question and DUA didn't consider introspection as having any value either… it worked out, or it didn't, and *if it didn't work out*—he'd sort it out—often *terminally*?

Part of the problem *though* was *Sir Nicholas Peres*, who, like the famous song, *oiled* his way around the floor and into every '*pore*' Politician's already open pocket.

Peres in DUA's *eyes was* responsible for the current incompetent Director General and his Assistant… DUA felt that Peres planned to take over as DG himself—just one more failure required… for want of a more impolite expression and DUA could think of a few; all unprintable— it never stopped him from uttering them, anyway.

The PM—*who's extremely well known distrust* of the Security Service relied as much on Peres' information as anything… *which to be honest* in this very dishonest world… was very good; from both inside and outside of the country thus raising the question of where the hell was the information coming from?

The question *was*, did the PM's care last as long as the funding for his party continued to come from the ever *present* Peres' presents extend to the care of the United Kingdom and not whoever donated to him?

Peres fed data from the US, Europe, Russia, Middle East and the UK—that was a hell of coverage for one man—enough in DUA's eyes, to crucify him and don't spare the nails.

Peres supported the *Layabouts* as DUA knew them—a change from the previous *Coal* group, who were always scuttling around, but Peres bought himself a place in the higher political and business echelons with his donations.

There were still some confusing issues from the 'Lunch' days, but the depth… and the width of the fall-off of information… following Simon Askew's death surprised everyone until it restarted with far better quality data.

With Simon's death… the world *turned*, whichever way you looked at it and wherever he looked… there wasn't obvious was the link between Simon and the distribution of information. How it occurred was clear in its existence, but not the method or who distributed it?

Simon, as a turncoat spy, *turned* so much, you might have spit-*roasted* sausages on him but his death only interrupted the flow which then streamed more than ever and raised his suspicions as well as his hackles.

DUA bounced this off Bishop, although trying to bounce things off Bishop if he wasn't interested, meant wasting time and *playing bouncy*, but he rang him anyway.

"Bishop. DUA."

"Yes, DUA?"

"Who was Simon betraying everyone to, Bishop? A question that seemed to incorporate everything he knew. Matthews OK'd his death after he finally found out, although knowing Matthews, it was more likely to be his way of getting that little PA on his lap?"

"Matthews is panicking, DUA," ruminated Bishop. "Might be an idea to give him something to *quieten* him down?"

"What do you have in mind, Bishop?"

"Sharp and *brief*, DUA."

"Let him panic, Bishop, he unraffles like kittens with balls of wool. Only thing I'd give him now would be a bullet *enema*. Killing the Minister of Defence needs a good reason. It doesn't make an ounce of difference what he is up to now, but who else was picking up Simon's information?"

"Thomas seems involved somehow, DUA, but I can't see how?"

"Thomas. Bishop? Thomas wouldn't put his nose above the parapet if he smelt '*Gold*', and that is not the smell that is coming from the Security Service, right now?"

"Thomas reports to Romel, DUA, and any information is going to Peres from Romel, I think?"

"It is certainly not coming to us, Bishop. See what you can get from Thomas?"

"Thomas knows we are out, DUA…. he will not tell me anything?"

"They forced us out, Bishop… maybe… tolerated… like the plague… although I think in fact, the plague gets a higher favourable rating than us, so it is hardly surprising that no-one wants to know us?"

"Thomas supports us, DUA. We need to support him. He won't risk anything for us or just for old friendships, these days?"

"Whatever he risks for us, Bishop, he reports to Romel. Thomas has kept his head down—saying nothing for years... I can't see him bursting into song for anyone – unless it is the Irish National Anthem."

"What are you thinking of, DUA,"

"There is another something or someone. Somehow holding this all together... Peres might seem the sauce of the month, but this turkey was gobbling long before he arrived, I think?"

"Who is it, DUA?"

"I don't bloody know, Bishop—one of us would otherwise have done something in the much better past climes we enjoyed, and that would have solved it."

"What do we do about Peres?"

"Peres is very dangerous… a lot less so, since Simon Askew left us but what I don't understand is why are there no known links to Romel, or the Russians from Simon? They had everything, but how?"

"What the bloody hell do we do about Peres, DUA?"

"We'll leave Peres for now... Peres and the Russians... both seemed to get all information Simon had, as did the CIA—who he worked for... unless it was the CIA leaking to the Russians and the Brits, who were then passing the information around in a controlled fashion... no idea. The proof was his death stopping most of the flow but then it started up again?"

"What do you want done about Matthews, DUA?"

"At the moment, nothing. The big worry in Matthews is his panicking... at most points… we need to... sort out Matthews and his underwear, but I want us clear on why we touch him... we will then take both out. Peres is dangerous with his knowledge about us. Matthews and his fear about us is paranoid, but we don't want any input from either into our areas. At the moment—we are stuffed enough as it is—we don't act yet to protect ourselves…?"

"They both have my number, DUA."

"Can you contact Thomas and get all the houses swept?"

"I'll do that now."

Bishop always enjoyed a conversation with Tom Maguire, who often seemed one of the few people with any idea of what was going on. This time the phone seemed to ring forever until Thomas Macguire finally noticed the number ringing, "Macguire here, Bishop?"

"Just had DUA on, Tom. He wonders when we can have a security clear?"

"I don't know, Bishop! Some 'knob' with links to the PM is demanding we check out his house on the Thames, like yesterday, and the guys are already out, checking the PM's children's places."

"I can do a sweep myself on your phones as that bunch is basically a Government Agency—I'll put that in as soon as I put the phone down—John might have finished work on the Embassy project. If he is free, I'll slip him in and bill it on the Embassy project, so no-one knows… I'll look forward to that crate of booze, Bishop!"

"Consider it done, Tom. DUA is getting a bit worried. Peres, prowling around and snooping, is getting up his nose."

"That's the Bunny, Bishop."

"He's causing the trouble, then Tom?"

"Romel runs around licking his backside."

"Sneak us in under the radar please, Tom… we don't want anyone bothering themselves about us?"

"Will do, Bishop. Two crates, was it?"

II

Algenald's dreams and memories were becoming crisper and crisper every-time Cynthia came into his office… something he would prise and prize in his dreams.

He watched her approach his desk, and just sat there swallowing with whatever he could find, although his tongue seemed to be a favourite at the moment.

Her chest—he still dreamed of, as did her hips whipping him in his sleep… he was sure she wore red underwear with a transparent patch for him.

He was virtually almost dribbling, as she came up to the desk.

"How can I help you, Cynthia?" He stuttered—touching his lower chin as the sweat ran down his forehead.

"Have you considered marriage, Algenald?"

He went into 'heart attack' mode… his shower was already wearing out with the excessive use it was getting, and now his heart was matching time!

III

Boy remembered waking up as a piece of metal was being removed from the quivering flesh constituting his chest—yes, they didn't possess a lot of time or room and assuredly not for some guy flown in from a dodgy project…. nice nurses though, but he would have swapped them for a drink in the same hourglass shape.

He dreamt that he wasn't fully asleep and slept as they realised he was awake—his brain with the drugs left him in some kind of reverse world and he'd had enough time trying to live in the current world by this point? An errant piece of shrapnel removed and two weeks laid up with concussion from the blast that hit both him and Huron leading to Mr Hoo's last fanatical charge as they weren't there to stop him.

Did Mr Hoo ever find dreams of sanity before he chose death?

Did he plan for myself and Huron to be dead in case *we stopped him from finding his last horizon.*

Now Boy woke up in a Ministry of Defence cell, underneath a Basketball Floor and a hanger in Kensington.

Everyone in the dark needs a wish and they carried him into the *Brain*—so called, as it concentrates the mind wonderfully.

No light and he became a nothing; his face blue, balls black and shoulders fixed.

They didn't come straight back to him—part of the torture after they limbered him up was to make him wait for the next session!

So he laid on the floor where they threw him, illuminated by the flashes in his mind.

He looked at the door; he was nothing to them… his thoughts were they will not crack me like that.

Pain I can take—let's see what they can take.

He sang quietly then—louder and louder—until an opening hatch passed light and words as if he was human.

They weren't beating up a punch-bag anymore but a person, and he focused on surviving rather than giving up.

A voice from a distance said, "We've got a hard one here Corporal—break him in the man said—let's do it!"

Now I switched from being '*he*' to 'I' an*d* back to first person rather than third person for these guys, and I had won the first round.

The door swung open with light flooding from outside, illuminating my body on the floor. I hadn't eaten, so the first blow was a pain in the neck—nothing in the guts or backside to come out.

One boot on each hand as they worked me over again until the bruises had bruises and nervous pulses illuminated my head.

I lay there for hours until I dragged myself over to the door and beat my heels against it. Irish had lived through this treatment in Northern Ireland and he taught me and I would survive by provoking them.

The door opened again, the light appeared from outside and another voice shouting, "Lad wants a lesson again, Sergeant."

"Well, let's give it to him," said a more distant voice, "let's sort this bastard out, once and for all."

Boy saw spots and nothing until he awoke on the floor and a kindly voice said, "why are you making this happen?" and she helped me until I could half crouch; then smashed me into the wall and kicked me as I fell down.

"I am Gris," she said, and kicked me again.

"Why do you want to pretend," her voice said, "we know you betrayed your country? All you have to do is sign the truth, and none of this need happen."

I vaguely heard the words as she disappeared and the *dark closed in again on me* and I lay there, illuminated by the flashes in my brain as a song I once knew echoed, and I still had lips to sing it.

The hatch was slung open. "Keep it down sunny or you won't need any love"

"What did they make of you before they fucked your arse, Sergeant?"

"I'll fucking teach you, son!"

"You won't teach your own son as you couldn't father one."

The door swung open—light flooding into the room.

When they had finished, and Boy came too again, he used his head on the floor to get to his knees.

He knelt with the pain washing over him, but he saw it in his head and he knew he had won!

Boy crawled across to the door, leaned on his back and started kicking the wall with his heels while he sang.

The door opened again, "Now keep it down sonny or we'll make sure you never roam again."

"I still think the lad needs a lesson again, Sergeant."

"Good. Let's sort this bastard out, once and for all."

"Put these cuffs on him and hang him from the hook, and doesn't he spin nicely?"

"You don't want children, do you sonny? They spun me around again."

Black spots made an appearance again, and nothing.

They came back and back.

I woke on the floor again, and a woman walking towards me, carrying a knitting needle.

IV

Bishop sat in his flat on *gardening leave*, when a garden was the last thing he'd possess, or want.

In a surprise move, they had placed the entire team outside the building—off-limits to everything, apparently whilst they considered the next operation with all but Gris still working for Matthews on some project.

The phone rang.

It surprised Bishop that Thomas Macguire called him.

"Someone *secretly* from Heathrow in Kensington on Matthews' orders, Bishop."

"Who, Tom?"

"Huron rang me—*talked about a boat and Boy*. Took both of them back to the US following an attack, and he wondered about the Boy. Said the Boy left for the UK and *disappeared.* You knew Boy... He was apparently down to ring Huron when he arrived and well overdue on the call. Huron is asking that we track him down and see if he is OK...? If it connects them, Matthews may have got to him—he could be the one in Kensington?"

"Thanks, Thomas. I owe you, and I won't ask how Huron knows you?"

Putting the phone down, Bishop immediately was on it again—ringing DUA and updating him, "What do you suggest, DUA?"

"*Leave it with me...* I need to think about Peres, and if Matthews has the Boy... we may need to take them both out at the same time... Matthews has history on me and the team, and that needs sorting as well—Peres is also prying and getting too close to us on history, and that needs stopping. Leave it with me, Bishop."

V

Peres had a riverside property.

Security conscious meant leaving the building to discuss issues.

A bugged house, perhaps, well the riverside attracts bugs?

He never looked in the ivy, which is where the bugs normally fight—in this case fighting for space for the devices and in conflict with each other amongst all the urns, cherubs and associated 'witchcraft' scanned daily, but dead spider's webs in the mock thatch remained a lump of NASA developed stuff, clinging like ivy on the walls of Sir Nicholas Peres' house. It did make you wonder, it really did, why the spiders seemed fat and didn't move much but a casual passer-by could adjust them if they didn't hear too well and rely on that inbuilt fear of spiders to protect them.

From one of those, Huron got confirmation of Boy in the country and in Kensington, courtesy of Algenald's displeasure.

Peres received the information from Romel at Mortlake after Huron had his updates, unbeknown to UK Security.

Romel used Kensington's resources for his own ends and the CIA used the country for its own ends.

VI

Kensington had originally been DUA's invention when Labour didn't trust anyone, including the US, and wanted their own Secret Prison to avoid Parliament, the Courts and those awkward questions as people disappeared during the Irish troubles.

DUA hadn't even thought Boy was back in the country until Huron, and now Peres/Romel confirmed it.

A routine scan showed no arrival by the Boy, so they'd picked him up on arrival and he never existed in the country—now placed in a building DUA helped design—staffed by *Northern Ireland redundant/moved over to the UK,* people, which made him wonder what Gris was doing at the moment, as she stayed separate from the team and was operating from Northern Ireland but now apparently operating in the UK without the courtesy of telling him and he did know Northern Ireland was in the UK but he considered it as a statement of fact not reality?

She was still part of the team, but hardly reporting to him.

Then Huron had rung him, completely out of the blue. He knew the information could only have come from the Prison so the CIA had infiltrated that as well?

He remembered the call, "DUA; the Boy is in your Secret Prison in Kensington. A contact has confirmed that he is there and having seven kinds of shit beaten out of him to get some confession, so Matthews can have him buried for life as a Traitor, if he survives; he is doing this to a US Citizen and CIA Agent."

"He is also doing this to one of my team, Huron, even if the Boy is now a double Agent, and I don't like that, I don't like that at all and that includes him working for you!"

"Can you get him out before they kill him, DUA, which won't be long? I worked with him; I like him, and we should free him. The CIA will take a very dim view of it, if he dies, and London Station will disclose Kensington to your top security committees, unless he is released and that will blow Matthews and you *sky high*!"

"Boy had always been innocent, Huron. Bishop pushed the Boy into Africa for a debt he owed to me, and a contract was out on the Boy anyway from the guy running the tanker hijackings. We killed the guy, the contract was cancelled—the Boy has done well—stupid to come back to the UK at Heathrow on a UK passport – *bloody stupid*! There are some other issues, and they need sorting out as well, before we can get the Boy out… it should be within days."

"You may not have that long, DUA. Don't let him die!"

"He'll be under my wing, Huron… as soon as I can move."

Huron rang off, although he was far from happy, but the worry was, if they went to the top would they find the Boy, his body or nothing and the Government records shredded?

DUA knew Kensington; He planned, created and staffed it with his authority there.

DUA agreed to Matthews' demands in the past, as Matthews had found the one thing he could blackmail him with.

A call to Bishop would take care of Matthews, while he took care of Peres in a few hours, and got the Boy out, alive, but would Bishop do it—Bishop had his own rules and if he considered they weren't transgressed often refused to follow orders and take out subjects.

He made the call to Bishop and heard a sleepy, muzzled voice, "Bishop?"

"Yes, DUA."

"I've just had Huron on. Boy is in Kensington, being tortured, and won't survive much longer. I can't get him out while Matthews lives. Can you take care of Matthews?"

"Give me 6 hours. Can you pull them off the Boy?"

"I can get him out, Bishop, but I can't do it while Matthews lives, and I can't tell you why."

"6 hours DUA, and if the Boy is dead, then so are you."

"Don't threaten me, Bishop!"

"It was a promise, DUA, not a threat."

Sir Nicholas Peres loved his title, which was becoming unbeknown to him, in US parlance, 'a cinch wearing out in this town'.

His informants were warning him that in the UK and Europe, people were looking at sir Nicholas Peres' history very closely, especially his EU title, but this fell on Peres' deaf ears and the '*none are as deaf as fools'* syndrome. He felt that once he headed Security, they would bury his past from public scrutiny and he needed to accelerate that process.

He needed the Government reshuffle and once he headed the Security Service, British Security would exist for 'Israeli Interests'.

Romel had been supplying him with information, and action for a long time and good information it was, often well beyond his own feeds—which always surprised him—given that British Security was never that efficient, with all its, and the Government's leaks.

The one thing he prized from this charade was his home in Mortlake on the Thames.

No communications problems, as people passed by on the river all the time, so it was always busy and there was one boat moving over to him now, and beckoning; lost… he thought.

He walked over, leaning forward to hear the voice say, "Sir Nicholas, what a pleasure," and there was a flash!

"Bloody fool," said DUA, and Sir Nicholas Peres explored the Thames' tidal flow.

Bishop walked up from Putney through the back streets. Through the backstreets although a longer trip than he needed, but a raincoat would go on at some point—no cameras—just a smartly dressed man, wearing horn-rimmed glasses, striding confidently along until he arrived at Algenald Matthews house, and took out his silenced .22 automatic.

His favourite for close work as the bullets stayed in the body he put them into and caused little other damage or noise.

He rang the bell, and waited until they opened the door, when he opened fire, shooting through the heart of a girl, and not Algenald Matthews.

He then heard a voice saying, "Cynthia, who is it? I told you never to open the door without knowing who it is," and the head finally caught up with the voice as he appeared. As both came out of a door, he put two bullets in it. One for the girl and one for Boy, and he closed the front door after him—the gun was Secret Service and untraceable, with some device which gave random markings on the casing.

The cell door opened again in Kensington, illuminating the body lying on the floor, and they carried Boy out, covering him with a white sheet as if he was dead, which wasn't far wrong—just premature.

Boy felt movement but nothing else, including the fact he was alive, and the voices didn't matter anymore. Were angels flying low and was he already dead—someone made a mistake?

Movement became days later, when he finally come around to find DUA and Bishop by his bed—probably trying to rent it out but if he was expecting anything like an apology from DUA, it was in vain!

"We put the Crown Jewels in debt for you Boy… remember that," was DUA's first comment, and I don't know that I bothered about the rest.

"They didn't break out anything of value, from you and you managed in your sweet way, to smoke a few plots out but I wouldn't try Israel for a holiday if I was you—you are out of my interest now, so just lie quiet for a while, Boy!"

That was DUA's last comment.

Bishop looked up at me and said, "I've done a lot of things, Boy, but I never intended this!"

I thought of one thing to say, and I said it, "Just go away, the pair of you. You have done more than enough!"

Bishop moved back again into his own reality and that reality is that you don't trust DUA and you don't believe he ever lets you go, although I wasn't in a fit state to understand anything.

VII

Thomas Macguire kept his head down… his mouth firmly shut unless he needed friends and favours—whiskey was a nice one—both as a friend and a favour.

Short years to his pension, was his mantra and glad of it, as he recounted the last few months— Peres gets assassinated—Gloria Nantucket gets sacked for being too good, and then she is back; told to keep 'Neville Jones' out, now in'. Kensington Secret Jail gone, people paid off handsomely, and put on planes to '*who would take them*'.

He'd enjoyed being out of this mess—recording his thoughts for his 'dead man's handle', tea, tot, and ginger nuts, with Eunice.

Without Eunice, he would have gone crazy years ago… it was her idea to use an old file to record transcripts for his protection, and he'd passed that tip on to Simon, for the same reason; thus understanding Simon's activities whilst Simon felt better for his records being in the filing department and untouched.

For Bishop he'd got the guy off the Embassy stuff to sweep the properties and now waited for his reward?

Checked out the team and BT checked the phones—Bishop, a good lad—always saw to his monthly reward for any favours he managed.

All should settle down anew after the excitement and progress towards a gentle trip to his pension.

Neville Jones never expected to win battles—he was surprised to come *second out of two* with his scalp intact and after some of them, used his hair conditioner for self-defence, but if anything was wrong now, he was '*kippered for breakfast*' for Owley.

He actually told me to grow up, thought Neville in horror.

At my time of life… being responsible for my actions and behaving as a senior police officer should. Who would want a corrupt life like that?

He wanted to see Antona and he wasn't looking forward to it… that was… was that why he kept ducking it, but he had to face her, and he finally travelled to Coombe Lodge and faced an Antona as blunt as ever.

The opening crashing verbal salvo was, "Why didn't you tell me, my daughter was a drug dealer?"

"You weren't honest with me, Antona, so I didn't tell Nat to go easy, although his knowledge of drug dealing in this area is worrying me, as we don't handle drug cases—in fact we don't even handle dogs fouling the streets, these days."

"How did she get away with it, if the local police were aware?"

"The 'local Bobbies' are on bonuses for low crime rates, and already hiding crimes under a softly, softly approach—you had money—the druggies moved further into the area… the police just did nothing? They avoid rich people who can afford decent lawyers. If they are charging anyone, it is better to go for those who can't afford them… your average… yes… Bobby wants, like every person, a decent job, with not too much work and to hit the bonus targets. They were more frightened of taking on your family. Once I put Nat with his knowledge in, there wasn't anything I could bargain with to stop him from annoying them so they go for Gold… he had his own motives too I guess, although I don't understand what they are?"

"She is in jail now for three years, with everything ruined—you did it!"

"No! You did it. You cared more about your house, than your children or husband, and you knew Roger was running an International Piracy Group that killed and wounded people, and hijacked oil tankers—he might have gone to the Ivory Coast had he lived, to die in some buried cell, but the Security Service was loathed to take any action to be honest, and hid his activities, which were in territorial not international waters—thank God… we have no jurisdiction there…? Anyway; *to our relief?*"

"What *happens* to me, then?"

"It is up to the individual countries to take action for extradition or compensation, if they wish? Then in theory they admit their back-handers for letting it happen… you're just living off the proceeds, until you become an embarrassment."

"So it is all buried, and you won't do anything."

"There is no genuine desire to take it any further, Antona, and I'll get slaughtered if I try, so it *lies doggo* with everyone sharing in the *doggy bags*."

As he looked at her, Owley's words came… back… if you could call it that… if he ever reviewed the old case in any depth, he would change tyres on cars, if he was allowed him to grasp that high. It was buried—the people at risk were so high up that they wouldn't have a Government if it came out, and they were now safe, and to refer all questions back to Owley was the requirement, but his pride could not let Antona think she'd got away with it.

Bishop still had nightmares about the words, 'I told you not to open the door', as he fired instinctively, but he hurt so much for the Boy, he didn't do the homework or check the site first, but went out to kill!

His incompetence bothered him. He wanted to kill. An innocent young girl was now dead because of it!

People he would love to kill were still alive, and he'd killed a young girl because of Matthews' power and desires… he couldn't kill Matthews any more—Matthews was dead but it rankled.

How much of his life was killing, with always for a good reason to his mind for the killing.

Boy was free. He'd killed an innocent girl as he again let his emotions take over.

He'd failed to do the job professionally but then again DUA knew she was there and didn't tell him so DUA obviously wanted the girl dead as well and contrived to have Bishop have no choice but to kill her.

DUA wasn't happy either—time spent working for Matthews, protecting him, killing for him, and then having him killed…?

Didn't look good on the CV—killing your Boss, although probably a strong demand for it.

The girl had found out about him and his team… she had to die as well, and he knew once Bishop arrived, he would have no choice but to kill her, but he didn't and would never tell Bishop, she was there, and she'd die because she would show off and be first to the door!

DUA knew Macguire had already got rid of the file linking him, in the 'clean out' of Matthews' stuff, but he couldn't get hold of the Defence File—still sat in Army Records—or so Macguire said, and it also meant Macguire knew about the file and the details, so where did the killing stop, if he tried to clean up everything.

Macguire had his own things to *hide*, anyway, so it was easier to let things lie, and leave Macguire alone.

He would not talk about anything of importance to DUA, anyhow—Bishop with the whiskey and contacts, was the conduit—DUA the blockage.

DUA still needed the other files destroyed, but now with his team disbanded on 'Pension Status/Gardening Leave', with even less leverage to get at the files, following the PM's reaction to his close friend and funder, being found to be an Israeli Agent and assassinated he couldn't get near them.

One thing that surprised him, however, was the Israeli attitude. You would have thought a quiet end to a failed project would be acceptable, but the Israeli attitude seemed to be that in a game amongst friends—it was poor form to kill a Spy causing damage to a 'friendly Country'.

At least DUA let Peres see the Thames for one ultimate time. *Some pleasant views*, providing your eyes worked.

Security never changed, however. The Squad would not stay out of work for long with offers already being made to Boy, Bishop, Gris and Prilloch leaving him as the '*only fish* swimming in the *big wide sea*', to learn of its monsters.

Security followed instructions from Romel via Peres, until Peres dictating Security Policy became a reality with him virtually running the Department, but as it fell apart, the only story within Security—Peres fooled the PM, not Security—fat chance?

Edinburgh still haunted DUA—a highland boy from Lothian who knew he was different somehow but more women for a Highland Regiment and a lot of quick and easy Scottish dances—some vertical, but far more horizontal; depending on your luck.

Prilloch—a son from a woman he didn't love—Meik, whilst not his son, came from a woman he loved who chose someone else.

He killed the soldier who fathered Meik and murdered Ailsa in a drunken rage and the guy had been his closest friend and he couldn't change that.

Just another death, to add to a total he never counted, but a son, and from someone else with an orphaned son from someone he loved.

He couldn't ignore either, but he—until another time—had stopped looking for relationships with women.

He moved South—making sure the sons were looked after, but while Prilloch he could understand, Meik was beyond him… Meik's father's temper and killing instinct, which Meik had inherited were the main thing, and trying to find somewhere or something for Meik's talents became difficult, but while he paid for Prilloch and Meik; all Meik could believe was that his true father left Edinburgh—abandoning him, and moved to London, with Meik now following those footsteps… hunting for his idea of the father who left him.

DUA never brought himself to tell either of them the truth, and he considered the killing of Meik's father justified, but if he told Meik—would Meik believe him?

Would Meik then stop hunting for his father, who DUA hung on a fence and left to die?

Alfred Stephens sat at his green leather-topped desk, thinking about his son.

Mark, in his eyes, was never worth anything, but *still his son*, and anything against his family was *personal*.

His son killed, justified revenge on the *'eye for an eye'* family honour roll, and that was in hand. Now the Boy appeared clear of any Security entanglements—Algenald had screwed up despite Alfred bailing him out, yet again—he was dead.

A straightforward matter to put the contract live.

Roger took a contract out on killing the boy and it lapsed with Roger's death but he put the word out that he would pay the fee—it was in operation again.

VIII

The CIA had put about £6000 into my account, plus the pay-offs for Survivors as we weren't meant to survive nor carry knowledge nor be protected if talking about West Africa as gigantic heads might roll and we were minor heads although all the compensation from the conning Banks and Estate Agents and the rip-offs meant some compensation for the trouble.

I was older in a lot of ways—compressed in some and squashed in others, but I now found myself like a target again and from original sources. The peace was almost a dream for a few weeks, but I missed the 'Lady' and the guys.

They let Mr Hoo betray and kill them—like—in a coon's age.

Would they? I couldn't believe it?

They knew Mr Hoo more than he knew himself, but why wasn't someone near him—bullet waiting?

The UK for me had always been dead… nothing… I just wanted out of the UK—nothing of dreams, apart from escaping them.

The back of a Nissan GTR was all that waved to me.

Mr Hoo taught me a lot on the 'Lady' in the early days… I had… I suppose… just drifted along with the choices in the dark sharing days at sea, but I kept seeing their faces now—I needed something else to see. To believe in and I did.

Faces were appearing too constantly around me these days, which made me take a break for a few days in Hartland—where to go though, and could I escape?

Hartland—a lovely place to me—decent B&Bs, Pubs that liked you to drink, and go home happy, and late.

I put the throttle down on the drive to the Chistle and was there in about 3 hours, out of the car and on the way to Cuddles, following the smell of a quiet drink and some kind of party, but once again I was stalked, and before I drank the excitement started to mount again.

'The Chistle' and 'Cuddles' were as 'chalk and cheese'.

Chistle was a splayed and played out, damp old Inn at one end of Hartland, and Cuddles, an old historic Inn at the other end of town. Chistle had about 20 rooms and excellent food—Cuddles, just the one room and a good time.

The 'Chistle' had good beds, if a bit damp, as they were tight on heating rooms, unless occupied, but 'The Cuddles' had warmth and was the *Devil's armpit* which warmed you through and through with his *punch-bowl*, partying like there was no tomorrow, where often felt like there wouldn't be a tomorrow.

Teeth cleaning after a night in Cuddles… more a toilet brush affair the following morning if you could find your teeth.

I walked around the back of 'The Chistle' when I finally made it back from Cuddles, and decided to go in from there—it was an old and a nasty habit, and now, I paid for it.

I saw a young girl in the corner of Chistle's car park, who seemed in some distress, although looking at her, bent right into her boot, the dress was the distress as it seemed to have risen to her shoulder blades.

I wondered over to the far end of the parking lot to offer a polite hand… it wasn't the sight of her that bothered me, as she kept her head well away from me—in the boot, but a scent I remembered… I couldn't remember where it came from, though, and that pricked my memory?

She came out of the car as I walked up—dark glasses and a floppy cap that must have been stapled on, hiding virtually all of her face. I waited for her to adjust her short skirt down—from where ever it had visited and reached into the back of boot to unstick what looked to be like a small umbrella, and that was the last thing I remembered from this occasion – waking up on a patch of cropped grass, a rugged hillside opposite me with a flow of water crashing into the sea, and a voice that I last heard in a hospital after Kensington, plus the face from the Cells that tortured me – minus cap and glasses, standing next to DUA.

It didn't take long for the words to spit out, "Some part of me you missed before… was it just a reprise, in case I forgot; before the next beating?" I said, looking at her with immense disgust.

"*Boy, that is enough,*" interrupted DUA, "Always in trouble, Boy, but where have your manners and a 'thank you' gone?"

From DUA—the most considerate person you could ever trust, if you were ever that *gullible,* was at once one of the grossest things I had ever heard… "DUA, what do you want. The sooner you tell me, the sooner I don't see you and your bunch of killers?"

"Where is your gratitude, Boy? We rescue you from the evildoers—not a word of thanks? You always were an ungrateful lad?"

Prilloch grinned at me with his permanent sneer.

Bishop added, "good to see you, Boy."

"Someone is showing a keen interest in you, my boy," carried on DUA, "and for all our faults, we still look after our own. Bishop and I don't want you go to waste in your den of vice here?"

"When did you care, DUA? You set us up to be Lunch, and I didn't know she worked for you as she kicked the immortal guts out of me plus your others recruits?"

"*I cared, Boy.* Gris was working on detachment, although she passed on your ID once she found out and we moved in. Someone put *your miserable carcass* out to lunch before you left for Africa, so you were dead if you stayed anyway—someone has hung you out to dry again—since you survived Africa. Bishop took the first guy out. The contract lapsed after that. Someone resurrected your contract, and we will take that team out—Gris went into that team so we knew what they doing and they are killers, so *Gris risked her life* for you!"

"Thanks Gris—now unless you are killing me, can I get back to my holiday?"

"Teach him something, Bishop! I am losing patience here!"

I looked at them both and said, "When did you find patience, DUA or you Bishop and don't bloody shout at me either."

"Leave, DUA alone, Boy… he is keeping you alive."

"My life to suit himself, yet again, Bishop, is more like it?"

"I can't change my life, and neither can you, Boy. The first contract started with your involvement in those Insurance files at the Brokers—the guys from the Oil Tanker hijackings, although we didn't know at the time. They will leave you alone now – dead with Roger Turner's death."

"Why the trouble now, Bishop?"

"One of them had a son killed in that last attack in Africa—he wants you dead out of revenge, so we need to take this gang out, and then sort him out!"

DUA cut in as this point, as he couldn't let someone control, or listen to anyone else, beyond a few sentences…?

"Stephens—Peres' records after he died; Stephens bent like a banana—he made his money in the UN. No-one will touch him for a time… he is dangerous—wants you dead."

"After the last trouble, DUA… why are you involved? It isn't necessary… I am pensioned off from everything as well—so why? DUA…?"

"After the last debacle—my guys are all unofficial—gardening leave, if they have a garden or not. A Pension—a '*thin line*' to walk—a flat in Wimbledon that a rat or evangelist wouldn't touch… I told you before, you are on my team – I look after you."

"The only thing you looked after, DUA—the attempts to kill me… how long did your last dog live?"

"My team works well together, and for me but all we did in the past is to earn money for others… who cleaned up afterwards—leaving us up '*shit creek*', and I think they owe us and not just a paddle without a boat?

"What do you want, now, DUA?"

"There's a job offer from Security for you… you owe us—you take it or we let these people enjoy you? Gris will marry you and go with you—I can monitor you that way… you can divorce her afterwards."

"How can I marry someone who tried to kill me?"

"Gris didn't kill you. She couldn't get there in time—her first assignment was someone else… you were trying to get yourself killed in your stupidity—do it again and I will kill you."

"What sane man marries his abuser, DUA?"

"Men have married their abusers before—you won't be the first. We've just saved your life, and without you repaying the favour—you're not even breathing tomorrow. You court Gris – marry her – take her with you, and you do it by Saturday… a whirlwind romance – nothing to waste, and you probably won't find the time to waste, either? Welcome back to the Team, Boy!"

I looked at Gris… she knew more of my body than I did of hers; about all I had the strength to raise was my eyebrows?

She nodded, putting her arm under mine… her other hand *down into my back pocket like a good wife*—leaving mine dangling around her backside, so I shoved it in her back pocket and *prodded on*—she then *steered me…? …?* Like hell, she did!

I prodd*ed deeply every time she tried*, so she either hiccuped from her backside up the street, with her body tossing her breasts up, or stopped steering?

I could pick the arm up later, when she had finished with it.

The drive back to the 'Chistle', *seemed like an eternity*—a wife I *didn't want*—a *pseudo father-in-law,* I couldn't stand, and a pack of hunting dogs *tracking me…* followed by another pack of dogs, *hunting them*; all it needed now was the hunt activists, and where were they when you needed them?

We arrived at the Chistle and immediately Gris said, "*I need the toilet*—I'll use yours—I don't like Public ones."

"I thought that was where you did your work, Gris…? You are marrying me, Gris, and do I live?"

"I will make you happy, 'whatever your actual name is'?"

"No choice, Gris?"

"I did my work… that is, what it was—a job, and I did it professionally?"

"You did it to kill and destroy—that, you say, 'is your job?'".

"You were dead. I told Huron—I blew my CIA cover for you. DUA knows they have turned me and *I am a double agent* and visible, because of you—*and I do like you*, so stop complaining as DUA works for the CIA as well. You have anything because this was a mess from Politicians. We had to bail out of their corruption?"

"Well, double meets double, or is *everyone seeing double*—a US Citizen, and CIA Agent and only Accountants get rich on double agents, as far as I can tell?"

"A truce?"

"Can we ever be honest with each other, Gris?"

"We can try, and I won't call you, Boy—actual name?"

"…? Ralf… Yours?"

"Griselda—call me that in public—you'll wish I had finished you."

I looked at her but this was too easy. I needed to find out why I was being sucked back into DUA's empire—even if it killed me which it probably would!

"There are the keys while I get a bottle of wine, for the evening, or morning, or whenever, because that bottle if you explore me again will seem essential?"

I left the Chistle; walking down the road and 10 minutes later on the way back, found an *arm in mine*—Blue eyes looked at me, and a piece of dress blew over my leg—the *cheating wind*, I think it is call, which showed my mood for the evening.

The show from the summer dress was obviously going to waste as she leaned forward to look closely into my eyes.

A beautiful woman with her head a fraction in front of you is a joy, but DUA had hers tied to him, and his Wimbledon Bishop.

I however still remembered this little this piece of magic kicking me around on a concrete floor, as I put my arms out to defend myself, hitting a wall before collapsing again…?

"Can we talk Ralf? It's not some sob story. Your people aren't the only 'dead men walking'?"

"They're all around DUA…? If still alive as the body count mounts. How many did we kill in the end, that we didn't drown?"

"DUA has every life in his hands, including yours—mine…? If anyone ever finds out the work I did for him, I am walking dead, as are you. He makes a point of not touching anyone that someone else won't kill, so we stay together, live, and he lives off us!"

"So you understand… yes… I'm called Boy, Gris, and you can shove it. Ralf—something was from somewhere else—can I want to remember; another life, another woman or object, as she said 'I treated her as'?"

"You treated her as what, Ralf?"

Boy stopped for moment… it was almost like some liturgy, "Someone I thought I loved and she would grow to love me. She walked out on me because the house was cold. She wouldn't work. I didn't earn enough for her, and her mother couldn't stop trying to attack and control both of us— she could have given DUA, a *'run for his money'*?"

"No, Ralf? You're feeling sorry for yourself—the*y have taken away the control*; the difference between stress and pressure rules…? You—free to live or die, according to DUA's Law—he recruits carefully – tries to blow them apart first – then he corrupts them and binds them to his team."

"That is what he did to you, is it?"

"Yes… *now he makes us*, 'man and wife'?"

So I now had a future wife, I'd never courted; a Security job I never sought; a guy who should have 'five *foot long fingernails*' and answer to the name of Charlie inscrutably managing my life.

Sex with Gris was the last thing on my mind at the moment. Although if she kept doing what she was doing, it could become the first thing, and in the street… as well…?

"I'm just practising, Ralf. It has been a long time since I needed to care for someone, apart from remembering how I hurt them, and yes, I do have a soft spot for you, and I also have respect for you."

"Yes… from where you kept kicking it, and me, against the wall!"

"Can we let bygones be bygones? You can't stop DUA, and neither can I, and he is corrupt; someone else can get him! Let's dump this bottle off, because DUA wants us heading down to Cuddles."

"Cuddles are and every slob over you__"

"Be there first—"

"—told we don't need trouble—"

"—you don't have a brain?"

"you're too beautiful. Tell them you came to keep me on the 'straight and narrow' until I marry you. We met in Kensington… it puts everyone off, especially Kensington. Guy who runs it is from Shepherd's Bush. Moved down here before his disciplinary in the police. Another one getting out before they took him out… runs a decent pub…? just don't take too many admirers out the back, and torture them."

"Was that necessary?"

"Yes! I enjoyed it—I suppose I need to move that ring from your nose, to your finger!"

"You only proposed today, on the spur of the moment, Ralf. The ring will be along later, and 'Chistle' knows we are a couple, and that is another £40 a day on your bill!"

"I'm glad you only charge day rates for abuse"

"I don't take what isn't there, and there are three guys shadowing us now…? In case you do understand, Ralf?"

"Too amateurish, I think. The dominant people will be ahead, and behind are to make us nervous and be stupid."

This seemed to lead to another dig, prod and frisk from my intended, but Gris was thinking again….

"Are you carrying Ralf—beyond the obvious?"

"No! Are you?"

"No! There isn't room in this dress. What have you got?"

"Two knifes—USP from Africa… Mr Hoo's training. Legal permits, providing, I never use the guns off duty. I am both Security and CIA, however, and the permits hold for carrying."

Gris stopped for a moment, looking into a shop window.

Flicking the front of her hair down, and her chest up, *after a bra twitch,* and then she instructed again?

"DUA was right, Ralf, this *surveillance is standard old rubbish* from 20 years ago. These guys trained for the 'Cold War'…? Confusion misdirecting your target—"

"—Mr Hoo, once again, drummed it into my brain. Convince him, he is better than you, and then when he doesn't expect it, chop him. Well, the chop, he was going to get, was Prilloch up his backside—filleting his kidneys—"

"—Ralf… we need to give them a chance, slow down!"

I stopped and kissed her, until she broke away, with the pair of us walking down the street like two mafia virgins in Italy.

She was by now several feet in front of me. I had enough of this crap.

I turned around; back the way we had come… she was so far ahead of me by then she had to run after me swearing—calling me a fool—just like a wonderful woman in love, after a tantrum.

I, like a good man, kept my hands in pockets and the stubborn attitude for all to see… hopefully screwing up every plan. What the hell was going on?

DUA might be good at killing unsuspecting people, but I was trained by Irish, and he trusted no one, not even his Priest.

Gris knew what was going on and DUA's Plan was like a neophyte praising a God—he didn't seem to know what he was doing?

I'd also got sick of someone running my life and my dying, if they got it wrong.

I was a lot more than these old 'has-bin killers' now, and DUA's efforts.

I carried right on back to the Chistle.

"Ralf…? Stop—they are being taken care of! The sides are DUA and Prilloch, Bishop is handling the 'Chistle', and you are to sort out the 'Cuddles'."

"Then why didn't someone tell me before, instead of treating me some idiot that needs a woman manhandling me… like a complete twit?"

"Everything will flow around if you turn around. You are blundering into things you cannot handle; it's sorted and planned? Give me a long kiss, and then we have made up, and head down to 'Cuddles', again!"

So a lover's tiff; for a woman I don't love, and a bunch of killers that I might put off getting killed… it sounded like my ex-girlfriend's mother, in one of her full diatribes before she built up speed with the exhaust gases, unfortunately heating the phone, and not the house?

We walk back to 'Cuddles', like lovers, following a fight, which with Gris going for the emotional stuff, would make you question my odds for survival, and the look on my face said a bit of it…?

"I am alive, Ralf, and I want to stay alive!"

"Alive for what, Gris?"

"Let's just walk, while Prilloch takes up his collection."

"Yes. Nobody takes a collection like Prilloch. There isn't a dry eye in the place when he has finished. I have just had Africa, my boy scouts badges, plus a bunch of killers, and a future wife I never sought, forced onto me all in one day, *so just call me 'Boy'* if we are going to be intimate… I am only small."

"Do I need the auto-biography already?"

"Yes! *Ralf was a name for old friends*, an old girlfriend and you are not that girlfriend—yes you are betting looking, better humoured, better looking… only thing was, *she didn't kick me around the floor* and enjoy it!"

"Do we go forward or back? I can't help what I did… it was my life—kicking and hurting the shit out of people… I stopped – *will you help me?*"

"Boy, was a name for people I trusted—I have to trust you."

"Yes! *Trust me…* DUA felt three were following us, with two of ours following them?"

"Where is Bishop, Gris?"

"He will be back at the Chistle in due course… you and I get the actual killer."

"Do you want a knife for your handbag? They are stilettos and *good for corns*—I am told."

"No. Ralf. I'll just use my future *wifely charms*?"

"I'd almost forgotten about them, and what they can do?"

"Bishop will stay at the Chistle for a few days afterwards, in case there is someone else."

"*Any other updates?*"

"The cars had seven of them. Prilloch and Bishop took out 2 earlier, who are floating offshore, with 3 following them, and 1 waiting for a dip… DUA reckons there is one or more in reserve."

"Christ? How much was the contract on me?"

"£200K, Ralf."

We carried on, walking down to Cuddles.

"Any idea what this guy is like, or what he will do when he sees you? *You were part of his team?*"

"Something has changed the plan, and I have picked you up for him to finish. Once they had you on the top of the cliff, the rest took off, leaving two to finish you. *It should go OK*, providing he doesn't kill you in Cuddles, but I can't tell you which one he is until he shows himself, or how he will try to take you. They won't understand how you got out."

We continued down the hill with her left hand resting on the USP, which with the silencer on, she seemed to push into my underpants, *scratching my backside* 'like anything'.

"Don't knock the safety off, Gris. I never planned on shooting me up the arse, and muzzle flash around my backside is not good either, unless I want to go suddenly."

"You should have put it down the front. It would hurt less, Ralf?"

"Hilarious, but I didn't expect you to be pushing it down there, so I can't get the bugger out. *When do I trust you*, Gris?"

The pressure eased on the gun, and I pulled it back up. There was no way you could trust any of this team, "How did I get found here, Gris?"

"DUA has contacts. He heard about the contract, and we followed them, not you. You were later—standard stuff. How they found you, we don't understand, but Security has changed little in leaking anything, anyone wants, and someone has been monitoring you. There is still a guy who Peres was going to make his Number 2; if he took over… he made a lot of jobs go bad by leaking to Peres and the EU Minister, to pass the information on."

"Who else is involved?"

"It seems like Alfred Stephens retrieved his bent contacts. Someone supplied information. DUA wanted to take Romel out, but he had DUA thrown out instead. We were all moved to other Departments and put on Gardening Leave… better in the tent peeing out, I suppose, but Romel was Peres' main leak in Security, and knows too much for us to let him leave, unless feet first, but no-one will sanction it, after Peres and Matthews. Too many deaths, and he has now taken on a Scottish' German guy, who even DUA won't touch. The guy makes Prilloch look like a Saint, and there are stories around about him, already."

"Is Prilloch connected to this guy?"

"He and Prilloch attended school together, and he is the only friend Prilloch has. Prilloch brought him down from Edinburgh, although DUA considers that a mistake, but DUA wouldn't take him on. DUA has some connection to his father, who was another of the 'Pontius Pilate Bodyguard'… DUA… still something wrong there… felt he picked up the instability from his father, especially the rages, where he go out of control as he became berserk. DUA won't touch him and he knows killers?"

"Well, we are coming up for the 'killing ground'… Ladies first for the initial underwear penetrating bullets."

"I am not wearing any, Ralf—it shows up under a summer dress."

"That's why they sold white knickers… *at least the sun is going down.*"

"*Jealous already*, Ralf? Your charm really has improved?"

"I live and learn, Gris—*just?*"

Boy and Gris entered Cuddles, meeting the grease as Dirk Rentley approached—oiling his way over.

"Evening, Dirk… whisper what you drink, Gris, being the passionate thing you are?"

"Bloody Mary, Ralf."

"Bloody Mary, Dirk—anybody will do, if Mary's out?"

"Hilarious, Ha, Ha," said Dirk and Gris, together.

"You two have obviously met, Dirk?"

"I'd remember if I had met your Lady, Boy."

"You're an ex-copper, Dirk and I do trust your memory, but let me introduce my future wife—the special licence and congregation for Saturday, before I am posted abroad."

"I never considered you the marrying kind, Boy—congratulations."

"I've met anyone like Gris before, Dirk?"

We watch Dirk stride off, and Gris rammed her palm into my gut and listened to my breath leaving, "you just can't stop going at me, can you?"

"Nor can you but something is bothering Dirk. He keeps turning around?"

I had an elbow in the ribs this time, although my thoughts were controlled and not by Gris who spun her buttocks on the way as she headed for the loo, saying, "Watch the door and see who hangs around it."

Which door, I wondered. And where were the nooses—was she studying Eastern cultures?

As Gris left, Dirk oiled his way back in again, "Interesting Lady. Boy," commented Dirk, as Gris shimmied for the loo. Looks like she won't get fat?"

"Any strangers in tonight, Dirk. A friend of mine came down from London. Did he arrive and miss me?"

"Funny you should say that, Boy. Someone said the same thing to me earlier and described you to a 'Tee'. He was around when you came in and then went out, as you came in with your Lady, which makes it a pack of lies. What are you involved in and I want it kept well away from this pub?"

"Nothing I want to be involved in again, Dirk."

"Have you known your girl long, only he described her as well, and said she was a close friend of his?"

"I've known Gris, from somewhere else, for a few months, but we didn't get on well when we first met. Now it seems to blossom, and should be good. Who else is around?"

"Two guys came in and approached him, and left again. I don't think they're friends of yours, Boy, and *I don't want trouble in the Pub*. You and your lady are fine as long as you don't cause trouble, but whoever these are, they are trouble, and I've been a Publican too long not to know trouble when I see it. What is it about, Boy?"

"*History*, Dirk, and you are an old copper who lived with villains. I can't say any more, but there won't be any trouble in the Pub."

"Good. Just keep it like that. Here's your Lady," and as Gris came back over, Dirk wandered off, out of earshot.

"I just spoke to DUA. There's no-one about!"

"They met up in here, Gris. The guy left as we came in. Dirk smelt trouble when the guy described you and me, as his friends, and then left as we came in… they… They all bloody know what is going on but me. I'm the target and you are all playing Mr Hoo in your delusions. They know you betrayed them, so you are a potential target as well?"

"I wonder if DUA reasoned that out and wanted us safe in here—out of trouble."

"The Chistle if stretched has various ways in and out. Cuddles has one back and front in, I think. They've must have gone to the waste ground opposite here with that car park and are waiting for us there is my guess?"

"You're sure of this, Ralf? They won't try and take us out another time?"

"I don't even know who set this up. Roger Turner is dead. I've no idea about the rest of why someone is on a killing spree. We need an update so can I suggest something you ate sends you to the loo again—make some comment and head for it."

"Why?"

"Dirk knows these guys are, I'm sure, and he knows your bunch somehow. He recognised you from the beginning?"

Gris looked at me for about 2 minutes… a foolish thought in the circumstances as I never change, no matter how long you look at me—another Irish teaching?

Eventually she uttered, "I must have eaten something that doesn't agree with me… back in a moment," and headed for the loo again, at speed!

No sooner had she gone, then Dirk was at my ear once again, "What's wrong with her? *Pregnant?*"

"No, she's not pregnant, Dirk… or not by me, if she is!"

"Sorry Boy, I am getting nervous."

"Well, you are making me nervous, with comments like that, and having decided to marry the woman, you and Cuddles are not helping!"

"I'll get the Champaign out and you ordered it all round?"

I let him make his profit. Like a true Copper. If he was earnings were good it at least kept his mind off Gris who now reappeared.

"Where has he gone, now?"

"To get the Champaign for our engagement."

"You've proposed."

"DUA did it for me!"

"The bunch are where you said—Prilloch and DUA heard them whispering, and reckon there are 3 there. The rest between here and the Chistle, and you still haven't asked me to marry you… something without sarcasm, please."

I then tenderly held her in my arms for the sake of onlookers and said, "you will not knee me in the bollocks again, will you?"

"Just say the words, 'will you marry, me'"

Still expecting the knee or a smack around the head, I said, "and it won't get much worse, the way we are going, ' please will you marry me', dearest?"

Boy's real thoughts were, '*Will you marry me, Gris*, since with my relationship with you… you… know my body better than I do? You've tested its endurance as well because you are a bitch.'

Before long Dirk appeared with the Champaign which would no doubt launch itself in soda bubbles onto my bill, as the door open and DUA came in.

Gris saw him, "Don't I get a ring," laughed Gris.

"DUA is giving you bodies instead. I think the head needs drying out before you wear them, although you can wear them as you want?"

"So where is my ring?"

"I'll get it later…? Off the bath!"

"Hilarious—I accept… as I don't have a choice…?"

Seeing us, DUA came up and said, "three down… we'll pick them up later, and Bishop took out one more who moved into your bedroom—he's still alive, just gagged and tied up there, so that is six out of nine with two out on the street and one still around the hotel but I seem to lose count; getting old…? Here's your *engagement ring*, Gris. Security owes me it for that lousy pension deal I've got; after we sorted out their problems for them."

He handed a box over to me and said, "consider it a down payment on what you are going to do for me… have a good time together, even if *it isn't very long.*"

I passed the box DUA have given me to Gris to open, and there was an antique diamond ring that must have lain in Security, from Queen Victoria's time.

Originally nicked from the Royal Household; knowing Security—been away for cleaning ever since.

She put it on her finger, and it seemed like the lights in 'Cuddles' went out.

Suddenly we heard the pop, which was probably Dirk's finger leaving his mouth, and DUA was there like a Genie looking at soda water.

Dirk gave DUA a strange look, but who didn't?

Breaking out the glasses for the toast, whilst Gris glittered around the ring like a blushing bride who has just nicked the church collection and legged it.

"Yes, Father-in-law, or shall I call you Daddy."

"Neither if you want to live, Boy. I had enough of Fatherhood, years ago."

"Who was your child and when did you kill them?"

DUA stared at me, but after the Lady in Africa, he could stare all he wanted!.

Another time lapse and no I don't read Japanese Tactics where you stay quiet because someone wants you to speak… load of sushi and Bishop might have seen action but all DUA ever saw was his underwear and he wasn't the old DUA I'd seen years before—I saw him now, looking old and before his time—and he was hiding behind the lines on his face.

"I want you and Gris to stay here, Boy… I have too much resting on you two, to risk anything else. I'll head back to join Prilloch, Bishop, and take care of those other three."

"How long do you need, DUA?"

"Give us two hours as we have one in your bedroom as well, and they can enjoy a late view from the cliff, as they go down it."

Gris and I mixed with the Bar after DUA left—watched carefully by Dirk, until he came over to us, "That guy who came up to you…? How well do you know him?"

"Fairly well. *Why?*"

"He came in earlier, looked around the Bar, then at that guy I told you about, and went out."

"He was looking for us," said Gris. "We arranged to meet him here, and got a bit delayed, because of Ralf here!"

Dirk looked at us two intensely and walked away, saying nothing.

"Your friend seems to have *noticed a lot*, Ralf?"

"Dirk came from Shepherd's Bush—*ran a Pub there*… if you don't see things going on in your Pub there—no Pub. He doesn't miss a trick, even if *a grease-ball*, but I don't think it involves him. He might once have been a crook or more times than they had ever caught him for, although more likely as an ex-Copper he took early retirement before the investigation. *Pocketed the cash and retired*. DUA probably appeared in the past, but he knows something's up; he recognised DUA but leave it be for now—he has a good business here and he won't wreck it for something that doesn't concern him. DUA wanted us out of here after two hours. Do you want to ring him?"

"No. They will block us on the way, if it isn't done. Best to stay out of it!"

"I think you are right. Probably time *we played lovers* and drank the Champaign."

We stayed for the couple of hours, ordered by DUA, before saying goodbye to Dirk.

"Dirk… we are making a move."

"No problem, Boy. Enjoy a good night!"

"Come on, Mr Snuggles; let's say our goodbyes to the Champaign as well."

"Who is Mr Snuggles?"

"A *teddy bear* I had. *I used to smash* to pieces regularly."

"Sounds like *your courting habits*!"

"Do you want to survive?"

"How much of my body is there left, Gris."

"There will be less than there is now if you don't follow instructions?"

"I proposed. Do you want this to be a brief engagement and Mr Hoo taught us a lot of techniques as we spent the time at sea? You probably can't match me if I want to kill you. How much is the ring worth, by the way?"

She looked at me, "DUA stole it years ago. *It is a diamond.*"

"How much is it worth, Gris?"

"More than you are."

"That isn't difficult, but where does it get me?"

"Inside me."

"I didn't mean that, but for how long?"

"Find out?"

We left the bar and headed out into the road.

IX

Neville Jones listened to Dirk Rentley speaking *quietly* but fast… He, like a lot of them, remembered the guys *they were told not to touch*, who were Government and were taking prisoners out of the cells and jails—never seen again.

Dirk took a Pub in Shepherd's Bush, and early retirement—before he took a much longer, and later retirement, if he had stayed in the police Force.

A lot of police officers had selected that early option in the first Met clear-out—supposed to clear them out, with no one realising; now you might meet them in Skelmersdale in a cheap hotel on the recruiting campaign… the senior guys—the ones running the rackets considered them paid off.

The big nudgers overtook the small ones, who stayed and faced the hearings, while they faced Politics and lucrative careers for being the biggest crooks yet untouched.

Eventually, it worked up… the guys at the bottom watched their protection from above, 'cave in', as more and more middle-ranking officers left the Met for a better job in another force, with no investigations, and it brought to mind, John Sotram who took the quick get out, full pension and an alternative career.

A lot of police officers also had back trouble in those days, and took invalidity pensions, with the knife always there for the bent who stayed on, when it would embarrass their betters, who, twisting the knives, applied open wallet surgery when they later retired sick.

Neville wasn't bent, but with information on his police and Political Seniors, who continued to this day, was a danger who needed forcing out or destruction, if they couldn't force him out.

Dirk had rung Neville for a 'CYA' and gossip to an old copper, except Neville wasn't that old, but Dirk knew the 'Bush', so Neville was happy to listen to Dirk, droning on, ad infinitum.

Dirk had also said a lot more…? Something pricked Neville's ears.

"She is wearing a sparkler that went missing from a trial, they involved you in—DUA is the guy— and I remember his face. I got out but kept the place in Shepherd's Bush until it took off, and moved down here, but I didn't expect to see DUA in Hartland."

"Why are you telling me, Dirk—this is all water under everyone's bridge?"

"The girl is a beauty, but I never saw her with DUA, before—this is bringing *'old trouble'*, Neville—back from when I got out… I don't want it back!"

"You got out, Dirk, like John Sotram, and the lot you left, was so corrupt you would need the country flooded to clean the stables behind you, out. You have stayed straight like John, who now nibbles on the edges, and runs like hell from virtually anything else that happens, but you took every penny and ran."

"So we keep our *mouths shut,* and *eyes open now*, Neville—I may not tell you… I will… 'old copper' to 'old bent copper'?"

"Smile, when you say that, Dirk… *I never took the money*, so it is 'bent copper' to 'honest copper', *if you don't mind and you are the bent copper*."

"This DUA guy ran a killing team for Security and took out 3 people at top levels recently. I've no idea what they are doing in the back of beyond and it is unauthorised, but the guy I am supposed to report to on Security issues—I didn't completely leave Government, is Romel Sebastian, who ' was an 'arse licker' for Peres, who never returned to Spain, unless the Thames floated that way, as he came from Israel, and Romel will want a report on this?"

"Dirk… I think you are reading too many thrillers—Romel is an Administrator; Peres is dead, and you are not on anyone's payroll—so stop lying and boasting. The Politicians are frightened, and that is something else we don't discuss, and I must forget everything you've told me, but there is something else you can help me with, Dirk?"

"What is that, Neville?"

"I problem on something in your old stamping ground—someone killed, just down by the school in Hammersmith, and no reason for the killing… estimates are: Male, 5 foot 6, sandy hair, clean shaven, Scottish accent and no-one saw it. Skull beaten to pulp. You understand the 'Bush'… why kill in a pleasant area?"

"No idea, Neville. I dealt with the Market, Bush Road, and the Green—your killing is Hammersmith, not the Bush, anyway. A mouthful of knuckles and a sore head is normal for the Bush – not killing."

"You understand Security guys, Dirk, in your safe area. I don't need violence in my safe area— Wandsworth, Fulham and Hammersmith are my dedicated areas, under Owley… now I get unnecessary murders in my area, while you get a bunch of killers in yours."

"Why are you complaining, Neville?"

"It doesn't stack up, Dirk… and the hairs on the back of my neck are rising—the team that killed in Kingston are now down in your area, while a brutal and unnecessary murder in your old stomping ground happens. That is too much of a coincidence?"

"Don't shout at me, Neville… I didn't start it?"

"I asked you a question, Dirk. I didn't shout but you obviously don't know so I think I will give John Sotram a ring and say goodnight to you."

Neville put the phone down, closing his eyes in old memory for old police officers who didn't stop causing trouble or meddling?

Old police officers never die, they lose their balls was the old joke and Dirk had run when justice beckoned, dropping everything everywhere where that made a profit and escaped including betraying anyone if he could as he ran.

Neville waited for a while until the noises at his back on the keyboard ceased, which meant his sidekick had stopped taking notes.

He picked up the phone and rang John Sotram.

"Hello," the usual non-committal answer from John Sotram, who wouldn't even admit to his name.

"Neville Jones, John."

"What do you want?"

"Forgetfulness, John."

"What do you want to forget, Neville?"

"Why none of your team remembered the faces of the people following Antona's children, when they saw you, and remembered you. Dirk Bentley remembered them, when he saw just one guy, and you were close enough to take their autographs, so you cannot recognise them, John?"

"I've no idea what you are talking about, Neville. We saw nothing. '*Been down the pub*, again', Neville, looking for clues?"

"I understand who the guys are and I've met them, so did you back in your police days also meet them but I didn't take the cash and the ignorance?"

"So what, Neville… nothing was ever proven—nothing happened—no-one talked, so *you shut up*, and don't cause trouble or I will talk to your Governor, and get you shut down?"

"That case is only closed for Security people, but for you, it is still open—a charge of withholding information from me, apart from Antona finding out you who was following her children and she will meet them in due course, and you didn't prevent the murder of her husband. Her taking action in a civil court would be something for you to think about."

"You can't prove that, Neville and I can get onto some people… they will have you taking dogs for a walk—on your knees!"

"I doubt that, John, so talk to me. Antona and Roger Turner were massively bent. As are you? I've dug into the past since then and your reputation doesn't get a boost when the guy you're protecting is taken out. So you want to help and I want that knowledge."

"These guys are killers, Neville and they backed off when we turned up, so we left them alone… we… what we supposed to do… we were there to protect the kids, the wife, and I was to be with the head guy—to cover him. Your guys should have been there, not us and protecting them. Your bunch pulled out after the murder, and ignored the threat to Turner before it, so don't accuse me. All you did was jail her daughter for 3 years."

"They paid you to safeguard them, John?"

"No-one paid us to risk our lives, Neville, and you can't afford the publicity to charge us, and that includes challenging my licence, but if you want a name, it was a Security killing, and you go find them."

"DUA—pensioned off by Romel Sebastian as part of the deal not to go for them as killers—the rest of the team re-allocated, closed down or sent on unpaid leave, so why are they together again, John; if not under Security or Defence control?"

"You can't touch them officially and you understand who they are so why are you going at me, Neville? Once again, you comprehend more than I do, and you are doing nothing and you are as corrupt as I am."

"What about the diamond they stole, John—Dirk recognised it?"

"There was a case where evidence disappeared, but there were so many cases where evidence went missing it became a joke, but one of them was yours where the diamond disappeared before the trial. Remember it! Well; this sounds like that diamond! Get it!"

"If it is?"

"Don't involve me because the top wags now were the ones planning to steal it to order and no-one else was to touch it and then the bastards from Security nicked it and no-one got a penny!"

"How did you get involved with the big-wigs? It is too big a crime for you, and someone stole it before the current MPC could—plus Bottomley and the crew. What did you understand about the diamond? They brought me in late as the fall guy—thinking I wouldn't check on the evidence before the trial and then tried to stop me from checking it. It had already gone with my Senior Officers blaming me by the time I could try to find it—Owley saved me on that one because they were trying to tread all over him?"

"*A too well known* Diamond of this quality couldn't go back on the market, Neville, it was being *sold to order*. Some bastard stole it, but the headlines were more interested with the drugs cut with fingerprint powder going back on the market, and that wiped the diamond off the Press radar and they forgot it."

"I do know that, John. The guys got off, the Insurance paid out, and the police paid for the aborted Court hearing, after losing the evidence."

"Well, if that is the diamond, Neville; it wasn't a copper who stole it, although the two big wigs set you up after they failed to steal it—intending to *steal it to order*—and this is the end of the conversation; comprehend?"

Neville put the phone down, spun his chair around and looked up at Nat—his sidekick.

"We've got this bunch loose in Hartland who killed Turner—another killer loose in Hammersmith… why do I feel it connects them? There is no reason they should be, apart from them happening at the same time. What did you get from the local bunch, Nat?

"*The standard*, Neville; no-one saw anything; no-one heard anything; no sign of a weapon… Locals are going around the Pubs looking for anyone who can remember anything—which means no-one."

"What do we have on the victim?"

"The guy had no record, Neville—minded his own business with no enemies. Recently down from Edinburgh—arrived last Monday; rented a room while he looked for a job, with cash down. Still had money on him, so it wasn't a robbery. Someone smashed his scull to bits—random attack."

"Anyone else around?"

"No one around apart from the dead guy."

"Why couldn't they do it somewhere else, Nat? I can think of some old time coppers, who would have loaded the body in the boot of a car and taken it somewhere else, so it wasn't in their area."

"What do we do now, Neville?"

"We must wait until forensics gets through with it and hopefully give us something more than a *'blunt instrument'*?"

"You are heading home, Neville?"

There is nothing we can do now, Nat… I am heading for bed before we get some 'head-bangers' out on the streets."

"I won't be far behind you, Neville."

"At least with Owley, Nat, we now have parking spaces, and the sandwiches paid for… I am heading for my cold hard bed, and *earplugs*."

"Good night, Neville… I'll try to keep them off your back until lunchtime."

"Thanks Nat… I am… I am usually up with the birds. Their choking usually wakes me up, but it doesn't mean you ring too early?"

"Why don't you find a woman, Neville?"

"If I find one who likes me, it's a good reason to distrust her judgement. Most women consider me as a collection of bad habits, encapsulated in the beer mantle of a police officer who never turns up on time, even for bed—never sleeps through the night or comes back to the house without smelling of drink, and looks at all of her friends like they should be in Holloway, which is where most of them should be… if she likes them."

"How do I describe you to any women, I know, Neville?"

"I am just a collection of foul habits, honed by too many years police work… you have an excellent woman, Nat—I can't afford your life!"

"Sleep on it, Neville. Someone—blind as a bat – no sense of smell… will find you!"

"And a good night to you too, Nat."

Neville made his way home and *slept like a drain* as usual, with all the associated noises. Gurgling, blockages, *wastage disposal*; finally disappearing into a cloudy dream, with Owley as the Arch Angel condemning him to hell for mowing the *'grass'*, before dealing in it.

In one of his briefly awakened states, he remembered asking Nat to charm up Gloria Nantucket.

Nat has the *Welsh charm*… Neville's charm went out with the Norman invasion, fortresses and slaughter of anyone who challenged him.

Mornings for Neville meant either he was awake for hours—full speed or he'd hit the beer the night before—slow speed and was *inspecting his own demise, often in what seemed to be slow motion.*

Awareness was his usual race between the eggs and the shower, with everything timed to confusion, and eventually he staggered out and headed for the Newsagents, to find out what the world thought was happening.

He finally found his way to the office, which seemed to be more difficult every time he tried, with as usual, Nat there before him, frisky and bright eyed, as if he hadn't left after, Neville… this struck Neville as odd to a degree, since Nat lived some distance away and his car was still in the same parking spot, *as if it hadn't been moved* and dry underneath, which meant it hadn't been moved after last night's rain.

"Had a phone call from that Antona woman, Neville; sounded upset, but wouldn't say why?"

"Can you ring your lover in Security, Nat? Tell her… tell her we know of the Security bunch of killers around Hartland—no further 'info'. I must ring Macguire later."

"I'll ring her, Neville, but you better ring that Antona woman. She was not a happy bunny."

Neville rang Antona—as usual she picked the phone up, as if poised by it.

"Neville Jones, Antona. *You wanted me?*"

"They have found Jimmy Mackintosh *dead* in Maastricht."

"Outside of my jurisdiction I'm afraid, Antona… I'd get in trouble if I move outside of Wandsworth, Fulham and Hammersmith—Maastricht would get me a whipping around every police Station, dead or not for ninety lashes!"

"*This is not a joke*, Neville, he is dead. They beat his skull in… no-one saw it… I think he was just found there when the police swept up after the drunks had finished on a Friday night. The police said, they thought he was so drunk they left him in the street and they rarely get out of the 4×4 on a Friday night, unless there is trouble… he bled to death by the time anyone noticed, the next morning."

"I can't do anything, Antona… if I try… my Boss… I'm pitched out of the force so fast, I won't have a Pension. I sit here and use my skills as I am allowed, and there is a police Commissioner and his sidekicks just waiting for me to make a mistake and Owley is my only protection."

"There must someone you can tell, Neville?"

"You got into this, Antona… I can't… no way… I can… I can't do anything as no-one is threatening you or is near your property… if anything changes, contact me, but I can't help you, although I will drop by later so someone is at least seen to be there, for all the help that will be worth."

The phone went down at Antona's' end with the impact echoing from Kingston.

"Nat, could you say to the locals, that a murder has happened to a Banker, connected to Antona, and after the last murder there, we wouldn't mind if the Patrols were directed that way, to avoid embarrassment if something happens again… I'd better ring this Macguire guy, as it is Security related."

Neville picked up the phone again.

Owley had been very specific, "Don't interfere. Communicate. Don't stray. Don't pass wind. Don't pass go, or *you will end up in 'jail'* and without a get out of jail, free card!"

The phone rang for a good while, as if someone wanted the call to go away, "Macguire."

"Neville Jones reporting as required. Your Pensioned guy and his team seen down in Hartland. Connection to Antona and the previous project found dead in Maastricht. Injuries similar to the person found in Hammersmith. Not aware of any connection. No authority to investigate beyond Hammersmith."

"Understood," the phone went down… Thomas Macguire wondered, as he always did, why he couldn't retire now.

DUA, he understood, would never give up—all he had was Romel Sebastian to report to, who would not even take a phone call from him if he could avoid it and wanted everything in email or writing.

He wrote the report in triplicate, as usual, making sure he kept his copy; filed in archives under an old 'dead man's handle' file so he had his cover, and the name of the file recorded in the event of his untimely death with the original sent to Romel.

Why didn't DUA go? DUA had a *clear run*. All the *old crimes wiped out*. Why wouldn't he just stop and go?

Maybe he'd spent so much time in this, he didn't comprehend when to give up… This trickled his own thoughts that deep down he felt the same and would hang on beyond his payoff time?

He put the appropriate copies into their respective envelopes and filed them in every sense of the word.

He would save his spare copy for tea time in the archives, and a ginger biscuit with his favourite lady, who understood his actions and watched over him this last 30 years as he moaned as she produced the tea, biscuits and tots of whiskey.

Much as every love to Neville became another challenge and another failure, he considered taking another chance but his visit to Antona verged on the professional?

Antona, he felt he needed like a house on fire, although not a fire to crucify him and burn his ashes for fertiliser?

Someone as crookedly honest, as he'd become, didn't belong in the police Force, nor did the interest in miracles, or in a woman who said 'I need you'… he booked himself out on a late night, and the desire for a beer waited. The beers from lunchtime needing cooling off, ready for later replenishment.

Neville often considered the women he'd known and often in depth when he felt in a lousy mood— well, possibly when he woke up in the early morning and needed another drink was the usual time.

All wanted to take over, train him and then always his fault when the relationship failed, as all the women he understood shouted at him, *before they or he left.*

They all eventually looked at him and decided no pension was worth him not being controlled; always the memory of it moved him and his legs usually toward the bar.

The bar was closed for now; he'd catch up later.

Neville probably took the longest route to interview someone that has ever been but eventually arrived in spirit if not brain and he knew he was finished if he didn't stop drinking.

When your success rate with women is relegation after relegation in the lack of desirable men, even a frog has more chance than you do.

Neville wasted the little petrol who could afford to burn as he drove around still he could breath into the tank.

When Neville finally arrived it was like a small boat pretending it was a liner!

Time to see Antona. He parked the car away from the door—ready to run.

The door opened, "I didn't expect you… but thank you."

"Old men take longer, Antona—I finally made it."

"And how long do you take, Chief Inspector? No! Don't answer that… I was just amusing myself—an old habit."

"How much do you want to go to the edge, Antona? I thought this business had finished—there is rubbish coming at me from all sides and I may not do a thing about it! The bunch that left you alone, after Roger died, are leaving you alone now but they've now appeared in Hartland and 'NO' there is no contact with them at the moment… No contact with anyone they might deal with, either – I know that they don't work for Security anymore, but they will embalm myself whilst I am alive and have my brain explored whilst I live, if I do anything. I can't even be here, officially, under my Boss's rules."

"I can offer you board and lodgings, Inspector, but I need protection, and you can stay with a girlfriend, whether he likes it—Human Rights Law?"

"*If I ever sell myself,* Antona, I will be asleep when I do it, but I do like you."

"When did you last *sleep* with a woman, Inspector?"

"*When I stopped dreaming about them,* but do I need this *conversation, Antona?*"

"You know what I did, and why. You promised me 'hell' for what happened, but you came here tonight?"

"There is still some kind of belief, I can live off, and yes, I lose my temper, promises, and virtually everything else, but I am human, somewhere, although *I wouldn't like to take bets on where.* If I wasn't, I wouldn't be the idiot, talking to you now!"

"You won't stay and *be an idiot,* then?"

"As an *out-of-date lover,* I might… may I… I would… can I consider you a 'girl-friend' with no judgement? That at least gives me a reason for visiting, as there is no jurisdiction to be here, at all."

"All my good thoughts went a lot of times ago, Inspector, and I cannot keep calling you that… you are the only one I can *trust*, now?"

"A *bad sign*, Antona… a terrible sign, but I do answer to Neville, although with usually a few expletives used before it, when I am being cursed—you might make an honest man of a *bent copper*, but I wouldn't raise your hopes."

"Call it a work in *progress*, Neville?"

"My love. You can call it what you like?"

X

"Can we trust Dirk?"

"Dirk is just a rich, bent, old Copper. Some crook described the Met police as the biggest protection racket ever and he was into it. He keeps a good Pub… what is the price for the ring and who would explore the Met again?"

"DUA has already fixed his price for that and it is your life, and his future."

"How many deaths is that? He got me out of Kensington—saved my life twice, but 'is there some heart left in him,' after he kept trying to kill me. Only when they went through problems did he act—how many did he order killed?"

"I asked Bishop once—he wouldn't answer. DUA, not only kills himself, but he arranges killings, and has done for years. He used to be part of what they called 'Pontius Pilate's Bodyguard' and rumours then, of them taking people out who crossed them, and killing within themselves… no. I don't cross DUA. Every time someone thinks they have got him, he gets out—usually by killing them, but he keeps us alive because people are afraid of him, and I mean they are frightened. He survives and so do we, once we come under his umbrella, and you are now under the 'bamboo infected umbrella' even if he pisses on you, so you get wet, but his water and thus *God's anointed and Holy!*"

"I take this as wifely advice?"

"Wife to be, Ralf? Don't blow the wedding. You haven't managed the engagement."

"Just bubbles then—least of all a wedding?"

We made our way slowly back, relying on the crew to *kill* and *disposed* of anyone else and I wondered just how many innocent people they took out to build the numbers up… including any pub staff knowing this lot if they interrupted Bishop, "When does this bunch forget killing?" Gris.

"They don't, Ralf. We walk back arm and slowly arm as we are told, with your gun, staying in your pants—let DUA handle it!"

"I don't want DUA near my pants, thank you. This *stinks*, Gris. if Dirk hasn't already talked to everyone he knows I will be surprised. By now, you are *praying* for miracles—he recognised DUA's face as soon as he saw him—knew the rest before we did. Dirk is burning the phone lines to protect himself, with DUA and us shipped down the line, including your *diamond*."

"They shipped this diamond down the line a long time ago, Ralf—Bishop told me there was evidence… *missing*. Insurance paid up and don't really want the hassle of the diamond being *found* as it was under-valued and not worth the effort. If it reappeared, embarrassment might hit major political issues. The case was corrupt and dropped; evidence didn't exist, and the Insurance Companies—as corrupt as the rest—nothing exists except perhaps as momento, and I am still on Security's books, so I am looking after this bauble should someone raise their heads and should such a diamond ever exist."

"As you looked after me?"

"Ralf! I hurt you—that was my job… there was nothing personal. I followed standard procedure, laid down by MOD rules – DUA didn't know you were there, and the people I contacted let DUA know… DUA has so much on me now from my contacting them, that without him, my lifespan is seconds… we all do what DUA says, because he keeps us alive – no other lives, so wrap your arm in mine, leave the gun alone, and we will slowly walk back to the Chistle."

XI

Romel Sebastian was considering his career over his late nightcap and thinking how he might better serve his masters.

If he was No.2 in Security and someone Carmella delegated everything to… things would change… they had to change anyway and he would be the person to change things but he'd get rid of Lance first with Carmella promoted to Director and Meik was the guy for that?

DUA didn't take care about who were running riot so he was no problem but he must stop them soon and Meik might hold a brief discussion with DUA?

Meik was a 'God-send' for these activities as he enjoyed killing, but you cannot make an Omelette without cracking eggs and his operation mattered more than a few useless people; Meik enjoyed himself as he did with Jimmy Mackintosh and Sasha Gomez was next, and that left Alfred Stephens and Antona Turner for the chocolate topping.

This insignificant tuppence police officer who was already dead as far as Romel was concerned would follow.

A pity Peres died before he finally oiled his way into nothing.

Peres as directed by his Israeli Masters took care of everything, however Romel as Number 2 would rule for his Russian Masters, but with the links to Peres and Stephens gone—cleaning up became a matter of urgency and getting the show back on the road again a priority.

It wouldn't take long, however—a few good leaks and some spectacular failures and everything would move again with Romel behind the impetus.

Even this useless bunch of Politicians would see the need for a new Broom, and he would sweep like the 'Sorcerer's Apprentice' with the broom stuck up his backside if he had to.

XII

Alfred Stephens sat there waiting for the reports on the Boy—now 6.00 am. The second brandy bottle emptied.

He was wondering about a third, which was why when the window exploded, and the bullet hit him in the head, he felt nothing.

Sasha who loved his Russian Women was in Luxembourg for another, when the offer came to go upstairs from the little bar on the corner—a lady from Leningrad. He didn't hesitate.

He followed her upstairs, and as she entered the room, so did a bullet enter his brain, and then another into the girl's head, before she had time to think.

XIII

Antona picked up the phone and rang Neville Jones. It was early morning, and she thought he wouldn't be there, but still wanted to make the call. He would get back to her—he had to get back to her!

She had Cookie and Albert, but she needed his bucolic stupidity, arrogance, and the aggressive nature of someone who was actually silent as a person, but as intelligent as she was. She needed honesty, stripping her apart and knowing what she was?

She could take a lot with her lawyer training, but she wanted *protection*.

A blurred voice said, "Did you really think I wouldn't be here?"

"I didn't know, but someone killed another of Roger's contacts!"

"Yes—Alfred Stephens."

"No! Sasha Gomez!"

"I don't believe you are getting rid of people associated with Roger, but I wouldn't put it past you if it suited?"

"Why do you hate me?"

"I don't hate, Antona… It disagrees with my bottom feeding habits—gives me acid, like a lead battery. You had everything, and you sacrificed it for your own greed… thinking about it, no, I don't hate you. Sorry for you, perhaps. I'm not the 'Last Samurai' or the 'Good Samaritan' but I do wonder at times how it feels to be honest? DUA's bunch are still down in Hartland, so it does not involve them—someone else is doing this?"

"I am the only one left, Neville?"

"No you are not, Antona—there is still a bunch—including me; out of interest. I've asked the locals to show a presence around your place, which might put someone off, but it didn't before. I will put in a call to Security, but I doubt they will do anything. They will record it as an end-of-story episode… I'm sorry, I cannot touch anything or anyone, Antona. I have to use Nat to order a cup of tea from outside the building. I am pensioned off, until Talbot and Stapleton resign or retire, or go to prison, which is more likely—Owley has me corralled. I cannot do a thing outside of the area allocated to me by Owley, even to feed the horses, which includes you!"

"I didn't need a comment like that, Neville—I am not a horse! You can come and see me as a boyfriend, Neville. He can't stop it under Human Rights, and I am an ex Lawyer; however I could do with a dose of honesty!"

"Joking apart, Antona—you have your revenge—I have forgotten how to be a boy, never mind a friend. I might manage an honest bent cop, but an honest man is stretching it."

"What can you do then?"

"I will make the call as required by my Boss to Security. All I can officially do."

"Will you come and see me? There might be rooms here for an honest, bent cop? Enough people around here to protect your morals as well—stay over as a friend, or become one?"

"It has to be better than what I live in, Antona? Just be the entrusting, crooked girlfriend, please."

XIV

Neville hung up and faced a cup of coffee with definitely more life than he possessed.

The door suddenly flew open, landing with Nat in full flight.

Neville didn't even turn around as he shouted to Nat, "When did you report to Stapleton, Nat?"

"Since you lost it!"

"I never lost it, Nat. You are too much of a crook to ever trust, and the one time I forgot that, you started working for Stapleton. What did he offer you… blindness on your expenses?"

"You would have put me back on the force, if it wasn't for Stapleton!"

"You are too corrupt for that, Nat, and the force, incompetent as it is, doesn't deserve you. You don't deserve Stapleton, anyway!"

"How did you find out?"

"If it had been Stapleton from the beginning, he would have nailed me years ago. By the time you started reporting, I wasn't doing anything, so your reporting was not that long ago."

"Then, how did you guess?"

"His information was too close to the truth to when things happened, so someone told him and you were the only one with the information. You also stop typing to make notes, which is silly as I'm not deaf?"

"You're investigating me. I'm making a formal complaint. You can't just do that?"

"Have you told your wife about the 'fancy woman' yet? The one over the road in the Arndale. No-one leaves after me, and comes back fresh before me, with the ground under their car dry, because after it rains at night, the ground gets wet, but you never really think."

"So you were checking my car out, Neville—I'll stop that."

"Owley gave us parking, Nat… your tires stayed cleaned and the ground dry under your car, even after you had driven home. I passed by on my way to the Chinese up the hill the other night, and there was your car still there at 22.30. I've suspected it for a long time, but you had your uses, Nat. Being a mirror for what Stapleton gets up to was useful but now you are reporting everything before I have even done anything, so Stapleton knows, or thinks he does what I'm going to do, before I even make a move."

"What are you going to say?"

"Does he know about the woman you are living with, and her drug dealing family? You can be a Desk Sergeant for Stapleton, for all I care. It comes with accommodation in a Station house, for when your wife throws you out."

"You can't do that to me, Neville. Stapleton wouldn't allow it!"

"I work for Owley, Nat—not Stapleton now. If I tell Owley of your basic corruptness, and shame of shame, betraying your own wife and living with druggies, I am sure it will appeal to his finer senses—if he still has any."

"You can't prove any of this, Neville, and you know it."

"With the loss of your house, wife, a criminal record, no job, no pension, and a jail sentence—I would think you gurgling down the plughole as the prisoners take revenge for all the fittings up you've done, and ram them up you, would go down a treat. Have a nice enema!"

"What is the deal, Neville?"

"There is no deal, Nat… you are a shit, untrustworthy, a liar, a con artist and polluter of my much reduced sense of honesty. I regard your running errands for Stapleton as an attempt for forgiveness, if that was ever possible. You carry on as before, but after the event. There are bigger fish than you, and I need them fed before it fries you!"

"Shall I tell Stapleton, you keep going out to see Antona?"

"Ring Antona—ask her who her boyfriend is… remember Kingston is outside of my police area, and part of my personal life!"

"You seriously want me to ring her, Neville?"

"I don't really care, to be *honest*, Nat, and that is a word I seldom use to you—what else, apart from your druggie dealing habits, have you to tell Stapleton?"

He heard Nat ring Antona, and utter some stuff about the local nick, and then Nat said, "Your Boyfriend sends his regards."

"Tell him to be early for dinner, was the reply," and Antona hung up.

"You really are an untrustworthy 'shit' aren't you, Nat?"

"You want me to report to Stapleton… I risk nothing for you, Neville!"

Neville picked up the phone and rang Detective Chief Superintendent Jonathan Owl, "This is Neville, Jonathan."

"Go ahead, Neville."

"Do you know of all those killings following on from the last Security project? It means someone is cleaning up, and it isn't the old gang as they are in Hartland. I am not involved, apart from Nat Jacobs reporting to Stapleton, and living with some druggies on overtime?"

"Yes, Neville…? I do know but that is my information, not yours."

"I can understand why you didn't warn me about Nat, but something new is happening—there is only Antona left out of the original bunch, apart from some kid, and DUA seems to have been protecting him, but Antona is now my girl-friend, so I will visit Kingston every night."

"I wouldn't expect anything less from you, Neville, now bugger off, and tell Nat, *I don't pay for his laundry*!" Owley's phone went down and Neville turned around, again.

"Nat. Owley says to tell you, he doesn't pay for your laundry!"

"*Bastard*!"

XV

Neville rang Antona, "I've just told my Boss you are my girlfriend and I will visit Kingston every night… being the supercilious arsehole that he is, he said 'he wouldn't expect *anything less* from me'. Does the offer still hold?"

"I would expect some *warning* of when you are going to arrive. It gives Cookie a chance!"

"Do you do '*doggy bags*'?"

"Only if *you sleep in a kennel*… you turn up like a normal person—you're eating habits, we can work on later… Albert will sort out the rest, and arrange the room?"

"It makes me sound like a *kept man*?"

"*Merely leased*, until something better turns up, is probably a more accurate description!"

Neville rang Macguire.

"Macguire!"

"Neville Jones. 2 more killed from the previous project. I am now staying with official approval at my girl-friend's house in Kingston, where Roger Turner died. Outside of my area of jurisdiction but I am a police officer in London, and *will act as one*. Please *pass it around*!"

"Understood, Mr Jones!"

Neville got ready—a kennel and a doggy bag would be his entrance and exit for being late.

Meeting a lawyer/crook closely, unless investigating them was unusual. He felt like telling Owley it didn't matter because Nat would tell Stapleton, anyway, and it would pass upwards, downwards and sideways like some kind of dance but to a degree he'd already done that.

He heard of some man in a book, finding a rich woman who took him in.

Antona might take him in, in more ways than one before he ever understood her or was that what she was doing, and doing it now.

Roger died, but they'd prevented him from investigating the killing—the only crime and evidence they found put her daughter away for 3 years for drug dealing—was there some kind of balance, if he ever found it or ever knew?

Neville understood Antona got the money from the oil tanker hijackings.

Now? Of the Group organising the hijacks—only she remained, and for what?

He'd might technically live off the *rewards of crime*, but what change was that to his life as a police Officer and it had always been *a career goal*?

Was this a deterrent to the local Bobbies, who would be told by Nat or Stapleton, anyway, to monitor him.

Now someone might *string him up by his badge*, if things went wrong, *without taking it off* first as so many had tried.

No authority anywhere in reality and strictly, all he might manage was ringing the local Bobbies, and they would be around a lot more, however he still a police officer mentally for *whatever that meant*.

Antona's house finally appeared in front of him and he managed, climbing out of his battered old car without his usual back-stretching and cursing.

The door; opened by Albert, who immediately took his bag, saying, "I will show you to your room, sir. Madam is in the study. Once you've had your shower she will, no doubt, be *pleased* to see you?"

I'm being trained already, Neville decided. Fit in or *be trained* to fit.

He followed Albert up to the room and was surprised to find a robe already lay out on the bed.

"There are some refreshments in the refrigerator for sir, but there will be a brandy downstairs, so I would suggest that sir *leaves* the beer until later."

Albert *butlered* smoothly off, leaving Neville to take his shower… a shower in the evening… Neville considered running for whatever home he had now, but there was no running backwards and forwards, to get his eggs timed by the shower.

His shower was just right as he finally remembered to take his clothes off—no standing under it in his vest and drawers as he washed his hair, underwear and himself at the same time.

He took his time enjoying *hot*, instead of *luck* dominated water—usually the way his shower worked in Putney, where you never understood the way the water was going to hit you, until it did—this was *enjoyable* for a change but he was hardly in his first bloom of middle-age, probably at the stage of the first wither and being smashed apart in a shower was something that never changed but did at least wash his underwear… often… not cleanly and usually in a fit of violence but it managed.

A bit of luxury before he died was appealing, but somehow didn't fit into his life.

He picked up an immense towel, that if his, would, either be *stinking* or *slimy*, and just felt it almost wrap around him, like a magic cloak, so even his toenails felt good—perhaps miracles can happen.

He'd bought casual slacks… Tesco's best; if they ever did have anything better he'd missed it and wandered back to get dressed, finding on the bed a package and a card… 'from your criminal girl-friend'; unwrapping the packages produced a decent pair of trousers, pants, and socks he would never ever find in a Tesco, and a good shirt… he turned the card over, and written on the back was 'criminal girlfriends don't have to follow the rules'?

He laughed, and that was the first for a long time—of genuine humour—she had him by everything, everywhere and didn't mind telling him she had him!

Port out; Starboard Home. He could live with it for a few hours, but a police officer never dreams?

A knock at the door revealed itself to be Albert, "Are you ready sir, only Madam is waiting?"

"Thank you, Albert," and he sounded a fool for saying it.

He made his way down, following Albert, who negotiated him to the Lounge and kept checking to see what he was stealing, in Neville's opinion.

"Please sit down, Neville. Albert will get you a brandy, and then we can talk."

Albert butlered his way to the brandy and glasses, with a rich biscuity deep aroma gently caressing the air, as he returned to Neville, who did not swill it like the cheap pub brandy.

He looked at Antona, and she looked back on him.

They were *two sides of a legal coin.*

Each *corrupted* by trying to enforce what they saw as the law, or what they could get away with in a court of law.

"Antona, I am being sliced, diced and hung up for smoking—possibly by the police as well, but definitely with the gang I know about… I think… maybe… I might be able to stop something happening, but I can't give you guarantees. I can only muddy the waters, and I have already done that, but I can't *dam* the flood, although I can certainly damn the people concerned."

"Neville. You could have walked away and you have already told me frequently your opinion of me, plus a few threats, or promises as well… what made you come tonight?"

"I've always had this silly belief in the Law… I try… I try to observe it, but if the law hits you, I have to watch but I don't consider the law wants to know you. Killers, Villains, Criminals all seem to want to know you, and most are working for the Government and that offends my sense of reasoning but I like and respect you for your courage, determination, and desire to provide something that is stable—I know, I probably have as much credit in your eyes, as a *spent copper*, but I am grateful for the chance to meet you, and at least be somewhere decent for a change."

"You are here, Neville. Albert will make that room yours, for the shower at least, and as a dressing room… no-one else I think… no, no-one else will come near me. You said what you thought of me—most of it accurate… I felt… I fell I suppose into a habit, not a personal desire, apart from preserving what we achieved—I guessed my son was on drugs as I don't really trust men but it wasn't him and why was my daughter so stupid!"

"An interesting train of thought but not one for a police officer to consider—that is for the courts to decide?"

"It was sexist because I don't like my son. He is brash, noisy and speaks his mind—he enjoys being rude for the fun of it. My daughter no longer likes me because I seduced Jimmy Mackintosh, after she failed to drive him away and she cannot face losing. I needed someone to love that night, but also for the money to keep this place going."

"I am not a Merchant Banker, Antona, nor will I ever be one."

"You are not Jimmy Mackintosh, but at the moment I need you here. You possess a kind of stability about you, a brain often lacking in others, and there are worse than you, believe me."

"A backhanded compliment, but I probably asked for it?"

"There is a room… this is your house until you leave—I am not speaking of love or desire, but of respect and a fear of the future—the possible future that I hope, you will stop from happening, but I like you, and you are someone I want around the house. Shall we dine? Cookie has done something plain."

"You guessed, Antona, that I am not used to proper meals, without layers of fat and burnt offerings… decent food doesn't feature in a normal police officer's diet."

"Let's start with the basics, Neville… I mean… that's regular meals, and you come here until you choose otherwise, but let me know first?"

"Thank you, Antona… I like the idea—I will need to be able to get about without calling for Albert to find my car, though."

"I'll tell Albert… although your car needs a service and he will sort that out—you are on a lease, and not a kept man, Neville—by your criminal girl-friend. You being here could prolong my life, and that matters to me! Let's eat this dinner!"

XVI

The times when Thomas Macguire didn't think of his pension, were becoming very infrequent, and matched his definition of his career.

Another memo from Romel, and another copy for the *Tea and Biscuits* folder, was his daily routine.

They were good 'Ginger Nuts', and at times like these, holding onto your Ginger Nuts, mattered more than.

In the past he'd have told DUA or Bishop, who knew how everything worked—DUA was now unofficial, and 'banished'. They transferred the squad; told to sit at home for allocation under Romel Sebastian; it would never happen until they withered away on the branch, like the rest, and Thomas had no authority to take them off the Waiting List.

They were there, being paid non-active rates and able, but not authorised, to operate… he sat there for a good twenty minutes, and changed his mind, ringing Bishop.

"Bishop here, and this better be good, Thomas!"

"Rest of the bunch from your previous operation, taken out—Copper knows, and he is shacked up with remaining target… someone is working their way around the lists of those connected to the Insurance Guru, you took out—don't know who, but Romel is starting trouble; using this Meik to do it?"

"Thanks, Thomas—2 crates was it?"

"Pension will suit me and the kids growing up, away from your bunch!"

"Take care, Thomas, and remember, we are always *behind* you."

"That worries me, Bishop. I would prefer you were in *front*, by about 15 miles."

"Goodbye, Thomas."

Bishop looked up at DUA, "Only one left out of the little exercise, excluding Boy and Huron, and Thomas is getting worried?"

"Why is Thomas worrying—nothing in there to do with him at all… something there isn't right, Bishop—Thomas shouldn't be bothered?"

"What about Antona, DUA?"

"I am surprised, Stephens didn't go for Antona, Bishop? Boy was ego for his son, but Antona really *knew* everything that was going on and could have slain him—this is being muddled, and by someone who doesn't know? *That is worrying me.*"

"What about this team hunting Boy, DUA?"

"Still don't know… when you do a high price contract with this lot—they have someone stay back, in case they are *unhappy* with the way the deal pans out, so it could have been something like that, but Stephens was set up by someone else to clear the air/take him out, and the timing is just *coincidence!*"

"*Calm down,* DUA… we just have to look and learn."

"There is still that Bastard, Bishop, who had me thrown out of Security, and Romel is up to something."

"I know that, and Macguire is right on that score, DUA."

"Sebastian has taken on Meik, Bishop…? I wonder what he is using him for… I don't want to take Meik out, until I know he is te*rribl*e, and I have no choice. You know me, Bishop and the history, and you have kept it quiet. I had one child as a 'by-blow' from the woman who loved me, and I loved the woman Meik's father took and later killed, as he did Prilloch's mother. I killed him, and he didn't even deserve that death, because it was too quick. It should have been slower. I've looked after both of them. One for being mine, one from someone I loved. He killed both of the women in his drink, and I killed him. Now I'm left with Prilloch and Meik… three bloody killers on my soul."

"Prilloch, I monitor DUA."

"I know, Bishop, and thanks… Meik I can't kill because I keep thinking, something of his mother will come back out in him, given time, and we are all killers—maybe he will change?"

"He is killing like an 'out-of-control' idiot at the moment and he is killing, DUA!"

"I can't do it, Bishop… Boy should have gone in there, but I had Gris keep him back—I should have let it happen. I am going soft, Bishop… going soft. Losing too much, and too many… I looked at how many on this Gardening Leave crap and they are getting rid of the good ones."

"You don't know how to go soft, DUA, but you have never forgotten how to go devious, and that is what you are playing here; in a long game?"

"They made Gris and Boy for each other, Bishop. 'Made for each other'."

"Leave the Boy, alone, DUA. I want the choice to be his."

"He is just another of your Bastards, Bishop, and you set him up for Africa, and started all this."

"You started that team, DUA—just leave him alone. He is being conditioned by you for something, and I don't like it."

"Mr Perfect Bishop, looking after his Boy and you say I am going soft?"

"You said you are going soft, not me. Leave him alone."

"He would be dead but for me. Shall I leave him alone?"

"You caused it, DUA, now leave him alone."

"Or what Bishop?"

"You die, DUA, and I don't need a gun."

XVII

The idea for Boy of sleeping with someone, he could last remember kicking him into a wall, no matter how she hugged him now, was difficult.

"I get the idea you don't love me, Ralf," Gris muttered, looking directly into his face.

"No Gris. I learnt the movement, as I swung… I said before, you understand my body, better than I do?"

"It wasn't personal, Ralf, and they'd have taken out—*our would-be killers*?"

"Thanks, Gris. They have taken out our killers—for a Big Mac? They gave us to those killers and now they kill them. So a bunch of killers are killed instead killing a bunch of killers?"

"I didn't ask for this, Ralf, and there are things I like about you—don't comment, or I will finish the job?"

"And you didn't run away, either, Gris. There is nothing like being *beaten about in a cell* to make you '*love*' someone. It is the memories emblazoned in my mind, which I can't love."

"I'm sorry, Ralf… what do you want me to do?"

"Go gently, and no kicking or fighting, in the clinches, Gris."

"I did what I had to do. They used me to do it. I let people know when I found out it was you. You are alive. I could have killed you? Brought in Blow Torches? Cut things off? DUA and Bishop killed massive people for you—they took out top people, and DUA carried you, to make you sure, you came out. We played by the rules until DUA gave the go ahead, and you were out. It was only hours once we found out. We played it by DUA's rules, and that is what we do now."

"Where in DUA's book did it say, 'kick the shit out of me'?"

"Nowhere, Ralf. I did the standard. Matthews wanted you dead, or confessing, but slowly. He wanted revenge for what the team in Africa did to his ego and his finances."

"Kicking the shit out of me, was good for me? Was hanging me and spinning me around, while they used me as a punch bag in the same vein, or didn't they find it first time around?"

"DUA says love you, and I love you… what is your problem?"

"I cannot find the card labelled 'Dad', to write his obituary on. The colour seems to be black that I want to use and they don't do that on birthday cards, so he can read it every day."

"We need a truce, Ralf, or both of us are dead?"

We carried on arm in arm like lovers, with her right hand, still resting on the gun and her left across my trouser belt, but at least she had stop pushing it down into my pants, so she could blow my arse off.

We walked into 'Chistle' to meet Bishop, standing by the Bar, "What do you pair want?" He said.

"Bloody Mary for Gris. I'll take the body, and I thought you would pick up those guys?"

Bishop waved his hand, and put the drink element of the order in to Basil, who as usual, gave me strange looks.

Basil was a London Barrister, who'd got out and bought a beaten old wreck of an Inn with damp.

He was as tight as a Jewish Balloon but stopped to give me one more funny glance and swanned off; extending his long neck and ears as he departed.

Bishop motioned us away from the bar, and debriefed us—ho, ho, bloody ho.

"There are three… I thought we missed two. They were Watchers and a Reporter who stayed well back and they've gone, we think.

"They weren't the mob then, Bishop?"

"You infiltrated them, Gris. What are they?"

"I never got a handle on them, Bishop. Servicemen or ex-services—they operated as if they were Servicemen."

"Why do you say that, Gris?"

"Everything as per manuals, instructions, and ranks and officers… like they were still Servicemen."

"Nasty, if true," said Bishop…? "Means we've another killing team—makes me wonder whether Matthews had some other killing team planned to take DUA and us out, as we know too much?"

"How would he get them, Bishop?"

"UN connections, I guess?"

"What about us?" Chipped in Gris.

"We are still in Security, although mothballed—makes me wonder whether Romel brought them in to wipe us out?"

"Bishop, this gets even more twisted as it goes on… I think… and I still do think these guys were basic—running everything from manuals. No experience in the 'Real World'—it just gets messier and messier?"

"Well, they won't be doing anything tonight, Boy, unless floating around, so you can swan onto your nuptials. Emergency licence already organised… Saturday. Government Service… foreign posting… met and fell in love… all arranged… 14.00… don't be late… DUA and I are the witnesses and that is the dream if it works. I don't know what name he is using or if he can remember it… Time I moved on—meeting DUA and Prilloch for a recap."

I looked up at Gris. "Engaged tonight. Married Saturday, on a Licence I don't know exists. One of us dead by Sunday, stabbed over the wedding cake?"

"Don't look on the 'Dark Side,' Ralf. We have tonight, and the wedding is Saturday, with no cake, so the only cake you are having and eating is me, and you can leave the decorations alone, I might need them later."

"Assuming I can get the gun out—which you keep pushing down into my pants—of my backside, I might get my pants off. If I put it down the front, it will shoot my nuts and wedding tackle off, no doubt with you on the trigger, so I really as a Russian Bolockoff!"

"We are a couple in love, Ralf, and women don't call their husbands, Boy and I need not shoot your bits off, I can just wear them down, so my hand stays there, until you stop behaving like a child, and flashing your weapons about!"

"I can see you two are getting like a house on fire," said Bishop from behind my back, "Don't scorch the linen!"

"Thank you for the obituary," Bishop.

"Time for my walkies, Boy. Enjoy Gris, it is the first time she has to love a man to death."

"Beating him instead, is probably quicker, Bishop."

"Leave it out, Boy… none… none of us are free, even DUA? Anyone it keeps her muscles taunt. Enjoy it why you can. Do what DUA says, and you might live. Cross him, and even I couldn't save you, although he won't live. Happy nuptials?"

"It looks like I'm 'fucked', in more ways than one, Bishop?"

"Take care of him, Gris. I like the idiot."

"He is safe with me, Bishop," We watched Bishop head out of 'Chistle'.

Bishop, funnily enough, had a soft spot for both Gris and me.

"I think Bishop was warning me, Ralf," commented Gris.

"Bishop has his own rules, Gris?"

"Get another drink in Ralf, I need to settle something after today, and that is my gut?"

"Did they tell you anything about Saturday, Gris?"

"No. Just that I had to be here, keep you out of trouble, and hang around."

"And then you get me as a prize? Not your lucky day, Gris."

"I don't mind you, Ralf. I've known a lot worse than you, and funnily enough, even DUA has a soft spot for you."

"What makes you think that, Gris?"

"You're alive!"

"You really do have the most seductive approach, Gris?"

"Maybe I am kicking a habit, instcad of people?"

"It feels like I haven't slept with a woman in a long time, Gris?"

"Well… let's see what you can do?"

"Thank you, Gris, I asked for that."

"Are you going to take me up to bed, Ralf?"

"Bed, I shouted to Basil."

And another punch in the guts!

"I would as well, Boy, came the reply—I'll put it on the bill."

We finally made it to the room, and I wandered around the room, trying to find any traces of blood, and then the toilet door opened, and Gris was in bed, with my jaw dropping so much as she flashed past, it was licking my boots.

Blue eyes looked at me over the sheets, and she lay there prim and proper like a 'Dutch Aunt' in what looked like a tent.

I stood there, like I was trying to sell something on an Aunt Sally stall to a winter's evening, as my tongue continued cleaning my shoes.

I headed for the toilet as well, and put the shower on—I needed something cold, which was how I finished.

They had trained an evening shower into me, and it was good to get rid of the day's rubbish… as if possible.

I finished washing the essentials and wrapped a towel 'round me'.

The problem was I liked Gris, and I liked her a lot as a person who was definitely a cut, kick and smash, above every other woman I had ever known but I just didn't trust her.

Now getting married on Saturday. Sleeping with a girl I last remembered kicking me around—well, she wouldn't be the first.

What would it be tomorrow… clown's make-up and a circus trip?

I took a step forward, knelt on the bed and kissed the re-arranged vision of a girl, now complete in an unapproachable tent and that image of Gris, has never left me, although most of that era has thankfully done as I got older and stayed alive.

She was the image, the desire, and a lot of roads led straight to Gris, and you slept well with Gris, apart from that constant nightmare of being run over.

We made love like cats in forgotten gardens with beloved fruits and smells… following our instincts, as we left the world and for moments were no longer part of this world.

Something sun kissed, sun dressed, and rippling through my mind uncovered as a fire blazed, engulfing us in heat before we exploded across the bedroom, as I surrendered, yet again, to my life.

We finally surfaced to the banging on the door of a cleaner who unlocked the door, let herself in, examined us and left.

Both of us felt we; wrongly matched in an 'all out wrestling' bout had won.

The sheets had definitely gone several shreds to every wind.

It felt like the beginning of 'spring and it's rites' and anymore of these rites would take care of any spring I had left.

Anyone who tells you they don't enjoy waking up in bed with a beautiful strange woman, is making a personal statement, but I wouldn't want to know about it, assuming both of you wanted to be there at the start and end.

My personal statement would be that anyone trying to kill us now would need a chair, a takeaway meal, an excellent book and a camp bed as they waited as we love each other. I could remember nothing in my life like it, or I have deliberately decided not to, which I could understand, opting to have it surgically removed from my brain.

I could love Gris, but not at least for a good while after the last session.

Gris had taken the first toilet trip and was now in the shower taking everything else.

I would get the wet towels, soaking wet floor, and underwear, but someone was hammering on the door bellowing, and was Bishop.

Gris chose that moment, wearing every towel there was ever likely to be, to open the shower door, wander over and say, "I think you might need some more soap and towels… can you ring for them? We seem to have run out!"

Bishop, standing there, smiled and said, "You are up!" and then vanished, returning a little later saying, "Towels as requested, and a further request that you do not come near 'Cuddles' again, from Dirk Rentley. He made this personal on the grounds of broken legs, and they would be yours. Two days with Gris will have to do, as you adjust to 'bliss'."

"And to you, as the butler!"

"Funny; mention that to a nearly married couple and you aren't yet and I use the phrase roughly although you two won't need the two bedrooms in your apartment but you will have my company, while you cohabit—albeit in a different room!"

My face led him to continue with, "The guys are still out there for you, Boy and Gris, albeit they may be inactive… maybe… maybe they have a desire… Well I have a desire to see you two living beyond the honeymoon but butler Bishop will be at your every beck and call."

"What happened to the Insurance Career, Bishop?"

"You happened! I am paid for being at home, as are the rest… my new home… it might as well be your home as you need me and they can pay for that. The bills go through easily, Boy; I'll help with your flat until they realise. It leaves you with your reserves, and your soon married wife, who will also claim for your flat. It will be a year before you have to put your hand into anything, but DUA's desire, as you claim as well, once you started active duty is that you find a house so everyone else can move in."

"Is this money an allowance, or do they pay the bill?"

"They pay up to £2000 a month travelling, hotels et al. A fixed allowance but Gris and I both claiming it would be nice but that is being handled by DUA and so far all he has is the money for Gris who stayed well under cover."

"I am only paying £1600 a month for this new flat, and CIA already pays the first 3 months, courtesy of West Africa, so that is a good profit. What made them agree?"

"Anything to get rid of us, I guess. We are 'persona non grata' to the Security Service, whilst you are flavour of the month if you want to be. They owe you for Kensington—you can get in, whilst we are quietly forced out."

"With you as our butler, Bishop, I think we'll need a bigger apartment. I've already had the Estate Agent onto me, asking whether I want to extend the agreement, as someone else wants the flat for a year plus, so I could take the option, Bishop. Head for Kingston, and with mine and Gris' allowances, plus the CIA money added we'd have enough for a month's rent? That sounds good for a decent place."

"What do you have in mind, Boy?"

"I can just about manage you as a butler, but can you do some research on the Coombe Lane area?"

"Why there?"

"I saw something the last time I was in Kingston… a 5 bedroom house for £7K a month. We can work around something with those amounts."

"You've come a long way, Boy!"

"Well, I am still alive, although not yet married to Gris, so ask me next week!"

"That was unfair, Ralf, and you haven't asked me!"

"Yes, you are right, Gris. How does a 5 bedroom house in its own grounds, surrounded by parks and commons with Bishop on the premises, sound to you?"

"5 Bedrooms means DUA, Prilloch and Bishop plus us. I don't want DUA or Prilloch!"

"Bishop?"

"DUA won't be near us, as far as I can tell. It is not his way for people to see him, and Prilloch couldn't live with someone, if you paid him."

"Do you trust them, Gris?"

"Without DUA or Prilloch… just fine?"

"Scout it out for us, Bishop."

"I'll have a 'dekko', Boy. As your butler I have to inform you of the expectations for you to eat food as you are staying here and they now on the afternoon cleaning shift so you'd better get moving before the leftovers?"

Bishop dumped the towels down and headed out.

"Do you want a new place, Gris?"

"There is still a contract out on you. We need the team—we need those bedrooms. I am still trying to come to terms with everything, and Bishop is about the sanest of the crew, so I don't mind him in a bigger house than we need."

"Fine. Bishop can check out the house, and we had better get ready and get downstairs."

We headed downstairs to find Bishop at the bar.

Bishop looked at Boy, once again as if he was summing him up… yes… well almost… alright but he was pleased as he argued inside his own head, with the way Boy had developed—West Africa had certainly put some Security hairs on his chest at least?

He could handle short and long-range guns, missiles, decide under stress, kill without thinking, or becoming involved, and he knew that area of Africa, which few people did.

'The Boy had come on well since Middlesex Street'.

He had warned DUA against action on the Boy, and that should at least blunt some of DUA's worst ideas and DUA knew the Boy had a lot more obvious stuff on him and so did a lot of other people… yes… DUA for a time had lost it and that seemed to trace back to his Scottish activities and the hidden files that Algenald always thought kept him safe but Bishop still regretted the killings Algenald and his PA—but in Government they thought they were Gods, or Goddesses who control Gods, and so often someone removes their wings and kicks them out from on-high out of the nest?

XVIII

Neville followed Antona into dinner, and found himself with her at his side and a woman who would sit beside him frightened him to where at some point she said, "do you always eat off a spoon?

Whether Neville ever considered that what he said provoked a response, he still continued talking, "I feel you are in little danger, Antona, but so is anyone crossing the street. I may have lived for nothing from everything I wanted to achieve failing, but they'll never stop trying to destroy me for the jewels they wanted to steal that someone else stole first before they managed it. They had deals they couldn't pay off, and those deals had a price and I can't prove that, although they want my head above a gate before I can and without my body attached?"

"Neville, if you don't relax, I will take your trousers off, now… I am… still.. as best I can be… a lawyer—I'll protect you in law and you protect me from the law and you open doors with a smile to anyone?"

By this time Neville was having trouble trying to be normal and honest, and it pierced him mentally as he couldn't get his mind around it.

Thought's like this didn't happen to a drunken old has-been copper… or did it happen if you weren't that corrupted enough —his mind was already in another Universe a tunnel was opening and saying this way or you will be a super-nova?

Neville found himself in a world where he could finally find a wardrobe to look at, and it was all laid out on a bed and all clean and dry, and he'd mumbled as he looked at it until finally something perhaps, intelligent evolved and he accepted a gift from his Crooked Girlfriend and dressed, which brought him back to the reality of something that was decent and then back in a way to Antona?

"I am not used to eating decent food sitting down, Antona. It unnerves me—most of my meals are eaten standing up and quickly, but how else are the police supposed to eat. Stuck in a van where the food arrives with bottles of beer and a request to move on?"

"That's why I like you, Neville, you are the takeaway, but yet consumable. You had a feeling from the beginning—before they threw you off of the case that I didn't kill my husband. They'd left me alive, didn't they? They don't kill on Neville's patch. Is that the attitude? I've survived, 'down to you'… then… who knows what them… you put the locals in to worry them, didn't you?"

"I didn't expect them to kill you, Antona, and I didn't really put the locals in it was more a political suggestion. It involved Nat in his drug dealing role and I didn't intend that either but it has attracted attention and he is probably supplying your daughter in jail. It is not what you're thinking. I didn't at any point, understand who had killed Roger, or who ordered it. They killed him on my patch… I am a cop… maybe… but you've offered me a bed, food and can argue lawyer to police officer without my having any jurisdiction."

"You are a police officer, you are responsible for the law?"

"I'm specially barred from interfering into this case."

"Who is investigating?"

"Anyone Owley selected not to investigate—not my business and I'm prevented from doing anything, anyway?"

"What shall we do?"

"Eat the best food I have ever eaten."

"What then?"

"I've reported to my superior, so as far as I am aware, to meet my legal and professional requirements, so I am not worried about them, but they killed on my patch and it reflects on me no matter what the restrictions… I don't understand what is worrying me… honestly… or not perhaps. I just know something is wrong, but I don't know what is wrong—things aren't right and I know it. I am tightly controlled and then they are letting go of me, but why. I now work for Owley but he is a Junior Guy to them and that worries me how he stops them. I know his reputation and that they probably can't touch him, but I don't know why? Things I don't understand also worry me, and I don't understand any of this."

"For Gods' sake, Neville, I lived with a bunch of crooks for years, and yes I lived with them and they gave me this property and when was Insurance honest? What I wanted was a life, but everyone treated it like a game in the men's cloakroom—all it needed was just one mistake, and I would lose everything. I gave birth to kids, and I watch everything slowly disappear as I got older. Roger had everything, but it wasn't enough. He couldn't stop wanting the excitement and he couldn't accept the things we had, including me. He was getting older and trying new things to prove himself and I never demanded that—I'm not of these 'and we all live in little boxes and we look just the same' people. He lived for Insurance, and we lived well from it, but adrenalin was his excitement. He couldn't come off the boil and started the Oil Tanker hijackings, and he did that as much from boredom—showing-off and money-lust, as much as anything. That is what he did to me—I didn't care anymore… he stole… organised killings and killed himself by his greed—no he broke every boundary because he considered greed would work for everyone and he would get away with it?"

Neville didn't think as he saw her face that she played a major part in it but just lived off it whilst tacitly encouraging Roger to do it… and yes, Roger did… and… Antona was… yes she was twisting… yes, she was twisting the truth that thought came easily into both of their minds but thought has its own direction and these thoughts certainly did?

Antona was as guilty as Rodger and the rest, but they were dead and she was already looking for a man to protect her and keep her alive and she was enjoying the money as it raked up with the tankers reaching China and paying off via Nigeria.

Within all these thoughts, he was also having problems with the different parts of his own brain and they were chipping in with their own arguments, wondering when something or someone would be intelligent enough at some point in this conversation to actually interfere?

Anatomy and desire in Neville, however, were fighting for a hearing like rats in a barrel and maybe Antona was the terrier he needed to kill the rats in his barrel?

Neville was almost tongue-tied as his mind whirled, and eventually his heart won as he spoke, "I am different—you will never see a lot of money from me, nor my running criminal gangs, besides what the police do normally and with you alongside me to work within the law maybe we can find something that matters but this is a set-up and we are being metaphorically handcuffed together and left alone until DUA needs us and please don't argue; it is only a matter of time. Yes; if you allow me I will sleep with you tonight and it sounds like an old 'Eagles song for the desert' but if I have to be tested every time before we make love then it will become questionable what I may still be capable of; I can at least still answer the questions?"

"Do what?"

"I haven't made love to a woman in ages or at least sober or I just can't remember. Only now, with you, can I consider a woman as more than a drunken moment?

"I will never be a drunken moment, Neville; nor are you!"

"I keep wondering… do I… yes, do I get a break and easy exit for my emotions and from my bunch and does that make me think it makes me more of a captive for all the manipulating?

"No, Neville. Alongside me… that… I think… is what they've tried to do. You will not speak of it now… later times are a better place for disturbing our food and that time is much later?"

"A simpler solution, I think… yes… I need you and already you are making my brain buzz?"

"Perhaps they will shoot me, Neville, and blame you. Who knows, and the food is getting cold, but you left your honesty in an unknown country a long time ago I think?"

"We… I don't understand, Antona… I really don't…? Why can't they leave the world alone; there is no way we understand each other, but I can live with that? How can they live with what they are trying to do?"

"Can you with live a caring woman?"

"I *can live with decent food, a decent bed and a decent woman.*"

"I think we can manage *two out of three*, Neville."

"*Thank you*, Antona," and Neville in his heart meant that."

Neville woke to the gentle awakening of a rattling tea cup at eight in the morning.

Antona alongside him made appropriate grunts and nasal assaults, leading him to finally getting up and carrying his tea into his alternative world.

He headed to the room allocated, to find Albert laying out a dressing gown and quietly leaving.

He could get used to this and become the '9 to 5' police officer without the 'glitter' of the lost ball.

Nat would be in the office, after his late night detective shift, which Neville did not have to sign for, and Owley wouldn't, but he admired Nat for trying to get his laundry through on expenses.

The lady did everything for him, in more ways than one in the Arndale, and Neville supposed that kept the druggie family away from her, unless Nat had involved himself in drug dealing, which would hit Stapleton, not Neville, especially as Owley knew about Nat's antics, but it had raised the question; how much did Owley know?

Neville hadn't known the truth about Nat, but guessed something wasn't right, and just ignored it.

They attached Nat to him 'in a way', that was normal for a bent police officer, and existed from time immemorial—in the right sets of circumstances, he could trust Nat to do what he expected and that was to betray him to Stapleton!

After what passed for an impossible morning with decent underwear; a decent shirt and a decent suit he felt he was posing as a decent copper instead of one left on the railway tracks to get bent?

Albert brought his wreck of a car around as usual and for a change he notice it had petrol that didn't display itself at the bottom of the meter.

He was also surprise that the car now seemed to roar a little instead of coughing when he started up.

His tyres are also seemed to have more grip which is more than he felt he did as he made his way down to the station?

The day passed with no bad news for a change and the same procedure with Antona beckoned, who still looked at him, basically—no matter what she said.

It was an unwritten rule with Antona, that you took your showers outside of the master bedroom en-suite.

He came out of the shower and again made his way to the dressing room to find a decent suit on the bed with the all trimmings, plus a written reminder from his crooked girl-friend that he was a crooked man, and with a little envelope full of newly printed notes plus a single sheet of paper marked, 'dinner is 7.00 pm tonight', please don't be late.

The night passed peacefully again, although he felt he was being deftly controlled and Neville dressed the following morning, still thinking about the murder in Hammersmith, the link to Maastricht and why everyone seemed to know more than he did.

Some guy gets his head smashed in Hammersmith, and someone else in Maastricht dies with the same 'style' injuries, but he could not touch it…?

What was the connection between the two… was… was there an 'International Serial Killer'? His movements once they'd traced them would pin him down if he existed, but did he exist and if so who was he working for?

You'd have to be a fool to do both, or just arrogant and felt you could keep bouncing of and off and inside your skull before the recognised it?

Security had disbanded the killing team—so it could not be them—unless someone else wanted them to kill or be seen to be killing and who in their demented dreams would want that?

Neville left the house to find his car, if he could call it that, waiting outside—at least that hadn't changed.

An easy drive, and an easy park, as he now had a sign on the area and Nat's car looked as perfect as yesterday, so he had been on night work again.

Nat probably left his wife a long time ago, and Owley knew that as well.

He made his way into the office.

"Any more feedback on Hammersmith, Nat?"

"You want me to look at those CCTV films, Neville?"

"Have a look at them, Nat. I doubt that you will find anything, as they all look at the premises and not outside, but you might be lucky!"

"What you are going to do, Neville?"

"Drive down and have a look at the site, Nat. There might be something we can use, and I need to look at it!"

Neville got up, walked down to his car, and headed for Hammersmith.

He should have done it sooner, but the locals had been in, taken photographs and had only just released the site, so there wasn't any real rush as there was nothing left that could ever be used, now.

As Neville left the office, Nat picked up the phone and rang Assistant Commissioner Stapleton.

Charles Stapleton picked up the phone, "Stapleton here!"

"Mr Stapleton. Nat Jacobs, sir"

"What do you want, Jacobs?"

"He is threatening to reduce me back to the force, sir."

"What is wrong with that, Jacobs? I have been with the 'force' all my life."

"I am a Detective, sir."

"I am not sure what you are, Jacobs. I handle uniformed officers and I am pleased to say, that does not include you!"

"I've supplied you with information for years, sir. You promised me protection, if I fed you information."

"I don't recollect being in a position, to promise you anything, Jacobs, but in view of information passed by you, I will allow you to hang up this phone, and never call a Senior Officer again without permission!"

The phone went down, leaving Nat now dependent on Neville, with all the years of words and promises, vanishing.

Stapleton picked up the phone and made his call. "Stapleton here, Sir Sidney."

"Yes, Stapleton."

"My informant has been neutralised, Sir Sidney... Detective Chief Superintendent Owl, has blocked everything to do with Detective Inspector Jones, and his Sergeant, in every way—there is no information nor control over Jones anymore."

"Owl has cast his pearls amongst swine, Stapleton... don't worry about Jones anymore."

"Sir Sidney. The evidence was never fully recovered regarding those Jewels. We must take steps to alleviate that position."

"There is no position to alleviate, Stapleton... those jewels never existed—a set of a very few dishonest police officers invented their existence to frame an innocent man—those jewels never existed in the first place, and the people concerned, were never convicted, because the jewels never existed... no matter what anybody thinks! Jones can do what he likes, but we stand for fighting crime and the stature of the Metropolitan police Force! Was there anything else, Stapleton?"

"No, Sir Sidney!"

"Goodbye, Stapleton!"

Charles Stapleton put down the phone, and his head at the same time.

It was bad with the Press inches these days.

They at one point covered the pages with a large condom Photoshopped onto his head after another case he had buried at Sir Sidney's instructions.

Someone knew those jewels existed; broke in and stole them from the evidence room. And that was before he could get there.

The jewellery gone, but the responsibility according to Sir Sidney Talbot disappeared as well, leaving others vulnerable even though the stuff usually went missing after the trial; but this time, before the trial?

Why Neville Jones hadn't gone with it, instead of being the interfering fool he was… something… that meant others were involved… Jones should never have checked the evidence existed.

XVIIII

Neville admitted to himself that he was achieving nothing with this murder in Hammersmith.

He ran the routine through his head and it ran like a nightmare; someone comes down from Edinburgh, books into a B&B; has his brains bashed out and in… not… not something for the tourist ratings or reviews but how did the killer what who and where to smash their brains out – any neighbour could do that for him as they went mental, yet again but the killer was doing it on the street and that was wrong and not because of the crime it was the operation that was wrong and that annoyed Neville because it lack either rhythm or reason but even more it was being done on his patch and that meant it was aimed at him?

Nat went through the CCTV cameras in the area or at least claimed he did, but all of them were premise security that didn't look any further, than into the property and chasing Nat was a waste of time as he would have to do something afterwards for failure to perform his duty and he didn't need that.

No-one saw anything, heard anything—nothing was the clarion cry.

The Scottish guy was newly arrived and minded his own business. There was no robbery.

Perhaps someone disturbed either the killer or something that night.

Was the killer just interested in killing… who knows, and he certainly didn't?

Local police were hardly interested; most only worked nine till five and wanted everything to vanish so they got home… so he got it, with Nat to provide assistance—worse than any help as he had to rely on Nat's word which worked in tangent with his expenses. Pay them and Nat performed… don't *and Nat sulked and you got shit all.*

The local police knew Neville by reputation, and that didn't do him any good, either.

Once again it was time. He should actually make a move!

Euphoria at his desk awaited, as if he ever dreamt of being a top detective which had no chance of ever happening but now he was a kept man and officially crooked?

He felt he was already in a kennel… taking the doggy bags through the grill and just letting her dreams surround him along with the need for control, but he couldn't—deep-down—let that happen… it revolted his feelings of failure?

Antona wanted a dog, and he didn't want to think about some things she expected dogs to do in bed but she expected him to be there on time for meals and that was required behaviour unless he wanted the kennel and a doggy bag as an alternative to her work-outs as she caught up on lost sex?

The following morning he headed back and found his feet were still functioning… it surprised him…?

Local police were aware he'd moved in—it produced a few more police patrols going past the house until they lost interest again, as he'd done nothing to ever give them anything.

Albert arranged the car's service.

His life seemed dictated by Antona and Albert, although for the moment he didn't mind too much—but how long for was another question and what did a well-dressed man with no money wear—charity shop gear as the shonky shops had gone; how did you find a suit that never fitted and £5 later and 24 hours even later, it fitted you like a glove and stood as if you had been wearing it for forty years and smelt like it but at least it was your poor suit and not a case of finding your own clothing in the charity shops – being looked after hurt… because if you opened your mouth the clothes hurt like an iron maiden closing?

He needed something else but Owley would be on his back if he left Antona and Nat was on a permanent 'Speaker's Corner' to anyone who would listen and why was it, him they were targeted?

Someone caring, instead of kicking him was also a novel change, and he was learning to enjoy it… he just felt… deep down… he was in a prison camp with an issued uniform, number and camp routine enforced but again Antona passed that to Albert so she was not involved although organising it.

He finally made it back to Coombe Lane and was pulling up outside when Albert, as usual, met him and said, "The Lady is in the Lounge, sir. I will bring a brandy in after your shower. I have put some beers in the Room fridge. I'll just put your… car away, sir?"

He never liked to ask Albert where he put the car, but it was there the next day, and always seemed cleaner.

The lounge was his first destination… he briefly kissed Antona on the side of her cheek, as she came to meet him like a returning husband, then upstairs for his shower to No.1 room, where Albert as usual had laid out a dressing gown and ca change of clothing, plus the fridge filled—which no-one discussed; but it felt always the mark of condescension as he followed Albert, topping the fridge up, again.

He told himself he really was adjusting to this life of decent food, decent drink, and a decent bed as he showered, dressed and faced Antona again.

"It seemed almost like some kind of dream with Antona greeting someone coming home from work and now as he went down to meet her she tried to involve him within her family.

"I spoke to Amand today and told him you were staying here. Amand said, "I'm staying at 'Uni', so why should I *care* who you go with, Mother… I was expecting tantrums *from him*?"

"I didn't do any harm to them, Antona, so they aren't directing those comments at me."

"Three years' jail seems a little *excessive,* Neville, for not doing any harm."

"I didn't break the law, Antona, nor did I *sentence* them—your daughter *was* a criminal, and that put her away."

At that point the door opened, advancing Albert towards him with a large brandy, "You might require it, sir!"

As Albert left… Neville raised his glass, looking at Antona.

"You seem to have the knack of making people like you, Neville?"

"Well, it wasn't there before, Antona? I would have noticed?"

"Cookie is preparing something, a little different tonight, Neville?"

"That is good of Cookie," said Neville.

Neville thought of his disappearing clothing—by now it was appearing in all charity shops throughout Kingston; it reached the point that every time he took something off, he never found it again—thank God he didn't have dentures.

Antona liked him, but she was making him someone or something else—control that was gradually annoying him as another piece of his self-respect disappeared—and he didn't have much to spare.

The problem was he liked Antona and didn't want to challenge it… but… it couldn't go on or could it?

She was the first woman, who looked at him without apparent distaste but as an ex-lawyer who would know what her training was for law or a fool for liking her but how can you like a lawyer who controls you?

She somehow did it so he liked it, or did he, or did she or was it just protecting her as she said? Who knows as he certainly didn't and he treated what she was doing as a payment to a bent honest copper?

His mind wasn't at cross-purposes—there weren't any purposes left for him to cross.

The love making he would never forget but what in fact was she offering that didn't have a price on and where did she learn those techniques?

He was… he admitted to himself, becoming fond of her, and after all these years, he was finally facing a future, and a life at the end, but he couldn't face something that had something he couldn't understand. Life for him was shit. He could understand that—not a decent life—that was for others, but reduced to a robot was something that hit his finer sensibilities which he didn't realise he still had?

The bar stayed shut.

Some large brandies were allowed, instead of his usual number of pint mugs but Alfred also kept the fridge stocked, which he needn't have done and Neville respected this and just had a couple in his shower with the water running down over his head, like a secret rite of passage—putting the empties back in the fridge—replaced before he returned for the next day.

He looked at Antona over the rest of his brandy and saw her smile… almost reading his thoughts.

"There will be a bottle of red wine at dinner, Neville. That should be enough."

"It will make a change from the red varnish I used to drink, Antona."

"I am pleased to hear it, Neville, but I need you to see if you can use Roger's old computers."

"Why do I *need* a computer, Antona?"

"I am a *technophobe* and Roger would often sort out things for me on the Internet… perhaps you know *someone* who could sort out the machines?"

"That is not a *good* idea, Antona."

"Why *not*, Neville?"

"No involvement from me in Roger's affairs by order, Antona?"

"What happens?"

"It is better they stay *locked* until they are professional gutted and wiped. I don't know even now, the full extent of Roger's activities and I don't want to know… I am barred from anything but what they refer to, as Hammersmith, Fulham and Chelsea. They will not see me involved in anything else—I use the machines and if there is stuff on them—big trouble."

"So the machines need destroying?"

"They do need gutting as 'persona non grata' to the 'nth' degree, Antona—I can't go near them. They are your machines, but I'd advise you to leave them alone—who organised them, Antona?"

"I hadn't considered it like that, Neville. It will be better to have them wiped and replaced. I never knew everything that Roger got up to, in any detail, and I don't want to now. I'll put it in hand, and get some new equipment in… Cookie is ready for us now—all meat in large lumps, so you should be happy?"

"My stomach isn't sure whether to compress or expand, but Roger certainly stayed slim."

"Roger was always a crook, Neville, and lived off his nerves. A better set of questions might be… why did Roger ever try to be honest, and who killed Jimmy, Sasha and Alfred Stephens?"

"They have already stopped me taking on the Tanker Hijackings, Antona and they won't allow me anywhere near this or anything connected with it… I have so many people watching me I don't need a mirror to shave, they just nod when the razor is *ready* at my *throat*. The last attack in Africa took out Mark Stephens, and several of the large boats, plus many people and the UK powers want that seen as the end, so it doesn't taint the 'arms dealers' and 'politicians'."

"They're finished then, Neville?"

"They've lost most of the resources, and Roger's death ended all the hijacking activities—it had become personal by the end, and appears to be staying personal… Roger organised everything even down to the half full tankers to take the oil. Without Roger nothing could happen, so I don't understand why the guys were killed afterwards, unless it was a Government sponsored clean-up, to protect those in high office—the Gods might know, but they aren't talking to me, so I do not understand unless I am drunk and everything falls into a dreamless mess, and that finished when I moved in here."

"What will happen to you now, Neville?"

"I keep my nose clean, mouth shut… do exactly what I am told to do, and Owley will watch over me—break his rules and he will break me—behave and I will retire… misbehave and it will be a pyre to retire on; *additional* fuel added as required by Owley."

Much later, Neville once again found those dreamless sleeps that escaped him in the past, but at least he was not likely to get fat or thin on Antona's planned diet.

Antona was now giving him some exercise—as a wife does on the once only basis, but he seemed married every evening and the sweet jar was filling up as he put a coin.

The food was superb and carefully planned. So something else laid on his stomach?

The next morning awaited Neville, with a cup of tea in bed, leading to a shower, with the clothes laid out in the dressing room for him, breakfast already cooked, and his car outside the door when he had finished.

Neville headed for work to find Nat's car, still pristine in its parking spot.

He went into the office, finding Nat sitting there as usual, *holding* a grudge, "Nat, you can either accept what is happening, or get out… they changed our lives. I am not interested in tantrums, and you are lucky you still have a job? Either operate as my assistant, or be replaced."

The look on Nat's face would launch the Titanic at an iceberg.

Nat knew himself to be facing a rock, and a hard place, and they would be a holiday, compared to what he had now—Owley wasn't interested in 'tittle-tattle'—he had his own sources, which left Nat minding his nappies.

"Latest instructions, Nat. An email from Owley to someone copied to me. He says not to do anything about the killing in Earls Court. He wants to see the connection first to the Hammersmith killing. The Maastricht police contacted him under pressure because of the similarities with their killing and the Hammersmith one. He wants me to sit on it; do nothing until he decides. He wants me to confirm that both of us understand?"
"Yes," said Nat, "I had a copy."

"No doubt Owley will notify me when he requires action. Is there anything else?"

"Not as far as I know," and here, Nat almost choked, before adding, "sir!"

"Fine, Nat, and forget the sir… you only do that to annoy me—I'd better ring the Security guy to pass the news on, as per Owley's instructions."

Neville rang Maguire's number, and followed the usual ritual, although it was now on first name's terms, "Neville here, Thomas."

"Yes, Neville."

"Another murder, similar to Maastricht and Hammersmith. Possibly linked. Nothing further at the moment."

"Thank you, Neville."

Neville put the phone down, feeling like an office boy, but Owley had been explicit. He must make the calls to Security and always to Macguire. Nothing ever came back from them, but he reported in, and they acknowledged it, almost as if Owley wanted Neville known to Security and what did Owley plan now and was it to get him out of the police force completely?

XX

The only dull face in the registry office was Dirk Rentley, who accepted an invitation but did not get the reception for barring me from Cuddles.

Most of the rest piled in, and Basil Smyth, who had the reception (paid for in advance by me), was the main smiling face.

Several nights with Gris, were bringing back memories of Kensington, and being attacked in West Africa… I was seriously considering asking the CIA to fly me back to the US, and I didn't need a drink to make me look white, tired and drawn-out, Gris managed that the night before.

I thought I was fit, but I was fit for nothing after Gris!

A honeymoon was out of question on the grounds of International Rescue, and the Insurance Premiums for Space Flight… if they ever caught me!

I said to Gris, "Can you go easy when I kneel, only I don't think I can?"

"You'll manage it, Ralf, but you only kneel in church. Here you try to stay awake!"

"That is worrying me, plus the wifely comments already received!"

"Can you remember the words?"

"Yes… it embeds them in my mind, I didn't do it, it wasn't me and I saw nothing, Officer."

"About the marriage, you fool?"

"I am waiting for the police to run in, take the wedding ring and engagement ring, plus us, and the words are, I didn't do it—where did DUA *nick* them from?"

"Don't ask me, Ralf! I don't know what he is doing, but they must have been too hot to sell—we get the legacy in return for something DUA planned for the future?"

"Yes… A forced marriage—stolen jewels and a fancy house, paid for out of gardening leave… and yes, Gris, I do care for you."

"Make the most of it, Ralf… I don't know what he is up to—we are being set up as a target for something he is doing."

"Let's get the big house, Bishop as butler, and then we can say 'the butler did it'."

"That is not nice or funny, Ralf."

"I like it."

We rather destroyed the mood, and received some very severe looks, when DUA signed as a witness, and Gris said, "I wonder what name he is using?" I burst out laughing—obviously down to nerves.

Gris and I finally left before being thrown out and headed back out onto the street.

I had this distinct impression, our wedding hadn't gone like others—no fights and no family duels and Gris and I now seemed to get on, genuinely liking each other, and confusing everyone who expected us to replay past endeavours—as if I had the energy?

We headed back to 'Chistle', minus Dirk Rentley who swept off like some Lord—dreaming about lost money and headed back to his pub, minus his customers, who were now in the Chistle for the day, and minus DUA, who had already disappeared.

Bishop, in his new role, as our butler, had already been making the calls to my current Agents, and those for the new house—people forgot that Bishop was also a qualified accountant and manager, and could do more than audit a few lives, using the reducing balance depreciation method!

For a married couple, and I have to admit, looking at Gris, she glowed as the centre of attention everywhere and she was lovely when she wasn't kicking people, although I could see that starting again, if I tried anything—enjoying family rows, with a few sidekicks and head-butts, thrown in.

XXI

Dirk Rentley felt bad to a degree, for reacting to the Boy.

He'd left the police years ago, wanting nothing that revived old and forgotten memories, least of all of Shepherd's Bush. He'd taken an honourable retirement from the 'Met' as the rest did, and the last thing he wanted was dis-honourable memories surfacing.

Everyone had done it in those days. You only survived if you did. Passing the cut upwards also meant an easy get-out.

The crooks were doing it, so why not they 'Met' in the bar and both were a bit richer?

Hartland he'd fallen in love with and lived with and in Hartland, and that meant without memories of things long gone.
He didn't want them brought back now, but seeing that face was really something that came back to haunt.

Back in those dark days, when Government was even more paranoid that it is now, these guys would turn up; people would leave the cells, released to freedom as they were frog-marched out with no paperwork for them in or out and no 'habits corpus' either.
Rubber truncheons and rubber stamps were in fashion for those days with no signature on them.

There were always rumours about the 'freedom releases', but no-one ever came back to complain and the standard answer was we released them.

They disappeared somewhere and didn't reappear, unless dead, so what was the problem, although just one look at DUA turned his bowels to water, and he was water-skiing, when he next sat down on the loo. He never wanted to see that face again.

Shepherd's Bush in those days possessed a large Irish contingent—especially around the Hammersmith and Brook Green area, with their clubs, pubs, and you minded your own business by staying out of them.

People lived there, ran their rackets and the rest and were 'people alone, and if you found a sticker on the back of a machine, the IRA certified as paying a donation, you didn't look beyond it, because it was quieter if you didn't.

Your Sergeant and Inspector did not want trouble when they reported upwards, so you didn't provide trouble if you wanted a career and not a job at the shit-end for your career.

Dirk let everyone know he could that he'd seen DUA.

It protected him and he needed protection, if this guy ever recognised him, because of that one they took out one day who ended up in the river, killed on a bridge over the Thames, and left to float downriver to Hammersmith again.

He didn't want it again!

XXII

We eventually escaped from the Gristle. Bishop driving with us packed in the rear.

The wails from my body echoed every moment I turned. In my brain, my groin; everywhere that could have somewhere to tune in to it.

Gris took to marriage, like *a hungry cat* to an open fridge door, with her claws fully extended… unfortunately, she had reached for me as thoroughly, and being abused by her, was nothing to being felt by her.

You had bits, sending messages to other bits that were failing to *respond or sending excuse me letters from their mother*. I kept missing the bit about the dominant male *or any male part of me…* no wonder I needed a butler, or Bishop to say the last rites.

Bishop looked up in the mirror at me and said, "you look a bit the *worst* for wear, Boy?"

"Bishop. I look like the cat adverts, when the cat won't eat whatever they are supposed to, crossed with an attack by a *rabid* dog."

"You are a married man, Boy."

"To a *gorilla*, Bishop, albeit a lovely and *caring* one—just call me her banana, perhaps?"

"Everyone has a stag night, Boy."

"Before we marry them, Bishop… not afterwards—I am still sitting on the *antlers?*"

"Stop complaining, Boy. All you have to do now is hold a job down!"

"I can't even hold my pants, '*UP*'! Can you drop me at the nearest *Monastery*? I have an urgent appointment."

"It will have to be in London, Boy, and your Lady is looking peaky and quiet. It seems you two are getting on, or off, as the case might be or is it both?"

"That is the point Bishop, and far too often?"

"We get on… at the moment. I don't remember 'getting off'—said Gris—and you are as bad as me, Ralf?"

"You okay, Gris," said Bishop.

"Keep your eyes on your Boy, Bishop… I'm uncertain he is on protection now, but I could manage it?"

"DUA negotiated us some good deals—Boy, met most of the demands."

"Tell me that again, Bishop?"

"Financially, Boy, you are the sole one of us bunch with any funds in an investment sense. You have about £100K and a car. We have monthly salaries and allowances, but nothing besides that, so you are the man with the capital, and Gris has the jewels on rent."

"Remaining awake is my priority at the moment, Bishop… I'm uncertain why I should try. I live with Gris and you, in the hope someone doesn't bop me off—I cross DUA and I am 'open season' despite Government procedures. Tell me about those qualities I have, Bishop, and without the oratory?"

"You and Gris are *together*, and you work for Security. We have 'Garden Retainers' and that pays off for the house, and here and there for the team to settle. You are inside Security, we are outside, and DUA manages the team, even yet he is outside. You are still a target, and will be for a while, but Gris and I will be there, and you two can live together happily forever after."

"It sounds very pleasant to be truthful, Bishop. How many games are being played here… you tell me, I am a novice—West Africa taught me I wasn't – was it sufficient?"

"West Africa was a learning spiral, Boy. Multiply that '50 times', and if you are still alive, come get me—*if you can discover me?*"

"*Locked up*, Bishop," said Gris, "I lack sleep if Ralf doesn't."

"The Boy needs to *survive*, Gris, and this is his hard chance to gain experience."

"You sing like a star on a *mission*, Bishop."

"I am your butler, Madam. That is my mission."

"Well 'butler' this car home, Bishop!"

I felt Gris put her head on my shoulder, and I automatically put my arm around her. For a forced marriage, we seemed to do OK.

Things seem to go quiet for a while after that, and it was about an hour later that Bishop cut in, "why don't you buzz the Agents for the Coombe Lane West house, Boy—it is convenient enough to Putney to make a brief viewing date."

"Well Bishop, my Agents are waiting to hear that I will accept their offer to leave this property… probably a good idea to get things moving? I booked the appointment to view".

At last, it became mute for a time but questions arose again, "Bishop. For the ninety-ninth time, do you *really* know what DUA has planned for me?"

"As far as I can tell Boy, he wants information on what is going on in Security, so he can try, and get back in, and if that doesn't work, he wants you to transfer to France, as he considers some ideas for West Africa."

"*Why?*"

"He is a *Security* guy… I think he is being hurt… by… people who know his trade… what is really *hurting* him is being thrown out, and he wants something to exchange with the US to repay that; if he can't get back in. He wants in and *controlling* again—it is all he knows… all… yes… all he's usually achieved before—for all his soul's delight; DUA exists for… for control?"

"He must have understood that taking out Peres would lead to concern?"

"He lifted out Peres, because Peres found out about us. He couldn't take Matthews out, because Matthews knew very high things about him, and wouldn't have opened the door to him… the camera was designed to trace DUA walking up the road and he sent me—DUA *couldn't* take him out and if Matthews *continued to rule*, Matthews would shut him off and overrule DUA so I killed Matthews for DUA and you!"

"How was it managed?"

"The arrangement was, I would take Matthews out, he would get Peres, and thus we would look at getting you out of that hole. Gris and you by default are considered part of the team. *We put ourselves out for the team.* DUA believes there is a duty and don't ask me what it is. Did you know he paid for Prilloch and Meik, after their parents died? A friend of his, got into a drunken rage, killed both their mothers, and DUA killed him—then paid for the sons upkeep. DUA is a very odd guy, and one I won't cross, although I might kill him if he crosses me, but he is very quirky; dominant, and thinks in a world of his own and I don't want to be part of it but I am."

"Did he tell you I knew him in DQs? I was part of his Class 53 squad, to be smashed into the ground and have no chance of survival."

"No. He never mentioned it, but I doubt he ever forgot. He has a memory for people that is unbelievable. He doesn't forget anyone, although he gets *greedy*, and that is when he goes '*arse over bollocks*' and needs picking up. It is often just better to let him play, touch your hat to him, and get on with life before his ends."

"How close is DUA to this Meik character?"

"He wouldn't take him on. He said the blood derange Meik as much as his father did. Prilloch he can control. Meik is out-of-control. Prilloch will do what is told. Meik won't and had been nothing but trouble as he grew up. DUA won't have anything to do with Meik, even though DUA cared about his mother and paid for him."

"That is a side to DUA that I never knew existed."

"DUA is so twisted and torn… there are sides to DUA, even he doesn't know exist. What is the top speed of Nissan GTX, Boy?"

"196 mph, Bishop. 0 to 60 in 2.98 seconds, but please don't try. I don't want Gris' lunch in my lap; my lap is still sore, and she has hardly digested it."

"Your lap or her lunch as she is lying headfirst in your lap."

"Keep your eyes on the driving and the road ahead, Bishop. You are on the hard shoulder and that isn't *Smart Driving*!"

"Then why did you buy it?"

"*I didn't buy the hard shoulder*, Bishop and can you stay on the motorway?"

"Just checking out the car, Boy."

"*And my grave?*"

"No, DUA does that."

"I thought Gris was hungry and *if anymore runs down my legs she will be starving,* Bishop."

"The car, you fool."

"I've never had a decent car before, and I had the money. I wanted something back from Africa after the guys died that had something of substance and not another con job."

"Well, you certainly have that, and they left pretty quickly, I was told!"

"Mr Hoo was on a death wish. Who do I contact to get into Security, Bishop?"

"Macguire is the general connection, as they consider you family. Once upon a time it was DUA, but you had an offer, and that way you bypass Sebastian. Already agreed and just waiting for your holiday and marriage to settle in. I'll let Macguire determine in due course, and you go through HR."

"You OK driving, Bishop?"

"I must pull in soon, for a break, Boy, and we can grab a coffee with some more plastic food. Up to you if you want to drive for a while, but it will spell me."

"I'll drive us back for a bit, Bishop… The short-cuts after Heathrow are a bit weird. It will give you a chance to keep your eyes free, for anything interesting."

"You are learning, Boy!"

"I don't get a chance, do I, Bishop?"

"Alive or dead these days, Boy, so let's keep you alive!"

XXIII

Macguire put the phone down… *writing* out his 'not to reason slips'.

He wanted his pension as soon as possible—or so he wanted it to appear to everyone—with luck, he wouldn't need his pension, but the image had to be there of the middle-bureaucrat, who never raised his head from his desk… who needed to pop down to filing for his mental health; put the latest slips in and sample those *Ginger Biscuits* with his tea and tot. Perhaps the only thing that sanitise the day for him and his background?

He also needed to talk to Eunice about Romel—she could always sort the problems out—no matter how much Romel was sitting on him but Romel Sebastian was becoming a major problem for him.

Under his orders, he must do *nothing* without notifying Romel… he didn't want to cross that though, in case he received a *visit* from Meik, *whose reputation was already spreading.*

Sebastian was up to tricks—he knew that from instinct: but if he just kept his head down; left it for others to rise above the parapet; take the first apple in the eye followed by every other arrow although everyone in Security seemed fruit ripe for picking these days and green but he would be OK and he was still wondering what they would do with the Boy… he hadn't put that on his slips but his pants were hanging with the shit he could see.

The less Sebastian *knew* about the Boy and his links to Gris, the better, although Bishop had said to him, "Boy is a lot more competent all round, since West Africa, and will be a good Agent." Mind you Bishop was careful in his descriptions and Thomas did not want to cross a bunch of killers?

Now… was it a case of where, when, and how they used him, plus his usual monthly case of something from Bishop for information rendered or coming out of a drain to find his transport was an old wrecked bike with a flat tyre… better to stay where he was and deny everything whilst he licked whatever socially accepted arse as it passed.

Luckily again, this was no business of his; they could do what they wanted, to whom they wanted to, providing they left his pension alone, and he stressed that to everyone.

He wondered what DUA's team—all unofficially retired these days, were doing, since he was getting reports from Neville Jones which made no sense at all, but given that the man was a drunk… it made sense, strangely—when you thought about it? Anyone, it was not his CYA!

He knew they and a quiet life were incompatible; still it was time to pop down and see Eunice to find his biscuit, whiskey, and tea stewardess ready for action.

He'd known Eunice since he first started, and she seemed to have been there for years by then— must be ex-RN with a cup of tea in troubled times.

Hairs now grey and in a tight bun, but no-one touched her tea, tot, and biscuits… it made the day worthwhile, and his spirits rose as he descended into the basement. No fancy new building for him or her, just down for his tea and biscuits.

Coming through the door he met her, which surprised him. He had never seen her away from her desk before, "I'm surprised you never took that job in the new building, Eunice?" He said.

Smiling at Thomas, she laughed, "My job is in my head, Thomas. No-one but me knows where to find anything—machines are OK but we missed some files when we computerised, and we don't have the budgets any more to transcribe them, so they sit here for whoever needs to see them, and get updated by me."

"I have an update for some of my files, Eunice."

"And for your throat and belly, too, I would guess. Is this a one or two nips in the tea, day?"

"More and more these days, Eunice. I seemed to need at least two nips in the tea with the current bunch in charge. The days of a one nip afternoon are long gone—along with the days when it was worth being here and doing something decent—let's ride the toughness of the biscuits and tea after I file."

Thomas made his way to his filing, putting his slips inside an old file, as he always did. The files had his notes, slips and everything else that he valued for his pension.

Eunice would have his tea ready—one nip had long disappeared from his afternoon tea, but she would not let him have over three nips.

It was like putting on a decent overcoat when it was raining. You still got wet, but you didn't feel it so badly.

He sat down with Eunice, his tea, and he talked… it never seemed so bad, after he talked to Eunice… he felt he could cope—she would just sit, pour and listen to him, as he drank his tea and ate his Ginger Biscuits, taking care not to spit out the crumbs.

Charles Stapleton picked up the news of the murder in Earls Court, and rang Sidney Talbot to warn him—it was the second in the London area, "Stapleton here, Sir Sidney. There has been another murder –in Earls Court, this time—the same '*MO*' as the one in Hammersmith. What do you want me to do about it, Sir Sidney?"

"Nothing you *can* do about it, Stapleton. Under the rules it goes to Detective Chief Superintendent Owl at Homicide and Serious Crime Command… I can't start getting *involved* in every 'two bit' crime in London—I have a police Force to run!"

"Yes, Sir Sidney. Sorry to have troubled you. At least that idiot Neville Jones won't be involved—that we don't need!"

Stapleton always wondered about his former Bosses' attitude. Two murders in the same area—the first in Jones' patch. It made… made him… wonder… was Jones involved – it was still local to Fulham and Chelsea… maybe it was time he updated Bottomley – he was as much involved as the rest of them?

XXIV

Boy, Gris and Bishop *liked* the luxury, and the feeling of a house in Coombe Lane.

The Agent accepted Boy's marriage meant something bigger was needed, especially as he now needed a butler, and bankruptcy loomed after the Agent had his cut, plus the lawyers and the Stamp Duty… well we can't all work for the Revenue but compensation seemed to *issue from MI5 and Lance who was still waiting for King Arthur,* finally accepted the boil needed lancing and *Sir Lance-DUA-lot was needed for those ingratiating boils*?

Bishop contacted Thomas… Boy joining Security—whiskey delivery required, et al.

They talking about working in Security when the phone rang, "Probably the Estate Agents again, Bishop… wants a larger deposit, and why don't I consider Buckingham Palace—he can get a discount on it?"

"Ralf Johnstone here."

"Boy. It's Huron. How are you?"

"No longer actively working for the CIA, Huron. How did you bugger me?"

"They call us the CIA, Boy, not CYA as your country's Security is. It does still mean something in the US."

"CYA or CIA, Huron… you almost had me killed the last time. What are you after?"

"We want you to join the Security Service."

"Why?"

"We know you have an open invitation to do so, and we need to find out why we have so much data leaking from your bunch? We passed the information you were in Kensington, to DUA, so you owe us big… I am also to remind you, that you are a US Citizen with an oath and that someone is shredding our interests across Europe, and Russia—need to find out who is doing it… get them stopped, pronto – savvy, my friend?"

"What do you think a 'newbie' can do, Huron? I have no experience, no sway, no influence, and no job."

"Well, give my regards to your wife, who has some influence."

"Gris. Do you have any influence with Security, only Huron thinks you do?"

"I grassed us out of there, after Peres! Throughout as the door slammed up our backsides."

"I take it you heard that, Huron, through your listening gear?"

"That will change soon, Boy. You are back on the payroll now with us. £3K a month to go towards your new house, with no expenses, and don't forget your green card tax returns. Another £3K, if your Lady gets back in?"

"What do you want *me* to do?"

"Find out where the leak is and arrange for one of your friends to remove the blockage."

"You want us to find the leak and *kill* them?"

"I don't expect you to find them and give them a *medal*."

"Do you have any *idea* who is doing this?"

"*No*… they are passing information—causing a lot of problems for us on some Russian work—we want it stopped! The EU stuff is not so *badass*—we have someone in the French Security Service passing it back to us, so we know – the Russian stuff we don't know about until they use it and then it is too late. We've lost several Agents – taken a lot of collateral damage… the bastards *stopped* and someone we can trust in the Security Service is our modest request?"

"I take it, I don't have time to think about this?"

"*You bet your sweet ass,* you don't. You are back on the books and working… stuff it and we will drop people off, and don't leave the country—you won't get *far* from Uncle Sam. Enjoy your new house… congratulations on your marriage. Take care Boy," and Huron hung up.

"They must have this place, and my phone staked out," I exclaimed—shaking my head, "he just told me to enjoy my new house, and I don't even have one; enjoy my marriage… who told him that one… I'll be getting tips on sex, next but they will pay £3K a month into the account, with £3K more, if I can get Gris back into Security—I am not just being *stitched* up, this is *weaving a blanket*.

Gris sat there thinking, "They won't let me back in, Ralf, but there is enough a month to pay for the house, with some spare, but you are still in danger, Ralf… we both know that!"

Bishop threw his *half-pint* in, "Gris is right, Boy. You are still in danger, and the more people tagging you, the better?"

"Why is it I am so wanted? I don't even have the looks?"

"Put it down to your bank balance, Boy, it looks obscene—anyway we move in next week, so time to do some shopping."

"I don't know when we are moving in, Bishop… or if—"

"And I want a *new* bed, Ralf. I am sick and tired of you lying on top of me."

"We only got married on *Saturday*, Gris—I thought they allowed it."

"Not the way you *snore*!"

"She's got you *sussed,* Boy. Better do what you are told and order the bed."

"It will be curtains next, Bishop—measuring for carpets, and you bunch have bugged the estate agents—haven't you?"

"*Us—never*—we wouldn't do things like that. How long did you take the lease for, Boy?"

"Still waiting, Bishop—how long are they going to offer it for, then?"

As if on cue, the phone, and the Agent were off, "Mr Johnstone… just had a call from the Vendor—he would like to change the agreement."

"We haven't signed an agreement, yet… we've only just looked at the property."

"We prepare him to consider an offer for the property of £2 million, but with this late change, the initial option would be to rent for 3 months, and then buy."

"If I wish to buy this property, what would be my outgoings per month?"

"The market is competitive at the moment—the mortgage would be £8000 per month at 3% on repayment, which is about the same as the rent plus £1000 per month. I could probably arrange a 5% deposit on a mortgage which would cost you £100K down."

I passed the offer on to Gris and Bishop, before my body and mouth froze, with bankruptcy removing the rest of my assets.

"Ralf, this jewellery is worth that at least, even if we can't sell it. With your money, some agreement with Security, we could probably do it, and you'd still have £6K for the initial furnishings."

"From *riches to rags* in a week," said Bishop, "Go for it Boy, and we will look to get some furniture there, by Monday."

Before my mouth froze, I rang the Agent.

"Mr Johnstone, that was a quick decision."

"We'll move in on Monday, as we are initially renting—we can pursue the other option, once we have moved in."

"Thank you, Mr Johnstone… I will move on it immediately," said the Agent.

"What am I missing here, Bishop… this is all too convenient, and they construct a solution, before a problem arises."

"Don't worry, Boy—the Agent will be on the ball."

"I bet he will, but I will have about £85K left plus the CIA money, so let's go shopping."

"I have about £60K as well, Ralf," said Gris, "I never spent what I earned anyway, so we have enough to start."

"We'll manage, Boy," said Bishop. I've just got *debts*, but if there is any more money floating about—I can use it, and be *grateful*."

If Boy felt he had problems today, they soon parted into insignificance.

Within an hour, Gris had complete measurements from the Estate Agent—abetted by Bishop… who had obviously done this before, and the pair were reducing Boy's bank balance by the second and increasing the balance on his credit cards to a level, that Boy stopped laughing at.

At some point, Bishop rang DUA to update him—DUA thought it was hilarious—joining in with suggested purchases.

DUA was also talking of being there on Monday, as well—it was like *Bluebeard* turning up as the 'guest of honour'.

Boy in a complete daze… still wondered why DUA forced him and Gris, together—an unfortunate choice of words as Gris, in a peevish mood, reminded him as she wanted her horse to perform again?
It had worked out so far with Gris seeming happily married and enjoying herself… Boy could attest to that when he had his breath back. Buying a house—once again Boy felt *shafted*.

DUA was still *laughing* as he headed out to the house on Monday—Boy had always had some spirit in him—ready to be *knocked* out.
A lot to learn from back in his DQs days.
Bishop said 'he had *hardened* up nicely with some nasty streaks eventually creeping in from the West African operation.

The CIA involvement didn't really bother DUA… some arrangement with the CIA… yes… it already exist… it would fit in… yes… covered?
Easily sorted out as long as they paid both UK and US taxes and under various names he guessed?

There was always the rumour of someone else in Security, being on someone else's' payroll… no-one had put the finger on… them… well, at times it came close…? Them, though… no… no way any of his people would do that… ho bloody ho? They would have gone with Peres and the others, otherwise… wouldn't they?

Causing *trouble* was always someone *high* up, but Peres really messed the waters up, as had Christie and Matthews—who really knew who was leaking what to whom, or why.

Bishop had got the Boy out to West Africa, because he was dead if he stayed, and he survived—which did really surprise DUA but then possibly another for his little echelon.

Gris, he also had a soft spot for, and he couldn't really sell the jewellery, so giving it to them was a friendly gesture.

DUA wondered… if he was getting soft, but he was like a dog with *no legs*, out of Security, *just crawling around*—Security was all he'd ever known, or enjoyed – maybe Boy could find a way for him to get back, so what goes around, comes around.

They had already booked into a local hotel for Monday in Kingston—a base, while the house was set-up… DUA with Prilloch in tow had now joined Bishop in the house… Boy knew Gris would not keep DUA and Prilloch out—that was fairly obvious…? Enough people were around now as they started laying carpets, fitting curtains and getting ready, before furniture arrived later in the day—a lot of the work seemed to be people standing still, drinking tea and doing nothing, with complete pandemonium surrounding them until DUA moved in, and the excuses that 'it will a take days for carpets to settle in, and be finished, changed to 'it's finished', as they legged it, following discussions with DUA.

Bishop made a call to Macguire for standard clearance, in return for another crate of the *good stuff,* with Macguire pulling people out of Embassies, so they swept the phones and house—it was settling in by late evening.

Gris, Bishop and Boy stayed at the house, while Prilloch and DUA opted to go back to the hotel.

Half the rooms would probably never get used… there was the distinct idea that DUA had chosen himself a room, but the house was that big—DUA might as well get lost in it, and Boy could let him stay, but never repeat that in Gris' hearing, until she accepted the *fait accompli.*

Prilloch, however, was someone Boy didn't want around, but to change that, he would have to go against DUA, and he wasn't prepared to do that.

The other idea for the team that he could change, was that the team lived off Boy, Gris, and that would change 'toot sweet'.

Selling the jewellery was a non-starter, so the collection plate would be out—*post-haste,* but Boy had to admit that with his name on someone's list for *permanent retirement,* with a whip-round for the flowers afterwards meant this bunch were good to have around, but it would be 3 months before he had to buy the house, so he could see how it worked out.

It was quiet after that for weeks as they settled in… Prilloch seemed to have taken over the outside of the house as a Gamekeeper, working for DUA—spending most of his time mowing and feeding the lawn, which ate better than they did, and Prilloch already had some bird feeders put up, in the shape of human scarecrows: handmade.

The butler tag for Bishop, however, soon lost its humour, leading to a cook being taken on, after Gris had refused to cook, and they couldn't face any more takeaways—they also given birth to the handy-person as you have to not be sexist these days although who cared as long as the person did their job and DUA used all sexes if they did what he wanted. Killing in not a sexist operation just operational!

Boy had machines delivered for the gang, setting them up with their own links, emails, various internet linked TVs, and the entire house now seemed to bustle and hum.

Gris and Boy had a few arguments—it was his money being spent at a fast rate, but the rest finally paid for their upkeep, following some very abusive verbal attacks from Gris, who had a tongue, Boy was discovering that could trim hair, and finish up plucking your nose in flesh hunks—marriage was obviously changing her.

Neville ended his week, returning home on Friday for another official proceeding with Antona—riding a lawn mower around the grounds being her initial opportunity for the course. Then, while he preferred time to contemplate the murders, he was murdering some guttering up a ladder… he needed… he really needed to connect to the murders, but every time he sought tranquillity; routed out yet again: watching people taking away old computers and fitting new ones—eventually she gave him Sunday afternoon off; to sit outside!

Allowed 2 brandies—no beer, a decent red wine with dinner to compensate—plus his casual slob gear replaced. As the makeover continued and she made sure he knew she kept him, and he recognised it.

The main thing holding was Owley's threats and without Owley he would be carved up in seconds?

Dinner—the usual superb food, to someone who thought KFC was gourmet was enjoyed and finally at ten that night. Albert let him have the messages.

He found out that Owley had been calling him all weekend and told he was away.

When he raised it, she said, "You needed a break—a soft version of Alcatraz, and no-one got in or out—."

Spare was an understatement for the situation he saw!

Owley had tried 5 times to call him—Albert was the initial one he tried for.

"Albert, those calls were from the guy who runs my life!"

"Not in this house, sir," was Albert's reply.

"Albert, I not a prisoner here. I can accept, and deal responsibly with phone calls—I am a police officer and I don't need permission to be one!"

"You needed a break, Neville," said Antona.

"The break I will get is being out of a job and the only job I know how to do!"

"Then ring him instead of going at me, and my staff!"

"I will buy a mobile, Antona – is about time, I got up to date!"

Neville knew Owley worked long hours and picked up the phone, "Jones, sir. Only just got the messages!"

"Nothing you can do until tomorrow, anyway, Neville. I transferred Nat Jacobs with immediate effect. Silvia Nescott will take over from Monday. Your killer has struck again in Earls Court and it increases your jurisdiction for this murder, to include Earls Court—don't go beyond it."

"How far can I go, sir?"

"The Maastricht connection means it may not be local, so you will liaise with the Dutch police… no gallivanting about all over the shop… find out who it is, and nail him. Keep me updated and keep in touch with Security via usual channels. Understood?"

"Yes, sir."

"Goodnight."

Their faces registered disapproval, leaving him feeling he had done wrong, but he was a police officer—they had no right to hide phone messages.

Antona, once again reading his mind, said, "Roger had a set of mobiles. Take one of them. I wanted the weekend for us, before you go back to police work… I will lose you, and I don't like that, having lost Roger. I wanted you here because I am in danger—you are more than that now… I was going to surprise you with a car on Monday but you can't do anything until Monday, anyway."

"Owley said the same, but he got rid of Nat for me. The new partner is Silvia Nescott, who is a real detective."

"Bring her over for dinner tomorrow—we have spare rooms and now we need an early night!"

Neville woke up to the usual routine—a lot better than playing rush the boiled egg, and sober up in the shower, as he used to.

His old car disappeared on the Saturday morning—replaced on Monday by a car to match his age, but not his embarrassment…?

Did he really feel that bad as it was suiting his face—being red…? he appreciated… yes, that he could escape at any moment, and wasn't going to—so did she—or did she really assume he would carry on, regardless and so would she… that would… yes, that would be the question...?

He went out to the car, wondering what they had done to it, and looked at the old red jaguar that he had always dreamed about. No fantastic expensive car—just pure old beauty – Albert handed him the keys, the car documents, and there was his old police Parking Badge stuck on the window.

His Parking Badge, like him, had fallen off on the floor years ago but he could get that fixed later, by ripping it off.

It didn't fit in with his image. They adjusted even the seat for him—he looked back at the house, with Antona grinning from the bedroom, and waved.

He got inside, worshipped the purring engine, and moved off.

At Wandsworth, he didn't want to get out of the car… he just sat there, but it looked a bit odd so he forced himself out.

XXV

Romel finally *achieved* a meeting with Lance Jagodzinski—the Security Service Director… to authorise the Stockholm Bank raid.

He was struggling to determine his—well it had to be someone else's' idea… the strongest approach to use… that the British Taxpayers, Russian Agents and Politicians were using it as a haven for illegal money, and the action was *activist, ethical* and *moral*, not a political or security action seemed the best but he couldn't be seen to be involved when it failed.

He headed upstairs to the meeting and found Carmella Salters, and Lance Jagodzinski… Deputy as well as the Director waiting and not what he had planned which was a solo meeting with Lance?

"Come in, Romel. Take a seat," said Lance, "I asked Carmella to be here because Russia is her *specialist* area, and we've had plenty of trouble there—leading the CIA to *withdraw co-operation* from us and I am interested in 'Why'…?

"That is all finished with, sir… we need to move forward—we can't reverse what took place, and we can't afford to hole up on it."

"We can review it, Romel… several Agents ran into cover before the Russian Security hit them—"

"And we know the information being fed back was not from the CIA," cut in, Carmella… who did not like the way Romel was trying to sweep problems into the long grass—as if they had never happened."

"This is all water under the bridge," persisted Romel, "we have been through this before."

"Romel… they should have got to the Agents by knowing the names and addresses—they didn't… there wasn't a track and clean-up procedure, either—why not?"

"There was just pure harassing—playing games and trying to provoke a reaction—which didn't happen… A lot of projects leaked from here, including all those that Simon Askew knew," and no-one knows any other source, which I find unusual as Simon never knew the details," said Carmella.

"Simon Askew was an ineffectual fool who should never have been assigned to the Service… he was the guy leaking to the US, and Russians," hit back, Romel.

"Simon was no such *idiot*, Romel… he was immature, badly treated, and then *killed* on Matthews' instructions—DUA's team, and Kensington, should never have been *created*, never mind used as a killing, and torture machine, for the MOD and apparently for you as you authorised without my knowledge several arrests without arrest warrants?

"Simon identified someone with global connections leaking beyond what Politicians dare do, and beyond individual spheres of influence—no-one at a junior level, had that information or clout, and Simon stumbled onto them and tried to get out."

"If you knew this, Lance, why didn't you take action?"

"Romel… the PM *prevented us* from taking action against Matthews, and Peres—it was *left* to DUA to sort it out.

"We can only *warn* Politicians, and when the Politician's ears are *shut*, we are powerless to do more than watch—unless you have people, like DUA's team—technically outside of this organisation; being controlled by MOD who then take action but only under the auspicious of the Minister of Defence.

"We didn't *allow* them to take action, but we understand why they did, and that is why they are 'out to pasture'… although you *forced* DUA onto the Pension List, which was not agreed, nor authorised, and I didn't find out about it, until afterwards."

"That is what I wish to discuss, Lance. There is the Bank, and we also need to get those Agents out of Russia… I am asking you to authorise those two covert operations, Lance."

"Romel… you know that we disbanded the covert teams, and we also would need Political authorisation to restart them and given our current Government, I do not see that occurring."

"DUA was under the *jurisdiction* of the Defence Ministry—technically not part of the Security Service—they escaped the reviews… I… recommend… I recommend we resurrect the DUA Team under MOD control again and use them for both operations; apart from DUA, who is on pension."

"You have obviously—I hope… thought this through, Romel were the thoughts of Carmella…?—I do wonder how far this had gone, however. The last three international operations were all leaked before our Agents went in, which meant that whoever passed that information on, knew before the operations began what the operations were, and that was internal information that was leaked?"

"Leave the personal out of this, Carmella."

"But you are always personal, Romel…?"

"You are admin, Romel, so why do you have the information yet you give us no information. How do you know those Politicians have their money in those Banks… this organisation doesn't have that information; also if we launch an operation to get those Agents out, and someone discloses details of that operation, those Agents will be lucky if they are dead, never mind caught."

"That is why we use DUA's team," said Romel, "They are *small, close-knit,* and the only external person to them joins the Security Service next week, and is married to one of their operatives."

"Romel," said Lance, "We *don't* know who is *betraying* us and if this operation leaks then our co-operation with the CIA is destroyed for years."

Carmella chipped in, "How do you know of the Russian Politician's activities, when we have lost most of the information we have been receiving from the CIA, and we have no active agents in Russia?"

"We still have low-level people in Moscow; Lance, Carmella, and the *Press*?"

"Romel… are you suggesting I base an intelligence operation on 'Press Inches'?"

"You do it all the time, Lance… all the PM's requests are based on 'Press Inches'."

"What does the DUA team have that we can use Romel?"

"Bishop is an experienced Manager; DUA is a ruthless organiser, and Prilloch is a dedicated killer, plus the couple… Gris and Ralf Johnston, who have a *strange* array of skills."

"I suggest we don't touch it, Lance… we give it to the *Cousins* and stay well out," said Carmella.

"At the moment, Carmella," said Lance, "the only thing we can give the US, is a *cold*, and that they will not allow that. The current bunch of Politicians and SIC, will approve nothing for us to do, and if we tried, Politicians will leak it to the French and Brussels, before we can move—we can do nothing officially, nor inform our Political Masters of anything. Resurrect the team, Romel and I need to consider how we can use them… they will report directly to me—the only way I can stop the leaks. Now I need to discuss other issues with Carmella—please don't let me *keep* you any further, Romel."

Romel knew they would not keep him around for anything else that might be useful, and left.

The team would come together; fail, and he had enough to raise questions on competence to raise, and they would remain unanswered.

"I'll get onto it immediately, Lance," he said as he walked back to his office.

"How much do you trust, Romel, Lance?"

"I don't, Carmella… I don't know if that is *personal,* but I *can't* stand him? I've never been able to pin anything on him—he is professional, gets things done, but do I trust him…? *No,* I don't."

"Why are you prepared to agree to it and keep it secret?"

"I know, as do you, we have a mole… I still think there are two, possibly three, in the organisation, although one may be junior and one just leaking to Politicians."

"What about DUA's team… how trustworthy are they?"

"Carmella; Romel is wrong if he thinks DUA's team will just settle down and become normal human beings. They move into a new house on a Monday, and by Friday everything is running as if they had been there for years.

"Thomas Macguire recruited their extra staff via Eunice… the staff report back via Eunice—who reports to me, so I know what is going on there."

"You don't trust anyone, do you, Lance? Who have you got, watching me?"

"You are watching yourself. We, courtesy of Romel, seemed to have destroyed ourselves in the quality of people leaving… I think the second mole is in HR and linked to Romel, but I can't prove it."

"I am not forcing staff out, Lance—who is?"

"So far the pressure that puts good Agents on Gardening Leave with spurious excuses has come from Romel and Ewa, while the incompetent ones have been kept on and promoted. One high up, one medium and one junior mole… I am fairly *certain*… I am also sure that someone is protecting these people—DUA and his team will have a *third* target, and that is to take out the rest of the *Traitors*."

"Lance, we don't have the authority for covert operations, do we?"

"Those operations are not *covert*, Carmella. They are Security Reviews. They are definitely '*not covert*'. They preserve your job and mine, unless you fancy retirement at a *third* of your salary."

"I *get* the message, Lance."

Lance watched his No.2 leave… *risky*, but he now felt there were 3 moles at least in his organisation—destroying not only his contacts with other Security Services, but destroying good people in the organisation—wiping out his plans. By-passing his chain of command, without him finding out what Romel did, until it was *too* late to stop him—he knew he couldn't run a paper shop but the Government offer him the position on that basis and he just let it happen; now his staff were running rings around him.

Eunice fed him details on Carmella, who should run the organisation on a day-to-day basis however she was too technically involved in Russia with her delegating everything that did not interest her to Romel, and ignoring it, thereafter.

He might try to replace her as Deputy Director, but that might replace him, if he tried it in the current Political Climate.

DUA leading the 'Tea Kitty Collections' Committee would serve for all he cared, and he would appoint him to it—with Prilloch back on the staff for the collections, they should get some decent tea bags and maybe less pilfering of the money—one positive, already.

HR had to take the Boy on from Monday, and the rest of the team would be brought to life then, but the team would report to him—alone.

Macguire picked up his slips and headed down to see Eunice… it had been a quiet week, thank you very much.

Ignored by Romel and virtually everyone else, he headed down for his Biscuit, Tea, and a little filing.

Eunice was there as usual, with the words, "kettle's boiling, and I'll just warm the pot, while you do your filing."

Macguire headed for his usual slot, and slid his slips in for posterity… Eunice knew about them, but she was the only one—protection for his pension, really.

He headed back for his tea. "There's a rumour that DUA's team are being restarted," said Eunice.

Macguire almost dropped his cup, "DUA's team restarted—DUA's retired, Eunice. The team split around Departments and so on but on Gardening Leave courtesy of Romel—what does Romel think about that?"

"He was behind it, apparently—had a meeting with the Director, Carmella, and was given the go-ahead. DUA in some ex officio role—getting around his being retired… chair-manning of the 'Tea Kitty Collection Team', or something like that."

"That should stop them nicking the tea money, Eunice?"

"If he sends Prilloch around, it will."

"I'd prefer it if they stayed on Pension. Crossing DUA and having one of his team come around is not something I want again."

"I understand there are two operations, and they want to use them on those, so they shouldn't be around."

"I still don't like it… it is bad enough with Bishop. When will they tell them?"

"Letters on the way, but the Boy will be told on Monday when he comes in, and he shares a house with them. I've taken on some staff for them, who are on Gardening Leave, so at least it is all family."

"Who did you get, Eunice?"

"Agripina Bocek, Larita Ciborowski, Valene Highshaw and Darius Innocenti."

"They are steady enough at least, Eunice… shouldn't have got rid of them in the first place, but Carmella couldn't give a damn about anything that doesn't interest her, and Romel is in tight with that HR Director—Ewa Pollart…?"

"It happened before anyone understood, Thomas—a lot of good staff forced out by those two clowns, and Carmella still couldn't give a damn as long as she can play, as she wants."

"Yes… she thinks the Service is a playground for her, and her bunch, Eunice—one of her junior girls hangs around Romel a lot… Deadra Dimitriadis, so he has fingers in there as well—guy is like a spider with his webs."

"Well, Lance has decided he wants the team back, and Ewa has agreed with no argument— surprising really, since anything she has control over is usually fought for 'tooth and nail'…?

"This worries me more than Lance giving direct orders, which has never been his style, Thomas. He is far more a negotiator than a driver—how he got the job under the last Government, I will never understand? Are you going to tell DUA, Thomas?"

"I will keep well clear… I don't know what frightens me more—Lance giving orders or DUA coming back."

"Romel giving orders frightens me more, Thomas. I don't trust him an inch!"

"I'd better get back, Eunice. My filing time is gone."

"See you tomorrow, Thomas."

"And you, Eunice."

XXVI

Neville was back in the office on a brisk Thursday morning, and pleased to see Silvia was late. She was good, conscientious and professional and she could be as late as she wanted to, if she carried on like that… he needed her brains, not her body.

She finally came in, "I stayed on last night… I wanted to see if the locals produced anything, and we have something in Earls Court, sir…?

"Someone saw the victim with another guy half an hour before he died. They were laughing, joking and *loud,* which is why people remembered them—the problem is, the guys *looked* the same – most of them couldn't be sure whether it was the killer or the victim they saw. It makes any identity parade a joke. Both were 5 foot 8, stocky build, ginger hair, and they *seemed* like old friends."

"Why do I *feel* we are missing something on this killer, Sylvia? Has anyone been looking for Nat, by the way? I am sure there is some unfinished business there as well?"

"The Desk Sergeant said, 'cameras saw people near my car, but they've changed the name on the parking space—when they tried to come in further, they challenged them and they ran off' – local Bobbies say they are drug dealers."

"*Oh, no*. Nat wasn't that dumb—he…? No wonder he'd never moved his car."

"I'm *missing* the point, sir?"

"A police car park is the most *secure* 'in theory', place you can find. Cameras, police cars, Bobbies nipping in through the back door—Nat arranged for our parking spaces by the street – for convenience he said."

"I am still *missing* the point, sir!"

"*Talk* to Stephen Black, and tell him we think Nat was using his car as a drug dump, and pickup, for—"

The phone ringing interrupted this explanation, and it was Gloria Nantucket.

"Gloria, I wanted to pick your brains, if I may?"

"Go ahead, Neville."

"Two people's heads crushed by a blunt object, and a connection to Maastricht, which Thomas Macguire considers is security related."

"No-one has spoken to me about Maastricht, Neville—No information at all on it, but Macguire is like a cat 'worried about his nine lives' – everyone forgets about him, apart from Eunice stroking him, until his whiskers twitch. If he thinks it is Security I would trust his gut feeling. He is such a scared cat that he sees problems in everything, but he is a good guesser – if he thinks Maastricht is a Security killing, then he is probably right."

"And if they link it to the other killings, then there is a Security killer loose, and killing for fun— Gloria, you are invaluable. Sorry we have halted your work."

"There is no work, Neville. Come back if you need anything else!"

"Thanks, Gloria!"

"Silvia. Get onto some forensic wizards of ours and ask them to look for plastic in the heads of the victims. It may be cling-film, it may be a bag, but I want them checking for something in the hairs on the victims' heads, which may have come from something wrapped around the weapon, and embedded in the skull of the victims."

"Doing it now, sir. I spoke to the Desk Sergeant while you were on… he is having the word put out that Nat Jacobs no longer works at the Station, but he would not go any further."

"*Shame*. Nat deserves it for drug dealing, and we can't get him on it, or prove it…?"

"On the murders, any evidence is w*iped* by now, and all we have is another plastic bag."

"No wonder they want them *abolished*."

"I think that is to do with the *environment*, sir."

"*People* are the environment, Silvia, and we will try to prolong that."

"I'll get onto forensics, sir."

Both Neville and Silvia spent yet another day just sat there with nothing happening…? Neville sitting there, thinking—all I need is another killing when I am off duty, to piss off, Antona.

As evening drew in, Neville looked at the clock and got up to keep his routine with Antona.

"Don't stay late to get the results, Silvia. They didn't do the work in the first place, and we won't have anything until they redo them, providing they still have the bodies and haven't shipped them somewhere where someone has cleaned their hair to make them look good, before burying them?"

"Go home, sir."

"On my way, Silvia."

Boy and Gris walked up to the desk at Security, and *identified* themselves—Boy with a UK passport, and Gris with her Security credentials.

Both filled in the 'lie about yourself sheets' for *external* visitors, and found themselves escorted to HR, where they met Ewa Pollart, whose opening comment was, "You seemed to surrounding yourself with Security people, Ralf?"

"No. I just sleep with one, Ewa. She is my wife."

"You seem very sarcastic, Ralf?"

"I am merely wondering, what business is it of yours? Are you trying to provoke a reaction? My file speaks for itself with stressful situations, and Gris, who is with me, is a person who tortured me in a Secret Prison. What is your point Ewa or are you just playing games?"

"I am the HR Director of the Security Service, and I will have respect!"

"No Ewa. You will earn respect… I don't need you—this is part of an arrangement, agreed under a legal agreement, and it does not need you! I am happy to walk out of this office and restart my legal complaint against this service – I do not need you."

"Against my wishes, the team under the responsibility of DUA is resurrected, and you will form part of it, as will your wife. The team will work under the direction of the Director of the Security Service—you will report to him. You are now operational within the Security Service.

"Goodbye and I suggest you alter your attitude, if you wish a career in the Security Service."

"You are most kind, Ewa. I'll look forward to avoiding meetings with you for as long as I can—your attitude is something I don't need, don't care for, and you can suspend me any time you like… let's get out of this joke, Gris, while I am still being pleasant." I turned and walked out.

"You need to control husband, Gris!"

"The Security Service needs to control you, Ewa," snapped Gris, opening the door, and caught me up outside the building… "You have made your point, Ralf. Don't push it."

"Of all the most arrogant, ignorant, bigoted fools—?"

"But you are improving, Ralf!"

With that blistering comment, Gris was lucky to make it down the stairs!

XXVII

Neville finally made it in the next morning, after the usual routine with Antona to find Silvia already ensconced and by the look of his desk had been tidying up there as well, "Silvia, can you contact the locals at Earls Court? I would be interested in anything they have, although this guy doesn't seem to leave many clues. Hammersmith and Maastricht have produced nothing, perhaps this might give us something?"

"I'll get onto it *now*, sir."

"I'll drive down, have a look at the areas. It might give me a better feel for why he kills… Nat should have found more forensics. Can you see what happened to them?"

"Doing it now, sir!"

Neville headed out to his car for the pleasure of driving it down to Hammersmith.

He knew the area to a degree—the Broadway was about half a mile from the site of the killings.

Standing at the corner, he could see the buildings opposite—the CCTVs all pointed *downwards*—the sites would have been closed… unless the cleaners had seen something.

Was it truly random, *though*?

He needed to see Earls Court, and the pattern repeated.

Neville headed back to his car, and Earls Court.

He noticed again at Earls Court, that it was a long road, with the murder happening at an intersection—he felt it was a pattern, but were the killings *random* or set up and what was the pattern—hardly a country dance?

It seemed the murderer was making *sure* he was on a long road, to let him see if anyone was near, and waiting for someone to come, or he was with his victims and knew them—was he grooming them to be killed?

Neville headed back to the office—with Nat gone, they would at least work as a team but Nat and he had always worked as a dirty, corroded team and now he needed to buff his act up and that was something that didn't appal him, anymore..

Neville arrived back—pleased to see the new car in Nat's spot.

Nat was probably still around in the Arndale—most likely in the car park.

He came back into the office, and Silvia looked up… "anything of interest, sir?"

"The places they were killed certainly have similarities. A long road, a join to another road, and he kills on the corner."

"Both guys were *Scottish*, sir. Both recently from Edinburgh. Both staying in B&Bs. Both have sandy hair, same height and build, and there the similarities end. Why would someone kill similar people in two different areas?"

"I don't know Silvia. I keep wondering if he knows them."

"Maybe he is Scottish himself, sir?"

"Why the same description, and why Maastricht—apart from the victim being Scottish, again."

"Maybe he travels, sir?"

"The guy in Maastricht, was a banker called Jimmy Mackintosh – part of an International Tanker Hijacking Group… a *long way* for a South London Serial Killer to go, when Bayswater or Victoria would do just as well, and be more at *home*."

"What could be the connection, sir?"

"I cannot think of a connection between Earls Court, Hammersmith, and Maastricht, unless he was in Maastricht, saw someone matching the description that makes him kill, and *killed* because he enjoys killing. Maastricht is the odd one out, but they *organise him*… that I think is certain."

"Who organised him, sir?"

"Someone, but I don't know who?"

"What is bothering you, sir?"

"I'm damn certain it is the same guy. I'm also damn certain he works for Government but DUA and his gang were nowhere near when the killings started. Someone has taken out all *the Roger gang* apart from his ex-wife and gone abroad to continue the killings—I'm missing something and that rankles as I can't or they wont let me see the relationships and who is preventing me from seeing them—now I feel I'm being used at the 'fall-guy' but Security know who it is. I'm damn certain they do and who has authorised the cleaning up and destroyed the forensics... I don't know and it appals me?"

"Do you need anything from me?"

"Nat said the locals had gone around the pubs with photographs. I asked him to double check, and I need to know if he did and they did? If they didn't go around, I need the police to go around the pubs with photographs of these guys and pronto, before everything is lost."

"Do you know Nat has gone back to Wales, sir?"

"No, I didn't."

"Compassionate request, sir."

"That was fast as his wife doesn't live in Wales but about twenty miles away and he hadn't been home in months. I wonder what he was *passionate* about, Silvia? It certainly wasn't police work, and he wife doesn't live in Wales… if you get bored find out why."

"Yes, sir."

Thinking about the killings, he knew there was a pattern, and it was Scottish, blond, recently down from Edinburgh, but why was he waiting at corners to kill them, if he was waiting until then and why he was killing across countries?

He returned to the Antona standard ritual, but refused to go into the house, sitting down in the garden to look at the view, and tried to wonder why the killings were happening.

It was not like a corner shop where you could pop out to pick up a late one if you had run out.

This guy was finding them and killing them, and he needed to think out how he was doing it. Was he finding them randomly or targeting them?

They were all down from Scotland, so did he know them before they moved down or pick them randomly from Kings Cross or the Coach Stations?

Antona came out to him and sat on his lap, which was fine as he wasn't using it now, "This is worse than Roger, Neville?"

"I am trying to stop people being killed, Antona. Not killing them!"

"That is unfair, Neville… I never understood, or I suppose, I never wanted to comprehend, what Roger did. He planned it—I lived off it and I cannot change that. I won't voluntarily give the money back… the Government will take it anyway, so who ultimately is the crook, squandering money for their own desires…? I kept the bar room *shut* until I felt you could treat it with *respect* – Albert has opened it!"

"I have an idea, Antona, and it is not about *controlling* me that matters—everyone seems to want to do that these days, anyway…? I can almost feel the person who is killing these people and I am damn certain it ties him to Security and he is an MI5 killer and MI5 are allowing it? They know!"

"Why would random murders have anything to do with MI5?"

"Maastricht, although I can't make it, make sense…? I know they are Scottish and apart from Jimmy Mackintosh—newly arrived—moving down for a job and coming from Edinburgh. Blond, 5 foot 8…? Someone has to know and is allowing them to kill within a *fortnight* of their arrival, but I cannot *find* the connection and until I do; people will *die* and that is because of me and what I cannot see?"

"You *care too much*, Neville… you can't do anything tonight?"

"I know Antona, but if I don't, who *will*?"

"Come indoors, Neville!"

"Yes, love."

"First time you've said that, Neville."

"I am learning, Antona, and learning I like you, but I knew that the first time I saw you. Maybe that is why I am here, and why I was so *aggressive* towards you. 'I *love* you'."

"You say that to a Lawyer, Neville… leave the words in the air and I will walk through them and enjoy them—when I have the time for leisure—if you stay?"

Neville slept the night soundly, as he seemed to do now. No phone calls, no distractions, a comfortable bed, decent food and Antona. She could put a ring through his nose for this kind of life and already had.

Neville went through what was by now a standard morning routine and arrived at the office to find himself in before Silvia.

He sat down when the door smashed open, and Silvia arrived, "Sorry I'm late, sir."

"Don't worry about it, Silvia. It is what you do that matters, not breaking your neck to get in before me. I leave that for control freaks and there are enough of them… I am not the Boss where the clock matters more than performance. We work many hours, and we need to do it in a civilised fashion, so leave the door on its hinges next time, Clockwork we can leave to the uniforms."

"I got a photograph of the victims from forensics, sir, and the locals are going around the pubs tonight, about half an hour before the killing times to see if anyone recognises them, and anyone with them? If there is another killing, we might need some more people, sir."

"I know that although until I have something, I won't raise it with Owley… he knows how I work and that I won't contact him unless there is *something*…? At the moment there is a *puzzle* with several bits missing. Unless our murderer thinks big, I still don't understand the Maastricht connection… why did he killed there—was it a random killing, with similarities or just a co-incidence?"

"We sit and wait, sir?"

"Yes. We can't afford a wild goose chase, so we take our eyes off the ball and miss something although I am missing something…? The 'pictures for now' and 'a bit of luck' I think. Warning people 5 foot 8, sandy-haired and travelling from Edinburgh to be careful might be one ploy but I would be laughed out of town if I did that, after the Press created all the mayhem and fantasies— more than you would get from a bunch of gossiping neighbours—still it is all we have to go on."

"Have you considered, sir… we could give a general warning to the British Transport police. Ask them to keep a general lookout on trains from Edinburgh, as people recently travelling down were killed. We need not be too specific, I think… just anyone seen hanging around regularly, when the trains come in should be approached with caution."

"It is nice, Silvia. I should have thought of that. Go for it."

"What are going to do, sir?"

"Pray the killer breaks his neck."

"Are you a religious man, sir?"

"Only when I swear, and I need to ring someone in Security—it happens from time to time… usually to report as per Owley's' instructions, but this time I need to talk to someone."

Neville picked up the phone and rang Thomas Macguire.

"Macguire here."

"Neville Jones. Thomas. Am I allowed to talk to Gloria Nantucket on a non-security brain seeking desire?"

"Why do you need to speak to her, Neville?"

"I've got two people dead in London, and another dead in Maastricht connected with Security's previous operations, but it is the same 'style' – I need to pick her brains, using no weapons."

"Are all 3 murders related to *Security*?"

"I don't think any are, but I don't know… two could be a serial killer, but they could relate the other death to the previous killings."

"I cannot let you talk to her about the Maastricht killing, but the other two are outside of our jurisdiction, and it is up to her."

"Are you saying the Maastricht killing was Security, Thomas?"

"I can't say, and I wouldn't if I could. It is up to Gloria, if she wants to talk to you."

"Ask her to ring me, if you would, please."

"I have your number—I will pass it on."

Thomas Macguire put down the phone… there would not be a slip to Romel on that one, just one for the dead man's handle in filing.

Neville never trusted his thoughts as often they sang to him and then he needed a drink to subdue them and then his brain tried to address the rest of him and re-act to a question which required another drink?
"Do you think he will pass the message on, sir?"

"He'll pass the message on, but he worried me about something… he said, 'I cannot let you talk to her about the Maastricht killing, but the other two are outside of our jurisdiction, and it is up to her'."

"Why does that bother you, sir?"

"If Security isn't involved in the Maastricht killing, why can't I talk to her about it? Does that mean that Maastricht is a security killing and the same style as the local killings? Is there a security killer on the *loose* as a serial killer?"

"How can you find out, sir?"

"Wait for any feedback from the Picture Show, and the British Transport police—I don't see any other choice… all the information from forensics is a blunt instrument about 6 inches long—able to smash a skull in.

"I pray there are no more murders, and that the Press don't find out before we can catch the bastard but it is probably a forlorn wish."

Neville then went quiet; sitting there for a good hour staring at the wall and suddenly spun his chair around to face Silvia.

"There is something we could do, Silvia… get the photographs reproduced and sent out to Scottish Clubs, Dance Halls and anywhere in London where Scots meet up. Keep it mild, and say there have been two deaths recently, and if anyone knew the victims please ring us. Perhaps we might strike it lucky, but at least they'll see us doing something."

"I'll get onto it, sir. The local Bobbies will know where to send them, in their areas."

"And it is the second request we've made so they might get off their arses. I'll wait for Gloria, if she rings although I've gone through this route before and I am just repeating myself?"

Neville was still sitting there five hours later, and he wondered whether they had ever passed the message on.

Wednesday night, and he'd got nowhere!

He put his coat on and headed home to Antona, and the nightly ritual, leading to the daily ritual and back in the office next morning, with still no call from Gloria again.

"Leave it, Ralf. We need to let DUA know, if he doesn't understand, already… let's head… yes, lets head back home. What's put your nose out so much, Ralf? You rarely lose your temper like that."

"I want to go berserk. She is an Agent. Something from the guys in Africa—it leaves a smell… Agents… they cannot… yes, they cannot trust anything, or anyone anymore—like a skin disease, or an STD you can never lose, because the stink becomes systemic."

"Let's get home, Ralf."

Boy and Gris arrived to find the entire team sat in the lounge reading their letters, which had been hand delivered, marked Secret, with one for Gris, waiting there.

DUA looked up as they came in, "They take all of us back on. Me as an *ex officio* as I am on Pension and they sticking us in an annex near Brixton underground station.

"I am appointed to the Tea Kitty Committee, with the rest of you reporting to me. What did they say to you two this morning?"

"Nothing much, DUA… Ewa was trying and succeeding, in riling Ralf, but Ralf raised the point which I hadn't picked up on, that she was more interested in trying to provoke a response from him and get feedback, than in interviewing him…?

"Ralf stayed on message and she got nothing, but she didn't even try for an HR interview," explained Gris—she was deliberately aggressive and attacking.

"She is an Agent, DUA… they cannot switch off—never leaves them, I saw it in some guys in Africa."

"Well, I've got to see Lance, Monday week, but we are *on* the Payroll from today, so there is a week before we report…? I know the place in Brixton, Boy—apply for one of the underground berths at the site. They owe you, and you'll probably get one —the rest of us will get the local car park."

"One other thing, if we can, DUA—?"

"OK, Gris… I can guess it; finally there is a request from Boy and Gris. As of now, you've taken on four staff, plus the upkeep here. They need you—I also need Lance to put more money in—so put your hands a bit further into your pockets. We are all officially off Gardening Leave, which leaves us with a lot more money coming in so I suggest that a £2000 house allowance (all-inclusive) a month each, to cover everything if appropriate but I will rattle Lance's chains for the sake of it and it won't break us. The house seems to work out well. Apart from that we will probably need a Gardener as it occupies Prilloch."

"Leave the garden, DUA," said Prilloch, "I can do that when I am not working. I want it looking good."

"Fair enough, Prilloch, but *use* Darius when you can—you will be busy."

"DUA… and then she was thinking some more… Ralf has some deal with the CIA, who will pay me £3000 a month, now I am back with Security. That puts me and Ralf on a lot a month each… I didn't agree with that, but it will happen and I don't want to tell Ewa."

"The Accountants can sort it out at the end of the year, Gris, but I don't intend telling Lance, you are *both* double agents—it would rather destroy his faith in you? If he still has any faith?"

"Fair enough, DUA… let… let the money be as it is for now. No-one has much money and we can let it build up."

"Gris. We are buying and furnishing, here—Gris has married an American English Citizen, so the income in the US, is neither here nor *there* but the taxes are—which might leave us a *nice* little nest-egg or the UK and US fighting over who can tax us the most."

"Guys," said DUA, "There is a week off now, so let's take it *easy* until we get the pressure and that will come. Given the largess of Boy and Gris, plus our contributions, I *think* another member of staff might be in order—I'll get Valene to talk to Eunice again – someone to help Larita Ciborowski to make a good housekeeper, and that gives enough coverage, if there is trouble."

"Just the one *question,* DUA… what were Darius, Valene and Larita's specialist areas?" I asked as more and more—this sounded like a setup?"

"Boy. Valene was coding; Darius was special tools and Larita was Eastern Europe to the Russian Borders, as an analyst."

"We are building our own organisation *through* you and Eunice, DUA, aren't we?"

I pushed it further. It was being set up and controlled yet again. DUA was hiding what was going on and I needed it opened up.

"They are *good* people, Boy, and you had better *update* your contact—if he doesn't know already."

Bearing in mind DUA's instructions, I rang the CIA to speak to Huron, "Good to hear from you Boy. What is the news?"

"DUA and team resurrected—all taken back on, including Gris. I'm finding out more, next week, why—based out of Brixton – DUA is in this, up to his '*pointed ears*'. We are taking people on for the house, but all ex Security on Gardening Leave, so we are *covered and controlled by Security*, but for what?"

"Sounds like you are building an army there, Boy. We've got a guy you might want to take on, as he will have direct contact with us and a high Security classification. There is information we can't give; even to you on some matters. We'll pay him, but you fit him in, somehow—his name is Marcel Datri."

"Bear with me on this, Huron. I need to speak to DUA," I turned around and shouted over to DUA to get attention.

"DUA, the Cousins want to have someone in the house. Name of Marcel Datri. They will pay for him—do we take him?"

"Prilloch hasn't got his Gardener, yet, Boy."

"We'll take him on, Huron—officially as a Gardener—what is his specialisation?"

"Deep engineering."

"Hilar*ious*, Huron."

"He'll be with you, *ASAP*."

"OK, Huron… at least… this house has seven bedrooms and at a pinch the utility—there are four of us, 4 staff and now, one of yours—he is going to have to *doss* down in the utility room… we are out of bedrooms… eight of us plus Marcel."

"He's slept in worse?"

"Fine, Huron. *No* more people please, though. This isn't the Lady?"

"See yah, Boy."

"What's the story, DUA? You was there *before*?"

"They don't trust Security, and don't really trust you… Lance will know… he'll know when the staff report back, and he will accept it, as it is outside of his control—he doesn't have any choice— I'll know more when I see him, but providing Marcel is *good*, we *live* with it."

XXVIII

Neville sat down in his office… Friday, and no more murders.

Forensics did check their hair and were curious why both victims had cling-film in their hair, but had put it down to a co-incidence—now their ignorance was too late.

They hadn't come back on why he asked the questions, which worried him, as they seem to do a basic job about anything, and if it hadn't been for Gloria, he would not ask them the right questions.

An *International Serial Killer* was the *last* thing he needed nor did people at large.

Silvia came in and didn't bother with the 'sorry I'm late apology'. She obviously liked her mornings. The same as he did—before he met Antona, and the regime now imposed on him.

Antona, once again, planned for the weekend, but he didn't know what and she still couldn't understand he was a police officer and not a toy doll dressed in blue to his mind.

His clothing standards had now risen from the Charity Shop to John Lewis.

She had broken him from the shonky shops so it wouldn't be long before he'd look like an MP on expenses or a Chief Constable on brandy at £45 a shot.

Antona meant well, but she was becoming even more overbearing as he wasn't resisting, and that was the price for living with a dominant woman, but at the moment he needed peace to think. Still, it was Friday, and no more murders.

If it could just hold out and he didn't believe that it would, but if they found someone of that description using Kings Cross Station and arrested him, any QC would destroy it before the trial started.

He needed something off the plastic, and he still kept thinking of Thomas Maguire's comment, which was almost automatic that Maastricht was out of his jurisdiction, as they linked it to the Security Service.

Who had authorised the kill in Maastricht, and why?

Saturday coming up worried him. He should out there patrolling, or the locals should.

"Silvia, can you *coax* the locals to have some 'feet on the beat' in my areas? This guy is targeting it—possibly on a Saturday? I have to give Owley an *update*, and it would be nice to say that."

"Will do, sir."

Neville then rang his 'nemeses cum' Boss.

"Jones here, sir. No positive news. Using locals as much as possible. Link to plastic in the hair. Think Maastricht is Security linked. Nothing to go on. BTP co-operating, as are local police, and thank you for Silvia."

"I get feedback, Neville. You haven't asked for more resources, but I am pencilling them in. I don't know if there is another killer, but killers are weird. Plastic in the hair was a good one. Gloria is good, and wasted where she is, but leave her be unless you need her, and they will release her to you."

"Anything else you can tell me, sir?"

"Not a lot, Neville… Security… yes, Security seems to be… going through a lot at the moment. Have an enjoyable weekend, and let's hope, a quiet one, and yes I knew about Nat's other antics, and he is helping police with their enquiries in Wales, before the gangs get to him. Goodbye."

Neville put the phone down, and never ceased to wonder how Owley knew everything, before he told him, still those were his instructions, so he might as well obey.

"Just been told to go home, Silvia. The Boss instructs, and I obey. Let me know if we get anything. They will pass the calls over, now."

"Will do, sir."

Neville headed home and Silvia *rang* her Boss in Special Branch, to *report*, which she knew went straight back to Detective Chief Superintendent Owl, but she reporte*d* and another person *watched* Neville Jones from the back of a long queue—had they but known or Neville knew?

Neville finally made it back home, joining Antona in the lounge, before his shower for a change… yes… why the change? What the hell was going on?

He supposed he just wanted to do something different, although he felt that was now also a routine and was being provoked to make him react—he was getting sick of control freaks working through a manual—he felt that if he told Antona he had been kidnapped, and ravaged by wild Indians on the way home, she would just nod, and ask him how his day had been, until he got it right in her eyes.

Albert, as usual, had delivered the door opening, car parking and brandy dispatch, as per schedule, and then Antona looked up at his face.

"You're getting *bored*, Neville, I thought you *would*?"

"I am just not used to being so *controlled*… you have done what you needed to, and I accept that."

"But you are not happy with it?"

"Who would be, Antona? I can only change so *fast*, and work is changing; as my own life changes. I won't go back and *blow* my mind on drink again if that is what you are worried about."

"I've tried to push it too fast, Neville—taking over, when there was no resistance, is not a wonderful decision… yes… yes, I think… it changes the rules. You can come or go, as you choose but let me know when you will be here for dinner, please?"

"Routine stays the same, Antona… I have… yes… a bloody serial killer… and perhaps another murder investigation, and if that rears its ugly head—I need to know what is going on and they need to know where, and when I will be. I am deliberately being kept in a dark hole like the games I had before as people play with me… why… bloody why are they picking me?"

Antona ignored him as she had started to do like a hard hearing wife, "Fine… now… have your shower—it is better if you have it, before the brandy."

Neville finally left the shower with a feeling that the day had thrown him out and headed for the clothes laid out for him by Albert.

XXIX

Downstairs… he found Antona holding a phone up for him to take—Gloria Nantucket, needs a word, Neville.

Neville dialled Gloria's number, "Mr Jones. I have just been told to ask you, with your Lady, to be in Richmond Park by Robin Hood Gate, tomorrow at 2.00 pm. Goodbye."

Neville nodded to Antona, "We have a blank invitation to be at Robin Hood gate tomorrow, Antona. 2 o'clock. No names."

"Do they want me there, Neville?"

"Security wants you there, Antona."

"Who wants the meeting, Neville?"

"No idea, but I suggest we don't disappoint them"

"Dinner is ready—let's eat, Neville."

DUA put the phone down… being summonsed, he could understand, but Bishop, Boy, and Marcel also being summonsed, *surprised* him… he *ran* his team, and they took orders—they didn't *join* in the decisions so who was behind this or were they just Politicians worrying about Blair's pensions.

Gris would also demand being present, which left Prilloch as the very odd one out, who would rather mow *grass*, than bodies, these days.

By some kind of *informal* order, they all gathered in the primary room at 8.00 pm every evening— awaiting updates—DUA said what they would do and gave explanations, and tonight his words were; core team were meeting at 2.00 pm in Richmond Park, tomorrow and don't ask me bloody why?

Lance Jagodzinski *enjoyed* taking his family out to Richmond Park.

The deer were there and providing it *wasn't* in the rutting season it was *harmless* enough—giving him a chance to *reach* his agents, elsewhere from Carmella, Ewa and Romel.

He considered w*ho* he could *rely* on now. It diminished in the afternoon and increased by the evening.

He speculated *at* the principal areas of trouble, and they were Carmella, Romel, a Junior Analyst on Carmella's team, and Ewa Pollart, but he didn't actually grasp the situation and his was the organisation that investigated and thought things out but they chose him because he couldn't and therefore was no threat?

Carmella handed over all Admin duties to Romel and th*us* dashed them aside.

Without *Eunice*, he wouldn't hear any evaluation of anything.

Virtually all the competent staff were torn out before he noticed, and so soft was it worked out, with Carmella ignoring any objections and sending them back to Ewa. He never learned until after it occurred.

Ewa and Romel were functioning as a well-oiled organisation, and Ewa normally declined to act with anybody, so that was another irregularity.

Romel certainly seldom took time for anybody, even though he was often seem talking to the Junior Analyst, Deadra Dimitriadis—another abnormality.

Now he expected DUA and his team plus Marcel Datrl… an established acquaintance from the CIA and former days… the Boy buying that mansion had been a boon—that centred the Team in one place, plus the ex-Security people and Marcel.

He kept turning his head for DUA, while his children and wife explored and played.

His wife accepted these encounters, although they were *seldom* professional, but they served as people *passing* him, dropped by to *gossip*, and proceeded on—no observations, slights or questions recorded afterwards.

He now saw DUA and a group of people coming towards him, "I'll monitor the children," suggested his wife.

"DUA, long time no see—you as well, Marcel. Give my regards to Huron, and yes… Ralf or Boy, as you prefer. Huron is from a long time ago, and so was Mr Hoo. The old times seemed a lot simpler—however, I've heard good things of you!"

"Thank you, sir," was all I could manage.

"DUA, I based you in Brixton because I want you well away from the standard people—any attempt by Romel to turn up on your back I want to know immediately, and that goes for Carmella and Ewa interfering as well."

"I understand, Lance, but are you really saying you don't trust Carmella?"

"Carmella has developed into a worry… it might be because it was a misreading to develop her but forced on me from the Peres days. Immediately she was in the position, she delegated all the Admin duties to Romel—ignoring them ever since, and Russia has just become worse and worse and it was her speciality area, so there is large question mark over her performance. Romel is *close* to Ewa, and by the time I found out about that relationship, a lot of good people were gone, with Carmella blocking the news to me."

"Well, Lance… Boy certainly appeared *not* get on with Ewa… he construed as an *Agent,* not HR—all she did, he said, provoked a reaction, and she didn't even bother to go through the basic ropes on HR recruitment, just applied the *needle*."

"If I spoke to Ewa, she'd declare she was *testing* him, and use that as an excuse to attack him… without evidence, I can't do anything *against* Romel, Ewa or Carmella, so I can't really *demote* or get rid of anyone."

"You say that you, as the Director, are *powerless*."

"If I have to fire Carmella, I will weaken the Russian Team a lot more—if they allowed me to fire her, without going myself, I would be very lucky."

"Romel knows too much as well… I *don't* know how, and he has his *fingers* in every pie—getting rid of him is virtually impossible, until I know how far his fingers go."

"What else is he up to, Lance?"

"He calls for me to support a surprise attack on a Swedish Bank where he says Russian Politicians and UK tax evaders have concealed their loot…? Extending into Finland and running an operation to get our busted Agents out is another issue, again and one I should allow but I don't like the feel I am getting on either. We leave behind one in situ, and I am damn certain—being observed for any hints that we might go on the rest, who are in safe houses, but I've made *sure* that we have no details of where they are on the files."

"What do you need us for…? We don't fit into this stuff?"

"I need your team for different operations… apart from your normal business—watch Romel, Ewa and Carmella—the priorities are Romel and Ewa…?

"Boy, will have my access and passwords, to monitor their systems—Huron has *spoken* for him and I know his CIA connections, but I don't have a *choice*, as the CIA doesn't *trust* us to cross the road—my organisation is a joke."

"What help will the CIA give you, Lance?"

"Officially the CIA will not exchange any information, and I am being forced to keep this from the PM and JIC, because even stuff to the Cabinet Office is turning up where we don't want it to. You have some ex Security Staff, who will work for you, and we can recompense the Boy afterwards…? Your cover is the planned bank raid in Stockholm—which will never happen, and that will also cover the raid from Finland into Russia, DUA."

"How many leaks do you think you have then, Lance—it sounds a lot?"

"There are four potential moles in my organisation—now you understand why I haven't bother to keep the CIA out… it is only personal relationships that are keeping the boat afloat, and we can't afford any more deaths. One point, DUA. There is a police officer called Neville Jones… his Security clearance will now allow full access to Gloria Nantucket, Thomas Macguire and your team. He is, I understand, talented and heavily controlled, but there is something going on which may also involve this Department, and I need to know that, before someone gets up and rings a massive gong to alert the audience and the Press."

"What are you thinking of, Lance… what would ring a *gong* over four moles?"

"If we have someone in this organisation killing people as a serial killer, I need them stopped—I won't ask questions how you stop them. Apart from that, best of luck, DUA, and I want you to meet our police friend. He lives near you, and they have offered their place as a communication and accommodation area, for when you cannot *use* your house."

"Thank you, Lance. How far do we go in *planning* the Bank Raid?"

"All the way, DUA… it must *look* as if it is going to happen—the one thing we do not do, is *have* it happen—it is the *cover* for the moles operation, but it must look *real* and use the people you took on through Eunice."

"Anything else, Lance?"

"Neville and Antona will allow people put up… in return, we don't look at the money Antona's late husband made from hijacking oil tankers in local waters off the West African shores—about £1,000,000, and enough to break her—lose her everything."

"Understood, Lance."

Looking around, Lance spotted Neville and Antona getting out of a red jaguar, and called over to them, "Neville—Antona… I want you to meet DUA!"

Neville and Antona came over to meet them.

"I understand, Antona, that there has been unpleasantness between yourself and DUA's Team, in the past—I wanted to ensure there are no repeats of this…? You are part of the team now, Antona… in return for no questions asked regarding her late husband's activities—Antona has agreed to *assist* with Team Accommodation and Communication, if we require it."

The *look* on Neville's face showed that Antona obviously failed to inform him of that.

"That is the introductions," continued Lance, paying no attention to details—as usual—I now suggest I leave you to discuss matters. Bishop, if you could come over?"

The look on Neville's face now launched a thousand ships by physically picking them up and hurling them into the sea.

Bishop came over to Lance.

"Bishop, we've not met before… there is an additional role for you in this—I need you to dig into the administration of the service—find out how far Romel's extended digits go. Carmella should do the job, but has passed it all to Romel—I need to find how far he has dug himself in.

"You know Thomas Macguire, probably Eunice, and they will be your starting point… I need to comprehend where Romel is getting information from, as it seems to be beyond his job—I understand he is getting operational information as a Senior Administration Officer, but I need a feeling for how much more information he is getting and from where?"

"I'll do my best, Lance"

"Thanks, Bishop—I'll leave you to get on with it."

DUA, Bishop and the Team moved away from the explosive argument between Antona and Neville.

"Why didn't you tell me, Antona?"

"My house is none of your business, Neville!"

"What did you do with my car, Antona? It was none of your business."

"Are you prepared to break up over this?"

"Break up over an overbearing woman who endangers my career, destroys my car, and tells me where I live is none of my business, is more likely to be the reason."

"You can have the Jaguar!"

"It is not my car, Antona. You just destroyed my possessions, then tell me yours are none of my business—you *dammed* hypocrite!"

"I am not a hypocrite!"

"What happened to my car? The one I paid for and you destroyed—I didn't pay for that car – it is not mine. It is a gift from a deal you did with Government, so you could keep money from crimes, you were part of – stolen money!

"Where would I ever stand in a court, no matter what the evidence was, as a Detective not only living from the proceeds of crime but driving around in it? Where is my car, Antona?"

"Crushed! Albert can tell you the scrap yard!"

"He can tell that to a court, as you can for theft, wilful destruction and bribery of a police Officer in the commission of a crime. You can join your druggie daughter in jail."

"You can't bring those charges… you just heard—they won't touch me for anything Roger did!"

"Roger didn't do this. You—Antona did… there is no agreement to prevent you and Albert from appearing in court, and as a police officer I must charge you with that crime."

"You won't do that, Neville!"

"*Watch* me, and the destruction of my clothing can go down with you as well! I am not some *puppet* you found as a child to play with. I tolerated what you doing, because I needed some control in my life, but I don't want an overbearing, convoluted, conniving *lying* bitch!"

Neville took out his phone as he headed back to the gate to call a taxi, leaving the Jaguar and Antona in the Park. They had destroyed his car, his clothing, and his habits but they had not destroyed his pride… that mainly went to sleep as it had done for a long time in his police Service Career, but now they were treating him as a fool who didn't matter, and that he would not sleep with.

"Marcel, DUA shouted!"

"Yes, DUA."

"Can you swing your gear around with Neville—I need him close to the team for—…?

"If you can get Neville's kit out of Antona's house, he can use your plastic mattress in the utility room—I don't need trouble between those two now, or any more than there is already."

"Will do, DUA, I can see the thinking."

"Neville, a moment?" shouted DUA. Neville, hearing his name called, came over.

"I need you to work closely with Bishop… you cannot do that at Antona's place—Marcel will swap with you for the moment… I… I need you to educate Bishop, and Bishop to educate you and you both use your police links for monitoring. It will be OK—your Boss *cleared* it days ago, and don't *look* like that—it appears no-one is telling you anything, and that will change… Bishop will give you a lift to Coombe Lane – give Marcel your car keys, if you still have them? – he can take Antona back."

Neville; still reeling from Antona's disclosures, plus the argument looked followed Bishop.

Blundering back to his own place wasn't on, nor to the pub…. too many times in the past. He had gone that route, but not now. There was finally something and no-one trying to destroy him?

Marcel navigated Antona to the car and drove her back.

DUA looking at Neville's face, wondered how he was now human relations when to him the people were never human, "You can trust Marcel, he has *bigger* fish to fry in the US. He'll see her back, and bring your stuff over—you need us, and we need you… there… yes, there will be a car there in the morning and an education in the Security Service tonight…? Or at least I hope so. Let it be for now… you try to be *honest*… we are *dishonest*—let's get things moving!"

Antona's *experience*, as Marcel approached rivalled Neville's experience… Perhaps… Marcel… a former envoy with a brilliant partner who never watched his enterprises should have watched them as he greased a course around Antona.

Marcel was sure with women, or perhaps not?

He'd worked the cameras *as a memorable face* that functioned like a lot for his friends at the CIA, and he knew most crap although something here wasn't that but what was it and his instructions were now hard on finding out what MI5 had in mind. This was really an MI6 operation, but they didn't seem to be involved?

Antona faced two questions? Should she let Marcel drive and did she stop trying to control the world so it suited her complete with boots and spurs to ride over anyone who challenged her?

These thoughts went as Marcel was in the driving seat before she though to move and they were on the way before she had even found her seat belt.

DUA watched this, as he watched most things… Neville needed a car organising, and it would be a damn sight *plainer* than some *red* jag.

DUA gave his crew a shout, "Lady and Gentlemen, let's roll. Briefing at 8, as usual."

DUA was worrying about going *soft*… maybe not *human*, but softer.

XXX

DUA thought of moles and with so many why didn't anyone spot them as they had possibly been there for years but who knows…? Did they and were people just ignored like Thomas was who were known IRA sympathisers?

Was there possibly a *fourth…? And how many double agents didn't he know about apart from his team who all seemed to be working for the* CIA?

Life can get interesting, so working out how far the wings had spread would be the first trick that attracted his interest.

Finding out why a *trusted* person had thrown away her duties and blocking every attempt at any complaint was the second and all to consider before a breakfast he never ate—he'd looked at grease and muesli and decided they didn't mix well and a Scot saying he couldn't stand porridge would mean excommunication if he could ever find a religion he could believe in?

The list just seemed endless… find out why an HR Director was in the Boy's words, an Agent, *not* HR.

Find out if Carmella *was* passing information to her staff that she shouldn't be. If so then who in her team was, and why was everything going back to Romel and all before teatime—another future, perhaps, as he was now in charge of the tea-making?

Did he know who he was facing, and why did this keep coming back to Boy—Africa was dead and so were most of the people involved—Mr Hoo had finally killed everyone but Boy and Huron.

He and Bishop set Boy and Gris as a target as he worked through Algenald's demands and the CIA plans with the CIA part and parcel of all of it, and the parcel would now allowed Boy and Gris' garden to be turned into a warfare defence zone—what had they got themselves into and more importantly what had he got himself into with no real way out and selling his Wimbledon flat hurt but the money would soften the blow and he could live in a mansion for less than his mortgage payments and he didn't need the space?

DUA thought on and to say a tremor disturbed his underwear was something he would never admit to as he considered that no Controller worth his *salt* would ever route everything through *one* destination—especially the Russians who used multiple organisations to the degree that they actually didn't know who was doing what and when we made their objectives even more difficult to understand.

That told him there were *two* destinations for the information at least… with one… yes, one… as *backup*, and why *hadn't* Lance raised that—he had the experience even if it was only low level and old.

Did he think they would be identified anyway, or *didn't* he even guess there were two independent sources?

The second *could* be Ewa, but she was too prominent. It had to be someone really deep in the organisation who was both trusted and buried and would be buried if he had his way?

It would involve him or more likely her for a deep *role—women* were so much better at getting into things—as HR did these days, but it was still too visible or was that the trick where she stood out so everyone looked at her and ignored everyone else including the real source.

He still thought she was too close to Romel, to be a *second* source, and that meant there was another mole, and Lance didn't even suspect it.

For Bishop, watching the Boy was seeing a son he never had, and it took him back to the possibilities he'd once dreamed of.

Boy would monitor things from the Computer side.

For Bishop, all Boy's other sides were gaping holes and Bishop didn't need much sleep—if anyone ever *could in this business*? So he was usually alert, no matter what and watched the boy like a hawk.

They met for the evening briefing, and DUA's instructions from Lance, before he suddenly said, "And this is where we *raid* Boy's money, a bit more!"

"There is n*ot* the money for you to raid, DUA. There is enough to pay the monthly bills but not a lot after that, as you bunch pay a fraction of the costs!"

"*Sell* the car, Boy that is worth £120K."

"Sell your flat, DUA—poor you as you tell us so we fund you—planning to *hoard* the money, while you try to use ours? Why should I sell the one *thing* that belongs to me, to further your career in Security?"

"Then keep the car."

"*Damn* right I will and it is a 3 month rental in my name on this house—not yours DUA, and I will cancel that, and this little joke goes up your backside!"

"Lance has said he will reimburse afterwards, but the money can't be provided now?"

"When did Government ever meet any bills so who else is arriving and why?"

"Four more people are joining the house, and all are on Gardening Leave—Jeffrey Cozens, Marlin Stieff, Cliff Kovalik, and Agripina Bocek. Cliff and Agripina are both Russia specialists, Marlin is Finland and Jeffrey is logistics. That gives us those, plus Valene, Darius, Larita and Marcel…. eight… plus… our five and Neville."

"Why and where DUA?"

"We base some people at Antona's house—Antona will pay for their food and accommodation… we cannot *touch* money from Security, apart from what we are paid—for now… I think?"

"Why not, DUA?" Shouted Gris—obviously getting really pissed off with DUA's *attitude* to our money.

"Any *extra* money spent, Gris, would be picked up immediately by HR—apart from expenses for the primary team, as we play-act Stockholm."

"DUA," said Marcel, "one reason I am here is to stop this Dictatorship approach… call it a vested interest in this operation—money, which your Service will happily repay in due course, or else; will be available under my signature for any expenses directly related to CIA interests."

"Thank you, Marcel… Antona will allow us to draw money from her reserves—with Boy and Gris' money that makes about £350,000 plus the CIA contribution—CIA will provide operational expertise, when we hit Finland, so I will leave Lance to sort that out."

"How do we find the room," exclaimed Gris, "We're packed out already here?"

"We are full, but Antona's place has enough room, and our core team are back on full wages from the service."

"What about the rest of us?"

"You get bed, accommodation, food, transport and a way back in. If we succeed—back pay as well once we succeed—do not advise your friends you are working again, or it will wipe out the complete operation."

The shouts rang out, "what if we fail?"

"What about surveillance?"

DUA ignored the question on failure, but he was already cashing in and relying on the house to fund him as far as he could push it!

"We need to be careful on surveillance—use standard procedures as much as we can—3 per target, no more… we aren't the CIA."

"We've only 13 people and some of those we can't use. Who do we follow?"

"Romel, Eva and Carmella… Larita, Cliff and Agripina can't touch Carmella or Romel, and I am not sure about Marcel? Has anyone ever seen you, Marcel?"

"Apart from the PR, I don't think so, DUA—Carmella is the prime choice to spot my beef."

"And if we don't succeed," said Jeffrey?"

"Then Security has a *cheap* bargain, Jeffrey."

"Always the same with Security, DUA… *succeed*, get paid and our jobs back. Fail and we will be lucky if they bury us."

"I believe your Pension kicks in then, Jeffrey—cancelled by your death? That is why you are on logistics—so organise your funeral, touching no other budgets!"

"Go stuff yourself, DUA—and stop complaining or you will get a long sleep from logistics?"

"When do we start, DUA?"

"Bishop or the Boy will map their routines."

"What are these routines, DUA?" Asked Neville.

"Couples, lovers, shoppers—all the usual tricks—leave the plastic dolls covered in the pram... they are infectious; you are not trying for an Oscar by cuddling them. Just paint spots on them."

"You are not a woman, DUA, so don't give instructions to women cut in one voice and he tried to remember it...? He needed to get control back? It was disturbing him. He didn't have absolute control. It was a bit like some woman in a supermarket who has lost the person pushing the trolley and he needed the trolley pushers?"

DUA didn't know women nor could he understand them and apparently nor could he tolerate them? What kind of history did he have to achieve that? The voice continued in his head, although he was now starting to hear fewer voices in his head.

"You don't know what you are talking about, DUA—women take out children who cry from prams and cuddle them, or they get more attention than they want. Get better dolls—don't attack us!"

"We are obviously thin on the ground, and will become even thinner once we start with Stockholm and Finland, but I need everyone mouth's tightly shut.

"No *telling* friends, family, old colleagues including Eunice... no-one is to *know*, or you *blow* the whole thing. We start Monday when we go into Brixton. Any further questions?"

"Would you *answer* them, if we *asked* DUA?"

"Probably not Jeffrey. The operation is now *live!*"

Boy settled down as the USB connection of Lance's keyboard liberated itself of old age, enjoying 'the *snip*'.

A keyboard with a software logger on the cloud, latest technology—a local *thunderstorm* from time to time might present itself as the future.

The file protecting Romel's illegally downloaded email client *became* a software problem linked to his keyboard, and thus a corrupted file that would require support to *delete* the inserted problem.

Why people thought that remote sweeps of PCs never happened because they switched PCs off was a joke, but Romel's PC was configured to prevent it being switched on, remotely—after Boy had finished, it wouldn't matter whether he switched it off, or on.

Most people's attitudes to passwords, though, were bad.

Did they really use the same passwords or password generation, protecting the generator with their standard password...?

Yes, they did!

As soon as the key loggers were in place, they would remotely access the data on the machines, and all of their complicated passwords—by tomorrow, would *log everything*.

By Tuesday morning, he would start reviewing the processes, whilst Valene would check the coding, and Darius was testing some CIA tools from Marcel on the data.

It seemed like a good day's work done *already*.

Bishop settled in with a few calls.

First to Thomas Macguire, "Thomas the team is *back* in Brixton!"

"Why me, for the call, Bishop?"

"I know about your *dead man's* handle… I want nothing written by you on us—Lance can *confirm* that, if you need it."

"I don't *need* confirmation, Bishop. I knew something was *up* from when we put the Bugs into Coombe Lane… you are working directly for Lance and he is bugging you already?"

"No… we are working for *DUA*—he is working for Lance, and let us see how those Bugs hold out—you won't get anything out of them, or Eunice."

"So DUA is back—do Romel and Ewa know?"

"Yes, and you not *reporting* back to anyone, Thomas."

"I never tell Eunice *anything*, Bishop."

"And they make the moon of blue cheese, Thomas, and sold in every good *Russian* store!"

"Why are you mentioning Russia, Bishop? Russia is Carmella's area."

"We go anywhere, Thomas… *nothing* gets passed on to anyone—*understand?*"

"*Understood* Bishop. I don't cross DUA… I want to enjoy my Pension, *alive*."

"Good… nice to be back, Thomas—I will be in contact!"

Thomas Macguire put down the phone to Bishop… reaching for his slips as usual—this time—all of them would go in the dead-man's handle file.

With Lance involved, he didn't need to worry about Romel, Ewa or Carmella, any more. He would drop them down with his afternoon tea, tot and biscuit.

Bishop started his delving into the administration of the Security Service at Director Level… it didn't take long to find out that Ewa reported to Carmella and was automatically diverted to Romel, without anything ever being *looked* at by Carmella.

Romel was now the de facto Administration Director—issuing all instructions under Carmella's name, and she didn't know or care what happened afterwards. Even if she wasn't a mole… she was a deadly Russian handmade and finished by them.

Trouble tomorrow would hit Romel, but they needed more people off Gardening leave, who were not known to the Russian team for monitoring and following.

Bishop rang Marcel, "Marcel, *Euston* has a problem, and it is not the trains… a lot of our people are known to Romel, Ewa or Carmella—either Russian or Eastern European specialists are unusable—damned to the eighth hell by the idiots who selected them, so they are useless…?

"You have a good point, Bishop—Valene, Darius and Jeffrey are the only *clean* ones I can think of, and we need them for their specialist tasks…? Bishop… we still *need* the others, for when we launch '*Eggy*', but we can't use them now, or members of DUA's team for surveillance, as that could *screw* up '*Easter*' as well."

"I appreciate the point, Marcel, but another 10 will take the team to 24… where would they go, Marcel?"

"I need to talk to Huron… with him talking to Lance but *someone* has to pay this bill, and a team of 24 is going to take a lot of getting through JIC, when they don't even know the team *exists*, or is *unauthorised*," Marcel put the phone down, wondering what he would say to Huron…?

Bishop rang DUA, and related the conversation—DUA's only comment was, "who chose these Agents in the first place?"

"*Eunice*," said Bishop.

"Eunice works *closely* with Lance, so Lance's priority is Russia—not the moles, and he is having us take on people who will be seen by the moles… some attempt to keep their heads down…? I think…? Why the hell can't these people be *honest* at some point? Who the hell is in Russia who is more important than these Security Service moles, and the information they have?"

"Who will you talk to, DUA?"

"I'll talk to Lance, now," and DUA immediately rang Lance, with Lance saying, "Make it quick, I'm busy!"

"Lance… why did you have us *take* on Agents we can't *use* for surveillance…? What is so *important* that one of your Russian Agents is more important than the moles? That you don't care about the moles you have us hunting—what game are you playing, Lance?"

"I am not playing any game—you can go *back* on Pension, any time you like."

"Through Eunice… you had us take on people who will bankrupt Boy and Gris and who *cannot* follow Romel, Carmella or Ewa since they know them… in your mind those people were to do nothing to the moles—except maybe frighten them, *OK*? Leave them active, but knowing they are being followed—keep them quiet."

"I run the Service, DUA—not you, so I decide and you follow instructions or you get out."

"The CIA knows that, and that the Agents out of Russia matter more than the Security of your own organisation…? The Russia project is not a *facade*, is it, Lance, but a *genuine* plan. Talk fast, and *honestly*, or we pull everyone out, and that includes the CIA!"

"One agent hiding in Russia has the mole list, but in code to protect themselves and make sure we pull them out… we can't crack that code, but they don't know that, although Romel and Ewa have pushed out every decent de-coder we had."

"How are the reports of this protected, Lance?"

"I have the reports 'my eyes only'--they reached none of them—I need the moles frightened to keep them under wraps while I tried to come up with a way of using your people, who I know I can trust because they only answer to you, to get the guy out of Russia."

"Marcel will be in contact, Lance…? Because of this, Lance, we need 10 more to handle surveillance without them knowing what is going on… we don't know how widespread Russia's tentacles are… there must be two independent destinations, Lance—this is not a set of moles with one information exit, there are two exits—probably working independently."

"What progress do you have so far, DUA?"

"Bishop is making headway, so is the Boy. By tomorrow we will know what they are doing without them knowing… frighteners on Romel, but no-one else, so they think he is the only one we've found out."

"Agree what you have to do with Marcel…. What is the cost, DUA?"

"They will want a cut of the asset… unless… *unless*… you give it to them you are up a gum tree with a fire burning at the bottom, as the crocodiles wait. Give the CIA what it wants—you don't have a bargaining position any more… you have blown it with your games!"

DUA put the phone down… Lance had no cards left—bluff called—luck run out… nothing worth saving, unless Lance could save himself.

The team were *monitoring* Lance as well—Lance would authorise the extra people or DUA would take the hit and wind up his team.

Gris and Boy wouldn't have lost a lot, and jewellery would pay for the inconvenience, if anyone could ever s*ell it*?

The day was drawing to a close, now, but a good day, he felt, and no doubt Eunice was passing on everything to Lance, from Thomas, despite the warnings.

DUA had already outlined the new 10 people he wanted—Sherrell Maten, Joselyn Dien, Akiko Hippley, Thresa Buchna, Dot Fischbein, Malik Boniol, Elisha Hargest, Warner Mckimmy, Loni Grocott and Shad Paluk—6 women and 4 men. The next problem would try to get them to work together, but he would pass that job to Neville and post them to Antona—it should interesting?

Boy finally crawled into bed alongside Gris that night, and she rubbed him down. Always marry a torturer if you want a good massage—they knew the areas to attack.

"Do you want children?" Gris asked as she pummelled.

"I don't know what I want, Gris. Once everything was normal. Now there are only dreams."

"Come to this dream, Ralf, and make it happen," she said, turning over on the very wide bed. Boy looked at her eyes, disappearing into them, and then quickly, somewhere else, a little more intimate.

Normally he would have taken time, and made sure she was ready, now he didn't care… all those thoughts of what she did to him were long gone—she was there, and that was where he wanted her to be!

"What do we do if I *get* pregnant, Ralf?"

"*Finish* this bloody project off and find somewhere else to live—somewhere just for us?"

"I live here, now, Ralf and slow down, it is not the final furlong, and I am not a horse!"

Boy and Gris finally made it downstairs the next morning, to find the entire crew laughing at them.

For Security people, they gossiped like rabbits, and bred like them, but so many years in Security, meant they were quiet in bed, unlike Gris, who was like a steam train with even the house shaking.

Even Neville was laughing, and he seemed to settle in—agreeing to help train the surveillance teams.

There was a lot of simple tricks he knew from his experience, and skills 'quid pro quo' exchange was very much in motion, with Marcel also handling training sessions with the team, and training Neville on some other routines.

Neville taught them basic documentation on surveillance with standard forms created and set up electronically by Jeffrey, who had also put in some planning software to keep track as a team growing to 23 people, needing managing.

Marcel finally spoke to Huron, who had been talking to Lance.

"Lance is still mumming and erring about the cost—I ran out of reasons. He just went on and on about how to pay for it. What he is prepare him to give up in terms of the assets recovered from Russia, I still have no idea… probably won't agree to anything until he has no get-out?"

"What is his plan, Huron?"

"Lance thinks he can get away with frighteners to keep the moles' heads down until he gets the guy… then he will then try to negotiate his way out of any deal… that is my guess?"

"What is Lance interested in, Huron… this is destroying the Service he is responsible for, and he does as little as he can to stop it…? Is he just taking on DUA and company, to show he is doing something?"

"Marcel… My opinion… yes… my opinion is that Lance isn't *interested* in Security, or the Service anymore—just getting out quietly. I'm guessing… yes, I guessing but is it his *target*? Lance was probably the worst choice for the job, and I think that was not an accident as DUA reckoned that Peres was looking to move in and wanting an a weak ineffective head of MI5 to be easily replaced but he would then have promoted Romel and that makes me wonder even more who Peres was really reporting to. DUA thought it was Israel but I really wonder… yes, I do wonder?"

"What do we do next, Huron?"

"Lance will receive a very senior call tomorrow, threatening to withdraw all CIA help, and telling Lance—he can't afford the PM and JIC finding out—he'll should just agree as he's gutless."

Was Romel also getting worried?

His keyboard wouldn't work.

He couldn't use another machine because the software installed was a special Client Server email system from his Masters.

His system files had even been touched when he had given instructions that he would apply all upgrades himself.

Worse… the id used, Support said, 'was Lance Jagodzinski'. How did he prove what they had done because he had no access to his machine, and he couldn't hardly approach Lance about a hidden email system that IT should not know about?

Support finally, were appearing with a new keyboard… he had tried to take a keyboard from one guy around him, but the IT Support Manager refused to allow him to interfere with other machines, on Security grounds—what the hell were they doing—?

They finally replaced his keyboard, and he found his master password wouldn't work—? He might not understand what was going on, but his language hit a level—…? As did his thoughts.

The message displayed was 'master password corrupted, please enter old password first, and then a new password'—He was *losing* it and that made it worse.

The 'been there, done it' attitude of support was even more annoying, as he entered a new password and rang Carmella, demanding explanations of why Lance had tried to destroy his system.

"Lance doesn't destroy systems, Romel."

"He killed my system!"

"He doesn't have the knowledge, Romel. Your keyboard has packed up. You are creating so much trouble over it—I am losing my temper, Romel. People that we need elsewhere—standing by you. Words defy me, Romel," and the phone slammed down.

Romel turned on the Support Manager… "I need my system back—I have lost work, because of this!"

"You have lost no work, Mr Romel… the duff keyboard corrupted files, and now you need to bear with it, while your system settles down," and I need to get on with my actual job.

Romel wasn't to report until Friday Mass, but with the changes happening he needed to pass an update through—only his suspicions, but they were due them, as well?

His system when it finally came up… seemed to be fractionally slower, but apart from that— nothing else was wrong…?

Still *worried*—he was in fifteen minds what to do next…?

Romel didn't believe they knew about him… should he use his fallback procedure at the Tate—it needed a shopping visit to Horseferry Road, first. Did they know about that…?

They wouldn't have cracked anything he did; he was too good and too careful…?

He would leave it for a few hours until people left—sit down and put a report together.

It took about an hour, and then he clicked on a non-displayed option on his system, entered the file name, and hit return.

The mail system would encrypt the file, delete the original and then once it was finished, print it out to his private printer.

Put that in an envelope—head to the local shops to buy lunch and a newspaper and then head for the Tate, would be the plan.

The beggar sat by the shop wall watching Romel approach him—Romel reached into his pocket for some spare change and threw a golden coin into the bag. This would alert them to an urgent message to the Tate.

The beggar at the Tate, sat at the top of the steps under cover by the pillars and it was that easy—Romel dropped the letter into the beggar's plastic bag and walked into the Tate… at least they couldn't say, he didn't warn them.

XXXI

A long day for Boy and Gris did not improve by finding a large van outside the front door, and equipment being unloaded, watched by a harassed-looking Marcel with Gris' ballistic comments following…?

Boy interrupted the tirade to ask, "What are you putting in now, Marcel—apart from *ear-muffs*?"

"Some equipment, I need… the machines… you don't have enough computing power for what I need, and I can't let you have the software, anyway—Huron agreed to loan this stuff for the Project.

"It looks like it needs its own power station, Marcel?"

"A bit of a beast, but it should cut down processing time."

"It is about *6 foot tall*, Marcel. This is more than a *beast*."

"Once it's up and running, we'll just leave it. We'll still officially pass data to Langley and they send the results back, but we can do some work here, in this bit of America. That software Romel is using takes a lot of cracking. There is top class encryption built into this, and Langley is working on it as well. If you had any reservations about Romel—it *justifies them*. No-one has this kind of stuff on a system, if they are just a Government employee!"

"We can prove it is non-standard… that makes it a dismissal offence, but we would still have *no* evidence to put him away, or track the other moles. We need them all *caught*… Did Lance agree to those extra people?"

"No! He is still trying to bluff with *no* cards, and against experts. He wants the people out of Russia, and he thinks if that happens, then all he needs to do is frighten the moles so they keep their noses down, and he can then walk away, if he wants."

"DUA said that there are probably two sources—to two controllers—they will not *risk* all their eggs in one basket! So we are looking for at least two major streams and not two people, which means more moles that Lance will accept."

"DUA is right, Boy… what Lance doesn't realise is, that they could still blow the missions, since we don't know the full extent of the penetration—we can guess at Romel and Ewa, but there could be others, without us knowing who they are…? The whole operation would be wiped out by them, and Lance has nothing, apart from Agents in Russian hands… until Lance is convinced of it, we are stuffed and he was never that bright to start with but Lance thinks he can call Huron's bluff, and Huron is not a guy to play games with."

"I know," said Boy, "I worked for him in West Africa… we better get a move on, Marcel. I need to shower and change before dinner."

"Don't take too long, Boy. DUA wants it to be a working dinner while he outlines general stuff on Stockholm, Finland and Russia… Neville and I are swapping around again, and Antona will be here as well tonight, so it is going to be a long, and probably, stormy meal."

"OK."

Gris and I headed up to shower, change, and get ourselves ready for dinner.

Finally, we all got there in one shape or another and DUA, as usual, went through the standard update, briefing and then moved to the Stockholm and Finland operations.

"This is the initial briefing on the complete operations. Because of the leaks, everyone knows as much as you need to so no further information unless specifically required and don't ask questions and discuss nothing outside of your team.

"I and Bishop will run things overall; Neville and Marcel the Surveillance and Transcription Teams, Darius the special tools training, and Boy and Gris will undertake work as instructed."

"What about the space? There are already too many of us for this house," interrupted Larita.

"We need to move some of you to Antona's house.

"Valene, Marcel, Jeffrey, Gris and Boy, Bishop, Prilloch and I are based here. Darius, Larita, Marlin, Cliff, Agripina and Neville based at Antona's house. You are guests at Antona's pleasure, so please remember that."

"One thing, DUA," said Bishop, "Agripina is sharing with me, so she'll stay here."

"Another thing, DUA," interjected Marcel, I'm still not sure whether I am staying at Antona's or Neville is?"

DUA looked at the colour in Agrippina's face, and said, "it will add a bit of colour to the place", which broke the atmosphere and everyone started laughing as Agripina grabbed hold of Bishop's arm; almost frog-marching him out of the meeting for a few words, which could were heard echoing through the house later on.

The meeting split up and people made their own way to Antona's house, following her car like a cavalcade.

Albert had been pre-warned and was waiting as they arrived.

They agreed that the team would eat at Coombe Lane during the day, and on deliveries at night, so Antona and Neville could get some peace, having made up yet again, and the team would just go there to sleep.

They set a large two door fridge in the bar and that would serve for any other meals and accessories.

XXXII

Neville, who was alternating between both sets of duties where he liked it or not, made his way into Wandsworth the following morning and immediately he saw Silvia's face he just asked, "*where?*"

"King Street, near Ravenscourt Park toilets. Skull crushed… beaten in—second in Hammersmith. The local Bobbies are increasing patrols around Hammersmith – Detective Chief Superintendent Owl rang a couple minutes ago – wants you to ring him!"

Neville picked up the phone and rang Owley, "Yes, Neville. What do you *have?*"

"Nothing so far, sir—everyone is drawing a blank. BTP are checking Scottish arrivals and people hanging around the platform exits. I can't be sure, but I think he is killing people who look like him. Uses some kind of cosh wrapped in cling-film or a plastic bag. Only one sighting with someone else and the witnesses couldn't identify who was who.

"Hits between 20.00 and 23.00 and all victims show signs of a good few drinks in them, but no pub visits, apart from the Earls Court killing. Could use a flask to drink from, and forensics are now going back and taking DNA swabs from victims lips and fingertips, to see if anything else, apart from their DNA is there, but the alcohol probably distorts any readings and it is a very long shot."

"What about Gloria Nantucket?"

"Without Gloria Nantucket, I wouldn't ask the technical questions—she has been the one with the brains, and only when I ask the questions she tells me to, do they remember they didn't do the tests or just filed the results—by which time they are useless. He obviously befriends them, but from where we are ignorant—the days he strikes—no relationship, either. We understand a bit about him, but nothing of any detail."

"What did you get from Maastricht?"

"I was hoping the evidence from Maastricht might provide links but the police *ignored* the victim; left him in the rain, and by the time they *bothered* to check, he had been dead too long and his clothing contaminated, so they just stripped the body without protecting the clothing. I've tried gentle warnings to all the clubs to avoid panic and make them aware that something might not be right, but as it stands… it seems… the victims, are *recently* in from Edinburgh, blond, 5 ft. 8 in, stocky build, and arrive in an area where someone befriends them, gets' them drunk, and kills them—all I can say, sir."

"Use Silvia as much as you can, Neville. Use the team from Coombe Lane, who will be in that area, if they can help. Sort out your problems with Antona—if you hadn't found her—you would be out in the Nat Jacobs' rubbish. You two need each other and this will need both of you. Keep in touch and stay off the drink!"

"From now on, sir, I will use the local forces… a surveillance team is being built at Coombe and I will run it, but I need full involvement with Coombe Lane and a watching brief on these murders as well, and your input is welcomed as it removes barriers."

"What Coombe Lane is doing is more important than you as an additional resource on the murders, but your local knowledge is what I really need, and I might come back. There are enough feet here to start a full operation and you are thinking again. Work with the Coombe Lane Team. Trust, Antona, and keep your nose clean!"

Neville sat there dumbstruck. Owley understood everything that was going on. He had always had respect for Detective Chief Superintendent Owl, but he had not realised just how far his claws stretched out when he swooped.

"Silvia, I need to ring Antona—we had another domestic this morning. Can you take a coffee break?"

"Will do, sir!"

Silvia left, and he picked up the phone. Antona answered it and said, "Yes!"

"How would you like a controlled Robot?"

"If you ringing me to insult me don't bother!"

"You don't own me, Antona!"

"I don't want to own you, Neville."

"Then treat me as human, not as a pet dog!"

"When you stop behaving like a dog!"

"In your kennel?"

"This is my house, Neville, and I do what I choose!"

"To anyone you choose, Antona?"

"Why did you ring me?"

"Owley told me I would be out on my ear with Nat, if it wasn't for you, and the killings matter less than the activities of Coombe Lane team. They wrap my life up with you and them, and I'm told I had better realise it!"

"Are you staying with me or in the room?"

"I'm training them on Police Procedures, Surveillance and Documentation at the moment… I am like a tutor, from when I get there, until I sleep."

"Maybe they need a lawyer, too. Albert will drive me over and we can come back together tonight."

Neville put the phone down. Perhaps the two of them working together might work…? Would he have made the phone call without instructions… probably 'No!'.

Would Antona make a difference? Antona was a formidable operator, and through her late husband with his contacts, someone who was not only at ease with anyone but also had a formidable brain. You did not cross Antona unless you could crucify her, leaving the nails in, with Owley to hammer the supports in as well.

Antona and Neville met up again that night, for the DUA dinner meeting and then headed back home, "Antona," said Neville, "Owley is building his own team, and will take it over from me."

"Does it bother you, Neville?"

"It does. I don't know what I…? I feel like a football being *kicked* around—I am not a Security guy --I am a police officer and all this security stuff seems like some *fantasy*…?

"My beat is London, not Russia, Finland or Sweden… I thought a mole was an *animal*, not a human being, and I am teaching these people about surveillance when I haven't done it in years. If it wasn't for Gloria, I wouldn't know the questions to ask the forensics team… I feel so *completely* out of my depth—I am being batted around, and I have no control over my career or anything else, now."

"Was that why you exploded at me?"

"Probably!"

"They are doing the same to do me, Neville—£500,000 of Roger's money gone. People I don't know, staying in my house—if I argue, I lose the lot, and could end up in Africa in a cell? Neither of us has a choice."

"Yes. You're right. No choice at all."

"Let's have an early night."

"Seems a good idea."

Arriving back, Albert, who was still trying to deal with people not used to being looked after, looked suitably harassed, and needed directions as he met Antona.

"Please to have you back *Home*, sir," was Albert's comment, as if Neville had just come back from holiday and hadn't crept in the previous night, "I am still trying to see to our boarders, Mrs Turner… do you wish the bar to be open?"

"Let them have two drinks, Albert, then close it. I don't want them serving themselves or we will have *nothing* left. Serve the takeaways in the Bar and then lock it afterwards. We have *warned them* to behave and we will need some more deliveries."

"I have already put that in *hand*, Mrs Turner… I will lock the bar after dinner. We have now put fridges in all the rooms and there is some beer and wine in them so they cannot complain, although no doubt they will."

"I'll leave it to you, Albert—you *know* what you are doing. I just wish everyone else did?"

"Yes, madam."

Friday to Neville came slowly.

Owley had now pulled him off the serial killer case – formally seconded him to Security and working for DUA.

Silvia was moved back to the Yard; he based at Coombe Lane—they patched a system through to the police systems, so he could be in touch—even if he wasn't involved.

Marcel's team were still struggling to get the machines working to process the data from Boy—now a backlog of 4 days.

Langley was working on the code from Romel's email system, with Valene keeping them updated.

Darius had gone in with Bishop, and the cameras focused on Romel, Ewa and Carmella's desks and repeated out to the team, once they were operational.

The glasses they wore also had cameras fitted which would record vision and speech picked up at 50 yards, if activated—all we needed now was to get the team in position, kitted out, monitoring and trained.

Romel was followed into church this morning, but apart from the confessional; nothing and then back to Security.

XXXIII

Boy had the feeds working; Bishop, the initial plans and reports on the information channels with DUA the organisation and surveillance in place. All meaningless until the US team pulled their fingers out with *nothing* achieved with any of it.

Marcel was already talking about throwing the week's data away, which Boy, Bishop and DUA fought to stop it, as they had frightened Romel, and if he made mistakes but then they lost that data it would be pathetic?

If Marcel had his way—worrying—on CYA for some reason they would see nothing but what the CIA allowed and Lance wasn't interested and in a huff?

Part of the reason was that Marcel did not want to admit his struggling team had still failed after 3 days to get a basic machine working. Shipping in boards and switching them to see if that worked— a simple solution when you don't want to spend money. If you believed these guys, it all worked perfectly before they brought it to Coombe Lane, so it was Coombe Lane's fault, not theirs. Their infighting was worse than the police.

Bishop had by now established the actual links into how the structure worked, and as he became known, other Managers tried to block him. A known killer working on Management frightened them more than an Audit. They didn't wait to help him on his way to the door, and out via 'the flying carpet' type of exit as they pulled every rug from under him they could.

Thomas was still passing information to Eunice, despite Bishop's warnings and Eunice was passing some to Lance, but everyone else seemed to be reluctant to answer simple questions of whom they reported to, and they would happily forget the question and answer another and waffle it away if they could.

Too many people had gone who queried what was going on, and the rest wanted to keep their jobs by saying nothing in a culture of career fear.

The monitoring was there now for everyone who contacted Romel, Lance, Carmella and Ewa, so at least they would get the information but Bishop was more interested in building bush fires to flush out the relationships whilst Boy was monitoring as much as he could but then losing it in the CIA systems.

It made Security almost seem clinical again, and they passed the lot back to Valene, Darius, Marcel, and then on to Langley with very little feedback on anything. Lance buried his head in the sand, as much as Carmella, so neither saw what was going on—content to leave it to Ewa and Romel, while they played at Politics and CYA.

Lance by now was receiving the next backside moving phone call—only his pride was preventing him from giving in—he could go to Carmella for backing, but if he did, the whole operation finished as Romel would know of it by closing time.

Lance put the phone down… this time the CIA *removed* all co-operation from the Security Service—the feeds already turned off… how long before people realised they were officially blacked from Security co-operation with the US, on the grounds of the leakages from his organisation.

All he needed to do was keep heads down until they took the people out of Russia—if that had to be done without Carmella knowing, then that would have happened…?

When he couldn't trust the Government or his own Security Services but who allowed it to happen…? Alright… he possibly did… but it was just a job after all and he was told to do nothing but stop it creating Newspaper reports and that was his instructions and what he did but he had an organisation stripped of US information and a short time-scale before people realised and he was out with the Politicians using him as a scapegoat.

He needed the moles out and the people out of Russia but he never sent them into Russia and MI6 was ducking every issue unless they could rush in at the end and claim the glory, but unless he agreed, the CIA would not support the operations which were outside of his operational theatre and so he was forced to use a team of ex-MOD killers.

He didn't expect to get the reports he was getting from Eunice and that they were frightened of more people compromised by the Security Service, and without the CIA, he would have to use

Carmella… and much as thoughts crossed his mind… so they promoted her beyond her ability… and gave in to her desires and she should have been there to review not organise the Russian information but the trouble with MI6 had led to the agreements and so his organisation strayed more and more into MI6's areas but MI6 was straying into his so who gave a damn but DUA's team's loyalty were to DUA—his team were funding the start-up of the operations… he would have to give the CIA the use of the Assets if there were ever any, or he was out—Carmella was out, and JIC would be told he had moles in his organisation and didn't try to find them and they would do nothing to find them either.

He picked the phone up and rang DUA, "Lance, DUA. You have the OK to go for the Surveillance Team… CIA will fund it for now."

"Thanks, Lance. I'll get onto it."

DUA hung up and then rang Marcel.

"DUA; Marcel. Lance has *given* permission to proceed with the Surveillance Team… we'll contact them, *ourselves*. I want to keep it out of the official organisation as much as we can. I'll use Bishop, and Thomas Macguire—until we know what the software on Romel's machine is doing, I want to keep as much away from Security as I can – especially HR."

"Langley are still working on it, DUA, but they have already come across hidden menu options that are very *sophisticated*, and merged with Romel's authority to make him able to go virtually anywhere in the organisation—we don't know how much of the organisation is compromised?"

"How many of this shower does he know about, and its history, Marcel…?"

"The only reason, he didn't know about you before, DUA, was that you were on *defence* networks, and he didn't have the authority to touch them, but it is possible he has been sweeping the entire Security operation for at least a year, and passing everything back to someone."

"We *don't* have a Security Service, then Marcel."

"DUA… the Security Service is so *compromised* that it is *useless*, with every operation known and blown—if Romel could access it?

"Langley twisted Lance's arm to the extent it prepared for both arms *wrapped* around his neck— after the initial results on that software—if he didn't capitulate. We are still working on the encryption, but the trick now is to identify his network, so when we move in, we get all of them— we need that surveillance team yesterday."

"We have the people, Marcel… *selected* them myself—Bishop is getting their details from Thomas Macguire as I want *Eunice* kept *out* so she cannot pass that on to Lance, and we will contact them directly.

"We'll start bringing the team in and only use those known… if we want to put the frighteners on; Darius should have the desk monitoring cameras operational by Frid—."

"and hopefully your beast will *work* on them, also it is getting a bit crowded, and Antona is *virtually* full now."

"Antona hasn't much room left, DUA?"

"Room for one probably, without people *dossing* down, Marcel."

"Boy and Gris' place is like a Palace compared to that, albeit a little crowded."

"You aren't sleeping on the floor, Marcel and bed sharing so I heard!"

Marcel ignored the comment. With all the packing in of people, he was packing in what he could and when!

"Antona has one spare slot… only problem is Valene and Jeffrey—the way they keep looking at each other, we'll have a spare room soon."

"Leave it with me… I need to concentrate on other things so I'll have a *word now*; I'll suggest to Jeffrey he is being moved—you should have a room by tomorrow—I'll talk to him now, if you put him on."

"I'll put you through to the kitchen… he's *bound* to be there."

"Thanks Marcel… this place is becoming like a 'love nest'!"

DUA waited while Marcel passed the call on, "Jeffrey… got a little problem—need your room and there is a spare room in Gris and Boy's place—if you can move in with anyone, there is no problem, but otherwise… decide… I must move you?"

Silence reigned as Jeffrey moved the button to silent and looked at Valene, "He wants to move me, unless I move in with somebody—wants the room for someone, probably Marcel?"

"He knows about us, doesn't he? No bloody secrets with this lot… do you want to move in?"

"I was hoping for a little longer as we developed. I can stay in Antona's place—?"

"Do you want to?"

"No!"

"Tell him to give us time to re-arrange things—we'll share," Jeffrey clicked off the secret button—DUA didn't need to listen in, he could guess the conversation.

"I need time to arrange things with Valene!"

"Should have *done* that ages ago, Jeffrey… I'll give you until Monday, and then you go."

DUA put the phone down. He was tiring of playing matchmaker, but people were dependent on them and he was tired of people moving between houses so you didn't know who was where; with whom and when as they played hopscotch between the houses so no-one knew.

It might not confuse the Russians but it was surely confusing him… did they consider it *Glands Week*?

Valene was one of the best Coder/De-coder/problem solvers he knew, while Jeffrey was one of the best operational logistics guys he had ever known. Put those in the same bed at the same time and you might have the next genius or a savant.

Anyway, that freed up a bed, got Marcel off the floor and juggling people would free up a room the surveillance team needed for planning, meetings—they could called him a cold-hearted bastard…

probably true—well a crook in the past as well and the past didn't seem that long ago, but he wasn't sure which was an improvement in his career progression if there ever was one?

They were thinking of him as a *shepherd* now, which is what he seemed to be these days, instead of the *butcher* from earlier days, but he could live with that unless the Butcher needed to rise again..

Still, the hardware wasn't ready yet, and now they were talking Sunday. The team needed information… he told Valene and Marcel to concentrate on Romel, but the rest of the week might as well go out of the window, for what was being achieved by the CIA.

No… he was being too ambitious—or was he, and why was the information going through to the CIA whilst all they got was CYA and nothing?

Was he being too ambitious? The hardware should be ready… the files were being captured—Langley was working on the code—He was expecting too much…? He doubted that.

The surveillance team would start coming in over the weekend, and two porta cabins were now being delivered to Antona, plus the Portaloos.

Thank Gods he had Bishop and Jeffrey, who seemed to take to it, like water off a vicar's rectum—Antona's staff had switched to industrial catering, as second nature for the crew assembled and assembling, there and problems were being solved, he was sure… wasn't he?

XXXIIII

Romel finally sat down at home—taking out the package he'd picked up from the *Priest* in the confessional this morning.

Running the encoding at work on the report had been a panic measure—this would give him the information he needed without the risk.

He selected another of the invisible options on the email, and waited while it converted the files—reading the transcription middle section, made him go back and read it again, from the beginning.

His masters—not content with him organising a false bank raid and destroying the Security Service, now wanted to launch a raid on Gris and the Boy's home!

There was some equipment there, and they wanted it either destroyed, or removed!

They were mad… there were four trained killers living there, excluding Gris, who was a very effective hands-on person in every respect, concerning the body.

Any action against them would blow the cover of any agents in the team before the actual operation started—all of DUA's team were licensed to carry weapons—this was stupid?

He still hadn't heard when they would start the Russian operation, named 'Eggy' or the Stockholm operation named 'Easter', but to raise a team and go against Coombe Lane was ridiculous.

There was also an instruction to only use the Friday Priest for communication.

This had to have come from Ewa, who loved to control and cause trouble.

They made him take the risks while she was paddling her arse to her bosses—reporting on him—the jealous bitch. Perhaps Meik should have a word with her?

He still didn't know how Ewa communicated with the Masters--Old KGB men, who would brook no dissent, still ran the 'Sluzhba vneshnei razvedki', but their information was faulty, and they needed that pointed out to them and maybe that might happen if he could find a way? His instructions and replies were via another route and without knowing her information routes he couldn't pass any information.

He got up, poured himself a drink and sat down to prepare the messages, as per instructions… with luck that should see it quickly buried, and Ewa slapped down. Then he could relax for the weekend and enjoy some music.

He got up, as he did from time to time, to check the street and other windows.

There was a BT van parked outside, with a green cabinet open… odd that they should work this late—probably a network fault.

He picked up his phone, which sounded fine. They obviously weren't working on this block.

Romel still felt nervous over what the Masters were planning and decided to stay in over the weekend.

XXXIIII

Antona and Neville by now had found that even their quiet weekends gone!

Five of the primary team staying in the house, but now 10 others were living in porta cabins on the lawn, with Portaloos dumped there as well, destroying attempts at normal life.

They restocked the bar, whilst Albert and Cookie ran it, but were now running a free pub for 15 people.

He normally stayed out of the bar as agreed with Antona, and left it to Albert to handle problems, unless they called him in.

They had covered the rest of the garden in assorted benches, tables and food deliveries, leaving it on the garden tables in the evening for them to help themselves and in the bar if it was raining.

Most of the time he and Antona watched TV, or went to bed, with Antona surprising him on quite a few occasions, in quite a few areas.

He had seen enough in his police career to wonder about arresting Antona for some things she did, but it whiled away those quiet evenings, and left no lasting scars, although he limped a bit, occasionally.

The one thing that surprised him was the two porta cabins and Portaloos.

The bottom house toilet was usually free, and they could free others up if there was a need, but the woman all stayed in one cabin with the guys in the other, and same with the toilets.

It was almost health and safety, but it wasn't stopping anyone from paring up and arranging things, and it made walking through the Lodge grounds. Interesting at night?

Sherrell Maten was interested in Malik Boniol, Joselyn Dien with Warner Mckimmy, Dot Fishbein and Shad Paluk, Akiko Hippley with Marlin Stieff, Elisha Hargest with Cliff Kovalik and Thresa Buchna and Loni Grocott… anymore and the local maternity unit would have to expand.

He and Antona were certainly doing their best, as were Boy and Gris, with Valene and Jeffrey joining in, albeit in separate pairs, houses, beds, and also in separate rooms, for the inquiring minds.

Antona to a degree was running an open house, with one bedroom, spare for use as well.

Running a brothel might be a closer definition, but the shapes and other things just kept making him wonder how they pared up.

Sherrell was big, while Malik was thin, and she was Christian whilst he was Hindu.

Joselyn was petite, while Warner was loud, but both RC.

Dot and Shad were at least the same size, but she was Jewish and he didn't talk about religion.

Elisha and Cliff were both Jewish, but she was from Israel, whilst he was from Russia, and the same again for Loni and Thresa. Agripina had taken up with Bishop.

The only people who weren't in bed together were Marcel, Larita, and Darius, and he would not ask about that since Larita certainly wasn't quiet.

They really could be done for running a knocking shop. No wonder they had separate cabins… it was probably in shifts, and not what they wearing them, either.

Well, it was the last free weekend, and it would start in anger on Monday, so they might as well enjoy it.

Antona had arranged for everyone to meet up, if they weren't already doing that at the weekend, although that wouldn't include DUA, Prilloch and Marcel with his guys, so Coombe Lane was covered, and it was only 10 minutes away from Coombe Lodge, so with the cameras installed now, both houses would watched.

XXXIV

Detective Chief Superintendent Jonathan Owl regretted pulling Neville Jones off the serial murder case.

There had been another 3 murders since then, although this time, one in Paddington, one in Bayswater and one in Queensway, as if they had queued up to die. Neville knew the streets.

Owley knew had to manipulate and kill if he had to, but when the Met police issued Warrant Cards to Armed Forces personnel and everyone else under political agreements, when did he know who he could trust and who was armed with anything?

All victims—the same description and around the same time of the day… were they attacked with a cosh like weapon… wrapped in some kind of plastic?

They had gone around the pubs in the area, to no avail. No-one saw anyone near them.

All were down from Edinburgh within the last two weeks, and all tradespeople.

Neville had checked out the same things he had, and Owl had come to the same conclusions as Neville, that the killer was killing people in his own image, which meant the killer was a Scot, 5 ft. 8 in, stocky build and probably from Edinburgh. About mid to late 20s, but putting a picture out would be the same as creating a riot, and he did not want copycat killings, nor did he feel it would be of any use. He now ran regular police Patrols in Kings Cross aiding the BTP and interviewing anyone who matched the description… he probably handed Neville a *favour* by letting him go to Coombe Lane?

DUA thought about the team… he was an organiser—possibly a *leader* more than a manager, but probably just a successful *schemer*, if the truth was *told*…?

The manager was Bishop—the supervisor was Antona.

He preferred the quickness of operations where it worked or it didn't, but with specialists, their egos were the main problem… this long drawn out preparation work wasn't for him, and Bishop now took over on the people side, with Antona managing the organisation of the houses.

The surveillance was rough and ready… they'd had a week of training and practice.

If they slipped up, it would pressurise the targets and they could monitor their reactions, but they still needed the surveillance team in place, the feeds into Marcel's machine and evidence to either imprison the moles, or exchange them… exchanges weren't on, with the information the moles had, however.

Pity they closed Kensington it was ideal, as a holding area for spies, moles and people you could not release or take to trial, but Matthews allowing it used for torture had been the last straw for the powers that be, and they closed it when it became public.

Prilloch's love affair with the back garden still seemed to be strong, which was good, because that was their weakest link, with all the trees and the 300 hundred yard lawn…

Once again, DUA watched Prilloch disappear into the trees on the left side—*sometimes* he disappeared for hours as he prowled around with that Bowie knife of his… maybe that was his belief and he had blooded enough with it in his day but he'd tried to care for something he never should have done. There was so much and… would… could… why think about it… why did thoughts of Boy keep coming back to him... he'd thought about everyone and in the Boy's case he'd given his best?

Prilloch's bowie knife was about a foot long, 2 ½ inches wide, and ¼ inch thick, and with the serrated edge on the back of the front edge of the blade it was how Gloria Nantucket identified the knife that killed Simon Askew.

Prilloch still carried it—only killing to order by DUA, unless it was an emergency—Prilloch didn't kill for pleasure nor was it love… perhaps it was just cold-blooded killing and with the garden and trees and the birds he had calmed down a lot.

The trees reminded him of Scotland to a degree, and the fresh air. He liked to check out twice a day… an excuse probably to get out of the house and into the garden. The birds usually sung in the trees and there were some rabbits around—he could relax—they knew him or just ignored him, to a degree. People were never his strong point, and he hadn't a clue about women apart from being different.

Now as he walked through the gardens, looking for his favourite birds, he couldn't hear anything… it too was quiet.

He always went into the trees to the left side of the house, working his way down and around, but the sound of the birds had completely stopped and he stopped too; listening until he heard wood crack about 20 feet way in front of him, and no-one should be there?

Prilloch moved to the shelter of an enormous tree and waited while the sound of wood cracking moved towards him, and then someone was level with the tree, carrying a semi-automatic AK 74.

Prilloch had the foot long Bowie plunging upwards before he even thought.

The knife however, skidded on hard body armour, but he just turned his wrist so the knife blade, serrated on the back end of the front blade, ran smoothly against the right side of the rifleman's neck, slashing deeply, whilst the handle guard with blade catcher rammed into the throat on the follow through, rupturing the throat, so he could not call out, as dying, Prilloch finished him.

Prilloch waited for the next movement… he could now hear the birds sing again further away from him… failing to hear anything else near him, he moved back to the house, and across to the other side of the trees, using the house as cover.

He could hear the birds still singing on that side—they were not there yet. The first must have been an advanced cover for the primary team, coming in from the far side.

He guessed that one would establish himself in situ on one side and wait if anyone was in the garden, until just before the other team were in position, and then open fire with silenced automatic rifles. They organised, and he didn't have time to warn anybody.

It looked like the team were now coming down the right-hand side of the back garden and moving too fast, so he moved forward, trying to calculate how long they'd have given the cover guy to get into place.

10 minutes would probably be a maximum, and then they would move in about 10 minutes behind him on the other side.

He kept listening for the birds.

They knew him as he spent most of his days in the trees and left food for them.

They weren't tame, but would just hop around him when he was putting food down.

They were his alarm, but these were probably Russians birds—the AK-74 had never really hit production like the AK-47, with the Soviet Government falling apart, and most of the rifles in fact, went to the Russian Army.

He moved from tree to tree, and had gone about a 100 yards when he heard the noise drop off, and he waited, looking for anyone coming through.

He could see four guys moving quietly through the trees. Two flanking—one in the middle and one behind as cover.

He moved over so one flanker would pass by his tree, and this time he went for the final attack with the blade catcher ramming into the throat to silence him, while the blade cut deeply into the right side of the neck on the backstroke, and he dragged him behind the tree, out of sight.

That left him to wait for the back cover man—once the other flank and central guy had passed by, looking forward he moved from tree to tree to take out the back cover, leaving just the left flank and centre guy?

Both were getting anxious and looking around.

Had the left flank listened to his ears, he would probably have heard Prilloch coming up from behind as Prilloch, playing the redskin, moved from tree to tree until 3 feet away, when the cover turned around to feel a knife thump into his rifle as he tried to bring it to fire before sliding upwards into his throat.

He could see the remaining guy just standing there, looking backwards but not sideways… Prilloch hidden behind a thick tree stayed hidden. The centre man walked back to the body that Prilloch hadn't wedged securely enough, to stay straight up and was now lying on the ground, until passing the tree Prilloch was hiding behind was his last move—Prilloch used the butt of his knife this time on the soft back of the skull, slashing at the throat with the follow-up as the gunman fell.

With the length of the knife and its deadly blade, it was a foregone conclusion as the knife ripped across the front of the throat.

DUA stood staring out of the window at the lawn… thinking about Prilloch and wondering where he had gone, now.

Prilloch was a killer, but controlled and DUA watching Prilloch running across the lawn—his long legs eating up the ground knew something was wrong, as Prilloch headed for the house.

DUA was immediately bellowing for Marcel, and by the time Prilloch was back, Marcel had joined him and the rest of the house was alert.

The phone would have been more expedient but DUA didn't bother, "What's the problem, Prilloch!" He bellowed.

"Some guys in the trees, DUA—I surprised them—"

"What was their plan, Prilloch—none of us had any warning until you took off like a *howling wolf*?"

"Marcel… they must have planned to come up through the trees to the house on both sides—there were five of them… we need someone to clean up—I only had the *knife and no time*?"

"I take it you solved the problem, Prilloch," said Marcel.

"Unless I missed someone—that would only be a driver, I think… we should be safe, but we need to cover Coombe Lodge."

"I think *Bishop* can handle that, Prilloch, with Boy as the *backup*? I'll ring him now."

After ringing Bishop DUA was already getting his brain in gear, "What beats me, Marcel…? How did they know we'd have most of the team at Antona's place to consider taking all of us with five people? Too *coincidental* Marcel—we're *betrayed* again, and by *people* on the team."

"DUA… they may have just been *scanning* the property—reacting to the fact that we had people going to Antona's place—probably more likely?"

"If Prilloch hadn't been *prowling* around, they would have taken us out with *no* trouble, Marcel. I didn't expect them to hit us this *quickly*… need a sweep of Antona's grounds, as well?"

"It can wait, DUA—Prilloch handled it."

"Damn it, Marcel… I'm running out of people with operational killing experience. Are you OK to handle the driver, Marcel, if I get Bishop, Boy and Gris to check out Antona's grounds, and don't keep telling me it is a one-off or an accident? I have a funny feeling the driver won't have hung around, and won't come back… let me ring Bishop again."

DUA picked up the phone and rang Bishop again but Antona answered, "Antona, I've already warned Bishop but we've just had an attack here by 5 guys, aborted by Prilloch—grab Boy, Gris and check the Lodge grounds, tell Neville and pass the instructions onto Bishop but… but no-one else."

"Why, DUA? Who do you think set it up?"

"I don't know, Antona… I think the driver dropped them off, and knows it failed as they haven't come back for your place… I just don't know, Antona. I think they had inside information? I think someone is also keeping them informed and the driver won't be coming back… it could be another driver coming in for your place, but we won't know where the pickup was planned until we check… I don't bloody know what is the truth…?

"Bishop's here, I'll pass the phone over."

"Bishop here, DUA and I have already started checking generally."

"We need to see if they cased Antona's grounds for a follow-up attack… these guys were carrying AK-74s, so they're not the standard gang, as those guns are their designed and re-engineered AK-47s, and mainly used by Russian troops."

"I'll grab the crew, DUA—check the Lodge—then head over to you… Larita, Marlin, Cliff and Agripina all have operational training, and Darius lives off weapons, so they can back up after we go!"

"Don't tell them, Bishop… somebody could have passed on the information that we had no-one here, and without Prilloch, the lot of us would be dead—it was too damn convenient!"

Bishop looked around for Gris and Boy—dragging them over to Antona and Neville.

"Just had DUA on—attack on Coombe Lane by five guys."

"I know, Bishop. We need the grounds checked with only us knowing."

"It looks like they were official, Antona—luckily they met Prilloch before getting near the house and we'll clear that up later… DUA wants us only, to know, and we'll have a romantic stroll around the grounds here."

"Where does he want us to check, Bishop," Boy asked.

"I know the weak spots, Boy and I'll outline them to you… we'll just go for a stroll—look for anything moved, footprints, broken shrubbery, cigarettes—anything different?"

"If they were professional wouldn't they have covered their tracks, Bishop," said Antona.

"Not unless they watch westerns, Antona. There will be something, if people have been here, but they are now short of five people who would probably have been heading here after Coombe Lane. Just wander around where I show you but then Gris, Boy and I, need to head back to Coombe Lane, but we will get Prilloch to prowl these grounds regularly in future—it seems to be what he enjoys doing."

"What happens to the bodies, Bishop?" Neville queried.

"Collected, Neville. This is a Security operation and they will go to Gloria Nantucket for investigation and processing, so don't ask her. We spread out and get this done. You also need… yes, need… to watch for anyone starting to look anxious. Bishop looked up at the faces. DUA picked the safest people he could but the people were forced on him by Lance and Eunice. We still don't know how far down the crap has gone in MI5?"

"There must have been checks on these people?"

"Yes, but by whom?"

"Some might have been forced out by Lance or Carmella because they are moles, but could they be got rid of quietly as moles because they were due to be uncovered, or that no-one knew they were moles, and they just got sacked like the others, for appearing to be too good… what a bunch… DUA is the only one who doesn't know… by the sound of it? We don't even know what damage Romel and Ewa did, or what they knew about the infiltration."

They split up both the conversations and their thoughts and moved on.

Bishop watched Agripina coming towards him and at some speed.

Bishop was fond of Agripina and that gave her some leverage from… something… from somewhere… someone who looked like her and had led to him hanging from a tree in a Malayan forest but that was as far as it went. They forced her out as a Russian specialist just when they needed them and no-one would admit to forcing her out so who and why and why was it buried? He enjoyed her company in bed? She was pretty, petite, stubborn, intelligent, knew Russia and the organisations just as well as the eyebrows she plucked.

Cliff was another Russian specialist, but Marlin struck him as the oddest. Why would a half US, half-German guy, become a Finnish specialist working with British Intelligence, although he could understand his relationship with Akiko, who was half US and half Japanese, as Marlin understood nothing straightforward and nor did Akiko? Cliff was just a Russian Jew, who hated Russia.

It might be worth a word to Huron about Marlin, but the grounds needed looking at, instead of him staring at the sky daydreaming, and he set off on his section of the grounds.

Prilloch would bring these grounds into his normal checking from tomorrow. They had never realised that Prilloch had spent most of his childhood on the hills and forests of Scotland until he prowled around Coombe Lane.

Bishop headed for the areas he would have picked to kill from—looking around for the spots he would have chosen.

There seemed nothing, and then he heard footsteps behind him as Agripina finally caught him up.

"I saw you meet up and then come out here—is something wrong?"

"No. Nothing is wrong, Agripina. DUA realised we had not checked the grounds out for a while and asked me to arrange it."

"Well, now you checked them, come back and join the Party."

"When I have finished, Agripina and I can do that faster on my own… I need to check out other areas as well, so please go back and I'll see you there."

"You've involved Antona and Neville, plus Boy and Gris—why not me?"

"Antona knows the place. Neville is a police officer, trained in surveillance—Boy and Gris are highly trained in unarmed combat and you have none of these skills, and at the minute, are just a hindrance… please go back to the Party and let me get on with it."

Bishop didn't need to listen to the explosion as he walked away and left her, but she didn't follow him and just stood there watching him.

There were now two people they needed to watch, and both Russian specialists, with Marlin as the third… all Eastern Europe specialists.

They would need checking and getting rid of, if he could not class them 'Persil'.

Bishop continued his walk and now saw the footprints—they had taken no care which meant they didn't expect to leave anyone alive!

They *knew* about Antona—they knew about Coombe Lane… someone had stood here for a long time, carrying something heavy by the depth of the footprints.

He followed the footprints back, looking for others and finally back to the road where he saw the tire tracks and footprints of at least 4 people.

He took one of the brown cameras he always carried and moving back from the road, shinned up the tree, spiking it into a branch about 10 feet up. DUA could pay for the dry cleaning, he thought, working his way back to the house and putting the other cameras in the spots they would come from. Then he headed back, joining up with Gris and Boy.

"What danger are we in, Bishop?" Antona asked.

"*None,* I think… if Prilloch hadn't finished them, we'd be dead, but it's *sorted* now and they know we can handle them… there will be a few long faces, somewhere. It was a five-man team, and they expected to take out Coombe Lane with no trouble and then head for here. Both out of the way places—shielded by trees… the shots ignored… Did anyone show any signs of being anxious?"

"Only one who seemed anxious was Larita, and she was your housekeeper before we moved here her. "

"We thought it was because everyone was pairing up and she didn't have anyone, but she was the only one showing any signs of worry…?

"One other thing we noticed though, was Agripina kept trying to ring someone, and both of them didn't seem to want to get involved in the party—staying on the outskirts for most of the time."

"I need to talk to DUA, Antona… someone knew about both houses, and Romel and Ewa didn't get it from us, or Carmella, as they don't know about you…?

"Only Lance, Eunice, plus Thomas *knew* about both addresses, although we warned them not to talk to anyone about this… it would have been a *massacre* if Prilloch hadn't taken his stroll—Boy, Gris and I need to get back. Monitor this bunch."

It took 10 minutes to get back to Coombe Lane and update DUA, whose immediate comment was, "Larita is one of the most trusted people I have ever met… I can't believe she is capable of this!"

"Someone on the team did it, DUA… Cliff, Agripina, Marlin and Larita are the closest to the Russians—Larita and Agripina looked uneasy, staying clear of the team at Antona's place, and Larita at Coombe Lane knew everyone and everything.

"What have we done with the bodies, by the way?"

"Bagged and tagged as it stands—waiting for the pickup, paperwork, and then Gloria gets them."

"I take it Prilloch is still checking the grounds?

"Can we check Larita's and Agrippina's mobile calls?" DUA.

"If Marcel's crew had the equipment working then yes—at the moment, it is open season."

"Monitoring the team's mobiles is an application on their mobiles, DUA—sent to our second machine from the monitoring box, not Marcel's hardware…? We put it in to monitor the surveillance team's location, their calls, and so we know who they've rung and when. If we bothered to look at it now, DUA, we would know, but the team isn't live until Monday so no-one is bothering to review the information."

"Get Cliff, Agripina, Marlin and Larita over here, Bishop—show them the bodies.

"Larita and Martin I planned on using in Russia if I had to, now I don't know, and I have nowhere to put Larita; if they have turned her—she knows everything about the teams."

"Let's get them over here and see who they know? The mobile numbers as well, if you can, Marcel, and who they are if we can find out?"

Bishop, Boy and Prilloch were off with some more cameras, courtesy of Darius… it was getting so bad, even the birds were powdering their beaks, and taking *selfies*.

We tracked back to the road, and once again Bishop photographed the car tracks—the rest of the cameras were pointing at the road and access points, but no-one was actually looking at the cameras, anyway.

The data was just being rammed into Marcel's big bag of tricks, and we had one guy stalking two sites with a knife, as our visual, while six guys, trying to install a computer weren't looking at anything else… the guy with the knife was now five to one on, as we were alive.

Watching the faces as we paraded our specialists in to look at the bodies was interesting. At one corpse, Cliff punched the air.

Agripina couldn't hide her feelings as each face appeared, but Larita, when she saw one, could not stop the tears as she sobbed—they both knew we weren't showing them the bodies for fun.

Bishop led them to the other side of the room—Larita knew everything… it would be a trip with Marcel to one of the US camps—Marlin made a point of spitting on every corpse.

Agripina looked at us, and said, "Do I go the same way?"

Bishop joined her and Larita, and said, "This isn't Russia, so you live. Marcel's crew will take you away, lock you up somewhere until this operation was over, and then swapped somewhere, in time, when your knowledge is useless. You set up a killing that would have killed 26 people, waited for it to happen, and the description 'missing in enemy action' would be apt for the pair of you—I would have shot you by now, but DUA stopped me."

"We have authority for self-defence, Bishop—that is *revenge*."

"If Security had done its job, DUA both of these would be *known* by now but we have seven body bags, and two potentials instead… we don't know who these two worked for, but it wasn't for Romel or Ewa, so there are other moles who had been getting rid of moles, and these are not reporting to anyone internally in Security… what a shambles—it makes our bunch of cretins look professional."

"What about the calls, Marcel?"

"Agrippina's mobile calls linked back to official Russian Security at the embassy, and so are Larita's calls—they were both working together and direct—not linked to our suspects."

Gris burst in staring at Marcel, "The cameras would have worked as well, if Marcel's operation had been monitoring the output"

"Marcel pulled everyone off everything to work on the machine, so we knew nothing," added Bishop.

"You said the machine was the priority, DUA, so I pulled everyone off as we are not live on surveillance yet."

"We have been living on surveillance since last Monday, Marcel. It is your machine that hasn't lived and is still not alive. Without Prilloch today, we wouldn't have a machine, a team or lives, because we didn't even have one guy monitoring-courtesy of your failing bunch, and Antona was just as bad. Partying, and no-one allocated to watch cameras. They caught us with our pants around our ankles and who arranged that."

"You can't just blame my team… we all fell down on the job!"

"What job were they on and which woman. If Larita hadn't seemed so anxious, Marcel; or Agripina hadn't kept ringing on her mobile when she thought she wasn't being seen. We wouldn't have guessed at their decision to stay clear of the party. Both of them knew and were keeping to the outskirts so the automatic fire wouldn't touch them. Maybe I should have let Bishop dispose of them—killed in operation."

"I can still do that, DUA… it would solve a lot of problems—I didn't talk in front of Agripina, or leave stuff lying around, so she learnt very little from me," said Bishop.

"Apart from the briefings, Bishop, which were more than enough, we have to assume everything went back to the Embassy, although Russian Intelligence Divisions are *renowned* for not telling each other anything if they can avoid it. Game-playing political points—they are more likely to kill each other—so we hope that by the time everyone knows, we have finished whatever disaster we are planning."

Things didn't go quiet after that, but there were, in the main general issues.

Marcel had become *involved* with Val—who would head up Surveillance, and his wife had found out and was now *divorcing* him.

Neville and Antona had *resurrected* another old war, and weren't talking to each other again, and finally Thomas had told Bishop and DUA about Meik being sent out by Romel on assignments, with three people dead, including Jimmy Mackintosh… the look on DUA's face being one of the hardest to understand, when he heard.

Neville picked up the phone to ring DUA and then left that until the 8.00 pm briefing.

Antona had *gone* off in a huff and wouldn't be there, so there was no urgency… tonight would be good enough, and it was probably a good idea to be out of Coombe Lodge again, and he drove over to Coombe Lane.

He headed into the surveillance room to see who was in—they always seemed to have the *best* coffee and always on tap, so he poured himself a cup.

Sherrell, Malik, Joselyn and Warner were all back—*drying* out with blow heaters and hot coffee after pacing out their patches.

Akiko, Marlin, Thresa and Dot were on site now, and Shad, Elisha, Cliff and Loni were on their way to replace then with Michal floating, as was Val for any night activity, but with this rain, they all were floating, still the coffee stayed on, hot and strong, which some of those relationships also seemed to achieve in the cold rain, as they huddled together as lovers. Any closer and they would need a nursery along with the coffee machine.

The state of the Surveillance Team, however, led to Huron agreeing to fund—*recovered* from Lance in due course for some apartments in London.

Romel watched by Val now rented an apartment at £795 pw, and another one at £390 pw in Marsham Street, and he wondered how would Marcel like that piece of shenanigans, as the CIA was using Val to *entrap* Romel, while the rest of the team (excluding Val) moved forward on Stockholm.

Huron had taken over from Marcel, who was *muddying* the waters with his divorce, and relationship with Val, and would arrive soon, with Marcel moved to Stockholm.

Life was certainly *interesting* on surveillance, if you could *remember* where you left your *underwear*, and with whom.

Neville smelt Security everywhere these days, but he still had Antona demanding instant *obedience* or *oblivion* again, if he did not do what do what he was told.

Owley was telling him his career depended on his relationship with Antona, who by now, wouldn't even acknowledge him… their bed seemed to get bigger and bigger, with Antona more and more remote… all the old problems of control coming back—now—she seemed to *hate* how close to the surveillance team he was getting, with all the women flirting with him.

Was she getting jealous or feeling she was losing control again?

The longer he could work away from Antona, these days, the *better*.

His clothes and old car gone, with the *only* thing left to him, a beaten up half house in Putney that he refused to sell, and things were so bad he would have to ask Albert to pack his stuff, so he could leave—he didn't even know where the stuff was.

He was *sick* of being manipulated by everyone.

He would talk to DUA tonight to get himself transferred, or he could commute from Putney as he had really had enough.

XXXV

8.00 pm, as usual, arrived for the daily briefing, and Antona *now* turned up.

DUA went through the general strategic stuff and then moved onto the Surveillance operations.

With Val moving out *unaccompanied* to the one bedroom Marsham Street flat, as part of the covert operation… Neville was in the three bedroom flat and in charge of Surveillance—they could not keep commuting between London and Kingston with things heating up and he wasn't thinking about members of the team who were getting heated in more ways than one.

Neville would be the *chief* resident and *Boss* for the Team, while Val would now concentrate on Romel.

Marcel would head for Stockholm with Huron taking over the US team at Kingston. Watching the faces was interesting for Neville, especially Antona's expressions, as she thought he had returned the compliment of not telling her what was going on.

DUA was a lot more understanding and more devious than people gave him credit for… Neville was out of Antona's place with no arguments, Val was out of Marcel's bed, and they would base the surveillance people with Neville.

"Are we changing the Surveillance operation, DUA?" Said a voice that Neville recognised as his own.

"We have a *third* target, Neville? We don't know who it is, but its not Ewa and Romel. We have fairly sound evidence against… no, I won't comment in case it is leaked. Whether it will *hold* is another matter… but we think we have found another mole? We feel that there is potentially someone else who is far more dangerous, but is Thomas Macguire the catalyst? We just don't know who he passes information on to—pass the *parcel perhaps*—we just don't know. There could be 5 moles now and possibly another one? We've identified 2, here; at least 2 in HQ. We could be as high as 6?"

"Are you *thinking* of Thomas Macguire, as a mole, DUA?" interrupted Bishop, "Thomas could have blown us out of the water, many times?"

"Romel is '*bang* to rights', Bishop. Ewa, we are certain on. Agripina and Larita's links were direct to the Embassy and we think that was outside of anyone else… we actually had 2 deep moles pensioned off by Security, run by the Embassy and dumped on us by Eunice and Lance…? What price, Eunice, Thomas and Lance?"

"What about the apartments, DUA?"

"Huron will be here, soon. He wants the flats kept for as short a period as possible."

The meeting folded and Neville saw DUA signal to him as he went to leave.

"You're staying here tonight, Neville. There is a sleeping bag in surveillance, and we will pick your stuff up tomorrow using Marcel, who is good at diplomacy.

"The team need keeping on target, and not in bed together, and that is your job."

"Brothel keeper… DUA?"

"Whatever, Neville… this needs managing and Val has disappeared again."

"Who is controlling Val?"

"Val will be back… so I am told by Bishop, who once again is hiding what he knows…?

"Val is to pick up Romel who I think feels he is busted. I'm sure about that after the attack as he stayed safely at home during the attack but I need Bishop to have a little 'tête a tête' with Thomas, and the thing that gets me is how does, whoever it is, get the stuff from Thomas—I am loosing this, Neville—how is the information passed on, and by whom…? We've deliberately been bouncing Thomas with rubbish, and looking at how much data passes on… it seems to be like Simon Askew again, where the Russians are getting information somehow within a few days and we don't know how. "Let's have an early night and see what shakes out in the morning."

Neville headed for his sleeping bag, and some serious head banging without the nagging banging him awake; waking the next morning with a neck ache and for a change it wasn't Antona. He finally got a shower and breakfast from Valene, albeit not in the same way and the agreeable thing… was… he was already at work or heading for his own flat, cleaned by someone else.

At least the morning was more peaceful, so far…?

Albert, not Marcel, turned up with Neville's wardrobe, leaving nothing left at Antona's place, apart from the car.

Neville was dropped off by DUA, the next day, and knew as he moved into the flat, an argument was brewing as Shad who was Buddhist and Dot who was Jewish, started on each other, yet again—he could not think of a more ill-*matched* pair. They were attracting attention to themselves instead of fading into the background for surveillance. It might be good for the others, but it forced him to haul the couple off, and split them up himself, after Val refused to do anything.

Val now wanted to sort out Marcel's throw-out by his wife, and whether she was going to be the woman who broke their marriage up.

Did Disney have these problems with their characters… he was left with a Surveillance Team, minus 3 people who should do their jobs—Antona throwing threats, ultimatums and tantrums as she felt he was moving out of her control—Val refusing to get involved in managing the team.

The flat at Marsham Street should have been a god-send with Owley approval, but was proving a disaster—waiting to happen.

Neville heard a car outside his flat, and looking out saw his 'Red Jaguar' from Antona, being put into his parking space.

She couldn't resist making a point… she was becoming as big a distraction as Val.

Antona's ego couldn't accept that she could not have her own way—Val worried about being blamed for breaking a marriage up, but everyone else got the bill.

Hopefully Dot and Shad after the *bollocking* Neville had given them would actually do a job, but he moved Dot to the 'three bed' flat to look after it—infuriating Antona even more.

Shad was back in Kingston as a 'gopher' between the two houses, and was told to roam around as directed by Prilloch, which should teach him to keep his temper, with a promised vegetable boot up his 'jacksie' as he didn't want a leather sole, if he carried on with his Buddhist *arguments. Which would be wasted* on Prilloch's bowie knife.

It made being a Spy seem a fetish for the evenings when you were bored, and so far Boy was the only person delivering anything by the sound of it.

Deadra Dimitriadis made her way down to filing, exchanging a few words with Eunice, first, before she went to look up some information.

Her instructions were to put details of anything she knew from Carmella's Department into one file, move to another file and anything she found there, went into a small brown envelope, which she placed in her original file and left there for three days.

As the three days were up on a previous filing she followed routine and dropped the small brown envelope off to a beggar at the Tate when she took a long stroll for a breath of fresh air.

Her instructions also required her to speak to Romel from time to time but her superiors regarded Romel with suspicion, considering him disposable—her talking to him was nothing but trouble making as far as they were concerned—she never really knew anything that was happening in her Department, anyway. She was just being pleasant and liked him.

Bishop had a Manager's interview with Thomas Macguire, who quivered every-time he saw him.

They went back a long way and Thomas always helped—maybe he was due an easy ride with Bishop, who intended to allow him his dignity and honour, providing Thomas gave him the information he wanted, otherwise he would screw his arse to the wall.

The office Thomas held onto like a limpet, was on the same floor as the Russian Department, and the old files that missed being computerised on the last project, *were* in the basement with Eunice.

Thomas kept himself *sane* with Eunice and he protected that, *filing* his slips, before he slurped his tea and ginger biscuits into a deep personal hole.

Eunice to Thomas, was like a Confessional Priestess—always ready to give him *absolution*— almost making it a religious visit, but now with Bishop visiting, that did not bode well, but at least he had time for a stroll down to the shop to buy a sandwich, and put something in his belly and buy him time.

He often saw Romel in the shop, although he deliberately moved away while Romel made his purchases, and then Romel gave the beggar his usual tip.

There were more people around these days as it was becoming a popular point for lovers from the flats, although the pair that were always arguing, seemed to have gone.

Thomas made his way into the store for his sandwich, buying the ginger nuts for Eunice—an old story to make the heart bleed.

He would buy the ginger nuts, and Eunice would lace his tea with an *extra* offering of whisky, so the balance *achieved* meant the world was at *peace* and he could lean back and chat about the day… not that Eunice was interested, as she often told him.

She would always sit there, half-asleep, *nodding* as he talked… often as if it was *something* he needed to get off his chest and she could offer kind words to—some days it *was*—then another cup of tea, another biscuit, top-up if he was very lucky and back to work for another two hours, and home.

He looked up from the Ginger Nuts in the shop to *recognise* a face—from *somewhere…* the look in the eyes seemed to say; he was remembered and noted, but where he had seen the face?

He paid his bill, with the pattern of grey stones *beckoning* him back to the office.

He always avoided the old caged lift with its metal grip—reaching his office to find Bishop at his desk, rising upwards to shake his hand, "*Good* to see you again, Thomas. Been a long time."

"Good to see you again, Bishop. It has been a long time and that is my desk."

Bishop moved around to the hard bone chair, "We go back a long way, Thomas… what are thoughts on the Service?"

"It has changed… maybe for better, maybe for worse, but outside of my control?"

"Information is control, Thomas, and I need to find out where information has been going, and to whom, in this organisation?"

"Don't look at me, Bishop. I just take calls, make notes and wait for my pension."

"Who gets your notes, Thomas?"

"Romel gets the notes, and I keep a copy."

"How many copies, Thomas, and this is Bishop you are talking to?"

"The third goes into a file in filing… old dead file—no-one would find it."

"So how do you know, no-one has ever found it, Thomas?"

"I used the old trick of two hairs… lick them, one by the spine and the other visible."

"When do you check them?"

"I meet Eunice then do my filing and I check then and have a cup of tea."

"The hair is always in the same place, Thomas?"

"Never moves, Bishop!"

"For how many years have you been putting the hairs in the same place, Thomas?"

"I suppose I have always put them in the same place, but Eunice opens the Filing Department— locks it when she leaves—I would know if anyone tampered with the threads! It would have to be between those times."

"Always white aren't they, Thomas, and every bit of information I have given you recently, has gone to the Russian… how, Thomas? Your and Eunice's hair are both *white*, and the hairs are always in the same place, Thomas and most files digitised and stored electronically—there is no need to visit, is there, Thomas, apart from your tea?"

"Deadra goes down there, I know… Eunice says she doesn't, but she has a *funny* way of walking— like there is some injury and you can see it in the dust—her files are close to mine, so she is doing what I am doing, I think and keeping her little treasure troves.

"I can't complain at someone else doing what I do."

"Did you ever talk to Simon Askew about this?"

"Why do you ask, Bishop?"

"Everything Simon *knew* kept getting around to people we don't think he knew."

"Simon asked me *one* time about where he could store some information he worried about, but didn't want to keep on him."

"I told him to go to *Admin*, but he wouldn't, so I told him to use an old file."

"Who else knows about this, Thomas?"

"Eunice *knows* what happens in her department… the walk in the dust shows her and Deadra's feet by the same files, so Eunice obviously checks the area after Deadra has been then… you can't be too careful these days, Bishop?"

"Eunice tells you Deadra doesn't go down there, and then checks Deadra's files, Thomas?

"Those feet go past your and Deadra's files, and you don't check the hairs on your files, do you Thomas?"

"I've always *trusted* Eunice… so does Lance."

"You are *too* trusting, and so is Lance? What does Lance *trust* Eunice with Thomas?"

"I don't know, Bishop."

"Then *how* do you know, Lance trusts Eunice?"

"They have been around together a lot—in the past."

"You told Simon to do the *same* as you do, didn't you, Thomas? Everything you are told goes into a file in the filing department—Deadra is also putting information into files, and Eunice is *reading* those files, and the only evidence she doesn't, is '*old grey hairs*'.

"Paint brush hairs, and a fraction of glue are probably the solution, while you *ignore* the blurred footprints that go no further than your and Deadra's files."

"*What* do you want me to do then, Bishop?"

"When you go down for your tea and biscuits, today, do everything as normal without recording our conversation, and you might get your Pension, and a Bonus."

"How do I *explain* that?"

"You *don't*… consider this a basic check on Security, and we are checking 'yours'!"

"You can't be *checking* on Eunice, surely. She's been here for years.

"She helped DUA pick people for the house, Bishop?"

"Which included 2 Agents controlled by the Russian Embassy; 2 Agents who cannot stand one another in a surveillance team, but the Russian Agents who tried to kill us, were separate from other control routes we know about, so if it is Eunice she is linked directly to the Russian Embassy, and not to anyone internally.

"You go down for your tea and biscuits, and I will give this small camera to set up, instead of doing it myself.

"Tuck it into one box opposite your files, so it can see everything, but is not obvious. That will tell us who else is looking at what files… if Eunice finds it, say it must have been Deadra who put it there. I will have to leave it at that and make a move back to Brixton. Take care, Thomas, and I mean that we wouldn't like to lose you."

XXXVI

Bishop hailed a taxi back to Brixton, seeing DUA as soon as he arrived, "Had to change plans… wasn't sure what to do—?

"Thomas told me that the old files are only visited by him and Deadra… Eunice's footprints, however, are in the dust up by his files—Deadra's files next to his.

"He told Simon to use it, as he does, which was probably how the information was picked up in the past."

"Afternoon Tea and Tot Dance, Bishop!"

"It looks like it takes three to tango, DUA, with spies dancing around the files."

"Is the camera in?"

"I told Thomas to put the camera in… we will know if he doesn't, but main issue is Deadra either dropping, or collecting, from the filing department—making Eunice the controller.

"If she isn't, then it is Thomas, as no-one else goes in, and he is lying about Deadra."

"Go on, Bishop."

"If the camera is placed correctly, there's a good chance it isn't Thomas, and the link is Eunice and Deadra, so we need surveillance on Deadra, to see where she goes and who she sees."

"Do you think she is passing information onto Romel?"

"She obviously sees Romel, and he is passing information—sabotaging projects, but not the level that Deadra would know about."

"So it doesn't look like a link to Romel, for Deadra."

"His work is more damage to the structure; projects being started, failing and working with Ewa to create havoc… not operational project data—he isn't getting that information, and Ewa does not really seem to have any real contact with him, except in organisational matters, so there is nothing really, that links him to Deadra."

"We seem to have 4 fresh streams, Bishop… Romel using Hammersmith with probably the beggars at the Tate and Horseferry Road, somehow involved.

"Ewa—we still don't have hard evidence on just Boy's hunch and her relationship to Romel.

"Deadra—we don't know who she passes information to, and the hidden mole—we know nothing about at the moment, but they seem to use different routes to pass information."

"What about Lance and Carmella, DUA?"

"Lance, we know uses Richmond Park to hide the information he gives and receives, outside of the organisation, but Carmella just 'couldn't give a damn' and they aren't interested in anything but themselves."

"We'll just have to see what the camera comes up with, DUA… I still trust Thomas as he could have caused us grief over the years but didn't, and he retires in 3 years so he isn't going to 'kill the Golden Goose' of his Pension now."

"I think you might be right, Bishop, but I am still not sure…?

"Ewa and Romel both stayed indoors the weekend the Russians attacked us, and I don't believe in coincidental lock-ins over weekends and certainly not for both of them."

"What about the Surveillance Team, DUA?"

"Marcel will arrive in Stockholm today, and that should generate some movement, however there is still the point that Lance made as a joke, Bishop…?"

"What joke was that, DUA?"

"Without Eunice, he would not *know* what was going on… so how is Eunice, who never leaves the filing department and only ever sees Thomas and Deadra, getting information to pass on to Lance that has any importance. Thomas and Deadra don't have big secrets?"

"She must have other routes for information, DUA."

"At the moment, Bishop, there is just Thomas, Deadra and anything general that is passing around, unless she gets emails from Ewa, and we would know about them now… no other way she can access information, as far as I can see."

"Agreed, DUA… I can't see that happening, so where else does her information come from—who have we missed…?"

"Much as I hate to say it, Bishop, it is looking more and more like *Eunice* is the deep mole and getting information from Ewa, Thomas and Deadra—spoon feeding Lance as it suits her."

"DUA… please don't tell me it was Eunice that decided which files to computerise?"

"If she headed up the team deciding what to scan, Bishop, then she would have been aware of every major project, and her team would have been the team scanning everything while a few important projects were missed and kept manual, with no budget to correct it. Eunice would also receive updates of every major project, if the files weren't computerised, with no Security in place to stop her?"

"I am actually wondering, DUA, whether we need Val to throw herself at Romel… it seems obvious his only connections are in Hammersmith and with the beggars."

"I am more *worried* about Antona playing up, at the moment, Bishop. Since we moved Neville, she is so counter-productive… Huron is moaning about the cost of two apartments—we might need to let her have Neville back, to fight every night, and put Val back in charge of the Surveillance Team, cutting the apartments down to one."

"I think Antona feels *frightened* without Neville there, DUA—she is the only one left after the rest of the Hijacking Team were killed, but she is becoming so jealous and overbearing, that she is a *menace* at those meetings and you can't keep *slapping* her down as she tries to cause trouble."

"I'll sort it out, Bishop—bar her from the meetings, if I have to."

"You sound more and more like a Manager, DUA—not the vicious 'son-of-a-bitch' killer, I always believed you to be?"

"Any more of this, and I will weep in my beer but as long as that stops you trying to *kill* Huron, I don't mind."

"I gave that up long ago, DUA."

"Well, don't adjust back, *now*. I need Huron alive. How did you get out, Bishop?"

"*Don't* ask, DUA."

"Well, let's see if we can *dig* these moles up. Have their little noses show about ground, and then bag them?"

"What about *Neville*?"

"I will *have* to talk to Neville and Antona—probably *twice* to reinforce it—see if I can get him and Antona back together, then ring Vance and Carmella to tell them Marcel Datri is on his way to Stockholm; see what that stirs up."

"That might push Deadra to action, possibly with Romel, and some walkies if she feels the need to deliver a message—make sure someone is watching her, and she doesn't slip through the net—we can at least try to trigger some action. I'll ring Antona."

"Best of luck, DUA."

DUA picked up the phone and rang Antona—waiting for her to pick the phone up, "This is about Neville, Antona. I need you and Neville to declare a truce!"

"I didn't cause this trouble, DUA."

"You have done nothing to make it go away, either, Antona, and I can't waste time on you two…? I need to pull Neville back out of the flat as Val's operation is cancelled, and she will take over the Surveillance Team again, so Neville has to come out of there—I don't have the room at Coombe Lane, and you two fighting, are wasting many people's time. Either sought it out, or he goes back to Wandsworth—Putney or anywhere, I don't care, and he stays off the project."

"Don't give me ultimatums, DUA."

"I don't give ultimatums, Antona… I don't have the time to waste—he is being pulled out of the flat—and I don't care whether he goes to you, Putney, or back to the police. Now I have to be at Heathrow, so the choice is yours!"

DUA put the phone down and left for Heathrow.

Bishop headed back to his own office. Boy's input to Marcel and Huron had been very good. Next thing was to talk to Darius, who handled the gadgets, and he was back at the 'ranch'. Neville was at the 'tower' until DUA rang him. Which given DUA's hatred of man management meant Bishop would eventually ring Neville as DUA would leave him hanging. He rang Neville. Found he was engaged—and probably not to Antona—so perhaps DUA had finally conquered his dislike of people management.

Neville had picked up the phone for another full-blooded row with Antona.

"Neville, DUA has just rung me to tell me Val's operation is *cancelled*, she is taking over again, on Surveillance and there isn't room for you at Coombe Lane—do you *want* to come back here, or go to Putney?"

"If we are going to carry on as *before*, I will go to Putney!"

"Do you *need* to?"

"I am too *old* to be a child, even if I *behave* as one."

"Then don't *behave* as one!"

"With you treating me as a child before I open my mouth? What are you *frightened* of, Antona… not men—you've have enough in your life, so why do I *frighten* you?"

"One *minute* you are happy, the next doubting, the next thinking, the next angry with yourself, and at *no* point will you talk to me about it. I don't know what I have done wrong, Neville, when you *bottle* it all up and *won't* discuss it—you have your own mental '*men only*' locker room—and you won't let me in?"

"Antona… I don't need… no, I don't need anyone *running* my life—it is already crowded with people doing exactly that. In my mental 'men only' locker room, they accept me as I am. They don't tell I am *wrong*; *patronise* me—try to change me; make demands; they just accept me. You will not do that. I can do everything, as long as it is as *you* decide, and you still can't stop, no matter what you *promise*!"

"What are you going to do then, Neville?"

"*Live,* Antona… just… just let me live!"

"Are you *coming* back?"

"Are you going to let me *live*?"

"I'll tell Albert to have No.1 ready, if you choose to come back!" Antona hung up.

Antona had always been in control of everything in the past, apart from Roger's earnings. She had controlled completely for her whole married life… her mind had shut away anything different—if she was ever honest with herself —that was a troublesome matter for her?

She could not live with someone who did not behave as she expected, yet Neville was one of the most naturally talented people she had ever known, when he allowed it to show through.

She would never keep Neville, but he was such a tangled mess she could not stop trying to run his life, dress him, decide what he ate—like she had played with her first dolls house—hopefully he would come back, but to a dolls house or it was now more a lodging house now than a dolls house?

Neville, yet again, had an 'accept or not' ultimatum. Whether it was by beer, a superior, a sense of justice or injustice, he was and had been controlled for most of his life.

Antona could not live with someone she could not control, and he was not prepared to be controlled, but someone had controlled him of all his life unless he was drunk and now that avenue was closed to him.

Would he go back to Putney? That was a *dead* duck, and he knew that.

Owley had involved with him Security for a good reason, and he knew why.

The powers that be, would never allow him to achieve anything but Owley did not waste a toothpick if he could recycle it, so he would go back, take it, and keep his mouth shut as he had done before, or lose everything in his life.

He was packing when he heard the doorbell ring, and opening it, found Albert standing there.

"I thought you might need some help, sir. Mrs Turner is not the easiest of people to get on with, but we have a balance in the house when you are there, sir, and I will re-arrange your packing."

"Thank you, Albert."

DUA made the airport—the plane was late, and he parked opposite the terminal, flashing his card to anyone telling him to move on, until he sounded like a recorded message, as they queued up to hear it.

DUA eventually spotted Huron's tuft through the crowd of parking wardens, although it was slowly sinking—probably needing superglue before it disappeared.

He didn't get out of the car to meet him, otherwise they would tow it away before he got back. He put the blue spinning lights on to keep the Wardens and the towing truck, which had just arrived, in limbo… then he got out of the car, and open the boot.

"Huron looked down, then at him and said, 'No!' I travel *inside* these days."

"We stopped the Cavalier class, years ago, Huron! It is all legal these days and we need to get moving before we get towed away."

"Always discreet DUA, but how else can I remember you?"

"My trying to stop Bishop from killing you would be a first stop, although I seemed to have to do that with many people at one time, but not paying me money I expected to see, would be the second!"

"We *needed* the woman!"

"So did Bishop, and they *strung* him up from a tree by his *feet* in a jungle, to show their need for her as well?"

"His fault for being *attached* to her. He was supposed to *kill* her with you killing him so you had an excuse?"

"He was just *attached* to the tree, not her… now I have to stop him again, from killing you!"

"We are all one team here, DUA?"

"No, Huron, we are several teams and likely to be in several parts, sometimes. Yours have divorced each other in the middle of a project, and we'd all be dead, but for my team!"

"DUA… Marcel has moved and so has Val; Neville relocated as well, plus Dot and Shad. Carry on, and we will run out of spots for relocations. It has seen more incisions than an operation, and I still need to talk to the Boy—alone—no recordings…. No nothing, but the Boy and me!"

"Why, Huron? He is over Africa… leave him be."

"*Alone*, DUA, and no-one, not even you there, when I speak to him!"

"Any apologies are long gone, Huron—the Boy has *grown* up!"

"Him alone, DUA, and I will not keep *repeating* myself—Him alone!"

"Your decision, Huron, but what really happened in Africa."

"You took out Peres, Turner and Matthews!"

"Then why the hell do you want to talk to the Boy… you not are in a damned confessional, and they were not related to your team!"

"Because I am in confession, DUA, and that is for the Boy… you have Romel dead to rights, so why the expensive action on the apartments? We know or will track shortly, the key contacts. So why?"

"We still don't have any information from your team… Marcel and his guys have produced nothing and we have only ideas—nothing hard and fast, or in writing."

"We know Romel printed out the message after he encoded it, DUA, and we have his pre-encoded and encrypted message but nothing, apart from that."

"You have it, Huron—we don't have any stuff at all, as it sits on you and shits on us!"

"So why do you need an apartment to entrap him, DUA?"

"Huron… we know that he made no attempts electronically to contact anyone, but managed delivery—we can't have people commuting between Millbank and Kingston, and doing surveillance in London—it's a bloody joke."

"So you have got him, DUA, but with no evidence to prove it… why the apartment—how is that going to provide evidence?"

"Romel is using a standard drop point, and that person won't only be *servicing* only Romel but *others* as well, and we can't follow that, *sat* in Coombe Lane."

"That still doesn't explain why two apartments *help* you? One, I can probably accept, but two, when one is a one-bedroom apartment—makes little sense."

"We have a ring in operation, besides the people we are after; they could be two separate operations, and we need two separate locations, although after your constant whining, we are closing the one bedroom.

"We know Romel left carrying something, when he went to Mass—we followed him, and no-one came near him on the way, or in the church—apart from the confessional. He left empty-handed. From the house bugging, we know he received instructions and information but not how except it was manual and thus we need to follow him."

"Your surveillance failed then—how do two apartments make it succeed?"

"We saw no-one come close to either him or a pickup, so between the Church and getting back, the drop made and we want the people."

"You are still not telling me how 2 apartments solves this?"

"If your guys were producing *output* we would have him, and we have now closed the small apartment as you *know*, so stop being bloody obtuse; however we need the drop and locations and they probably have a team out there, who could follow us?"

"What else do you need?"

"We need to know whether he was behind the clean-up that has left only Antona alive, out of the people involved in the West African Tanker Hijackings—did Romel order it, or is he just a Gopher…? We also don't know if Romel or his Masters were involved in the operation to attack the US interests in West Africa and cleaning that up is an operation. That would mean Antona was working for the Russians, and another mole in our operation—God's teeth, Huron, I need *help* from you, not an *answerphone* message about apartments for rent."

"You need a holiday, DUA… you are a bit restricted where you can go—they are refurbishing *Alcatraz*, if you are interested—I could get discounted rates for your crew."

"I am more *interested* in who ordered the killings, and killed Mackintosh, Stephens, Gomez, and why, Huron…? It was *finished* and *closed* down by then."

"What was the deal with Antona, DUA?"

"Antona donated money to this project, and we moved her onto Security, which prevents it coming out as she is *officially* off everything public—look Huron…? I might was well tell you… her husband's hijacking ring *went* so far up the Political Chain, it had 2 Ministers, the Met Police Chief and a host of Political backers in the firing line—this country would be in mayhem, if we had taken this through the courts…?"

"So you *covered* up, and justice doesn't exist for the Government, DUA?"

"Government quickly *ceasing* to exist was the rationale if it had got out—not what we wanted—hijackings were closed down, and so were the people…? MOD orders; as they all squawked chicken and looked the other way, including the Ministers up to their ears in it, but it forced Algenald to take action after Antona's husband threatened to blackmail him over his gambling debts, and destroy his career."

"But you only took the small fry out, DUA—the big, you left alone to protect them."

"I am a naturally a butcher, not a shepherd, Huron, and so is Bishop?"

"I think we've covered this enough, DUA. It will be *good* to see the Boy again, and I have spoken to Gris, but never met her."

"Bringing them together, worked better than I ever expected, although I am sure Gris thought she knew every inch of his body from her Kensington days, and has caught up on any other bits she missed since, Huron."

"Pity you closed it down, DUA… it had its usages."

DUA ignored the comment and took Huron back to Coombe Lane; settling him in Marcel's old room, leaving him his routines—DUA could never remember them but—yes, start the next round of phone calls…?

DUA rang Lance, first.

"Lance, we're putting people into Stockholm—Marcel is going in first, and we can work from there."

"Thanks, DUA. Keep in *touch*!"

DUA rang Carmella with a similar comment, although she tried to get details of where in Stockholm Marcel was, and when were they going to go into the 'Russian-finish' stage, provoking DUA's reply… "we are *nowhere* near starting, never mind finishing—Stockholm is just the first move, the rest is months away."

"We should be able to move faster than that, DUA, and I don't enjoy being left out of the loop!"

"We agreed we would handle it this way, for various reasons, and Vance authorised it—talk to him as that is how we are running it!"

"Well, I still don't like it—Russia is *my* area and I should handle it!"

"Russia *was* your area, Carmella, and then you took promotion to Administration Director."

"Romel handles that—I need not get my hands dirty!"

"How much can you trust, Romel?"

"Trust Romel…? There is no reason not to trust Romel—he is excellent at what he does—I have complete confidence in him and everything I know, he knows."

"Then I'll leave you to update him on Security and the need to know, Carmella."

DUA put down the phone and sighed—that was somebody else who would be out of a job when he had finished.

Now to ring Antona again, "Antona, DUA. Neville will be back with you tonight."

"How do you know that—we haven't agreed it?"

"Because if you give him a chance, he will come back, and then you'll behave…?"

"You don't own me, DUA!"

"I own this project, Antona, and you are causing so much trouble that I am sorry we don't have Kensington anymore to put you in. Continue, and I will find some way for you to kick your heels behind bars, where you will not interfere with this Project and you can make out of that, what you want."

"Why, Neville?"

"Neville is an important part of the project—I don't have room for him at Coombe Lane as I've said, so I need him back at your place and I need your problems sorted—or one of you has to disappear… it now looks like I need him, more than you!"

"He needs to learn to behave in a civilised manner!"

"What was the problem, anyway, Antona? You knew what he was like when you took him in—you knew there is no way that he will meekly have his life controlled by you. You two are Adults, so for pity's sake, sought it out… I don't have the time to do it for you, and he is coming back, but I need the pair of you, quiet and working together for now—. In 6 months' time, you can go hang yourselves, side by side and I won't care, but for now, I need peace from your quarters."

"I'll talk to Neville, if I can. Does he know of the fresh changes?"

"Bishop told him earlier, and Albert has already gone there to pack him up."

DUA heard the sharp intake of breath from Antona—the nostrils obviously wide and flared with eyes narrowed to slits—the phone slammed down, and he left it at that.

Something was obviously still there, although it seemed to be still temper than tempered feeling, but he needed a re-enforcement call to Neville and reluctantly picked up the warm phone again and this time Neville picked it up.

"Neville, I won't change the plans, from what I said, and there isn't room at Coombe Lane, which means Antona's place. Are you happy with it? You can go off the project with no problems."

"I still have the half house in Putney, DUA. I'll commute from there. It is a straightforward route to Coombe Lane, and it will be against the traffic."

"What is the problem between you and Antona?"

"I am too old to be a child—I don't like being told when I eat, go to bed, what I should wear or what car I should drive. I have my police wages, and half a house which needs a lot of work, but at least I have my own life, and not a series of instructions. Albert has taken my stuff back to Antona, and I have said, 'I will go back and see how it goes' – there is the No.1 bedroom, and I can use that."

"*Will* you work with Antona? I need both of you working together, and Marcel is now a problem with his antics, and still no reports from his machine—I am getting fed up trying to sort out emotional tangles."

"I need to talk to my Boss first. He pushed me into Antona and told me my career died if I didn't stay with her. I want to see what he says now."

"Fine. Let me know when you've finished. You have been a valuable member of this team, and a full-time job in Security might be one way out, with your police experience."

"Thanks, DUA. Much appreciated!"

"I'll leave you to tell Antona once you decide."

Neville rang Owley… normally 'Owl, Jonathan Detective Chief Superintendent—Homicide and Serious Crime Command' to most people. "Neville, sir. Quick word if I may?"

"Go ahead, Neville."

"It isn't working out with Antona, although I am going back."

"If you go back on the booze, it finishes you, Neville and so will I?"

"I wasn't planning to do that, sir… I am enjoying this project too much to slip back."

"What is the problem with Antona, Neville? DUA gives me reports, and he has spoken highly of you, and you're being prepared to work at anything."

"Antona wants to control my every movement, sir, and I am too old and too independent for that. She literally wants to dictate the time I eat, the clothes I wear, when I go to bed and virtually reminds 24 hours a day that I live off her, and hers."

"What are you going to do then?"

"Work at Coombe Lane, try Coombe Lodge again and commute back to Putney if it fails—I will see the Project through, sir."

"Fine… providing you stay off the heavy booze I have no problem with that. I had hoped the pair of you would brush the rough edges off each other but I could in fact, do with you here, Neville…? Still, *I need to know*, Neville, that you have left your past behind, before I take that risk. Your killer has struck another three times since we spoke. Same 'style', same timing, same districts, same targets. Do you have any thoughts?"

"Target Selection is the obvious one, sir—all Scottish, newly arrived, and that means either trains or coaches. Trains are Kings Cross, Coaches are probably Victoria. Where are the murders concentrated, sir?"

"Hammersmith seems to be a regular feature, Neville, and we still can't trace where they have been drinking before, but not in the pubs. Shepherd's Bush, Kilburn, Paddington, Bayswater and one on the Embankment just down from Victoria are the areas—all between 20.00 and 23.00; single blow to the head; usually a street off a long road and hit on the corner. Same operation every-time."

"The only pub he used, sir, was one of the first victims and that was down from Earls Court. He hasn't used pubs after that, so maybe he's using clubs and not just to hit them with; these guys don't survive long and they aren't well known so he is meeting them quickly and through possibly two holes as they come in. It sounds like Kings Cross or Victoria to my mind?"

"Interesting point, Neville. I'll look into it, but stay off the heavy booze… OK!"

"Yes, sir!"

The phone went down and he sat there thinking about what he was going to say to Antona before the full-blown argument started, and any words were useless, even though they had already talked. He rang Antona. "Neville, Antona."

"Yes, I have already had DUA on, plus Bishop before that."

"I spoke to Owley, and he said if I go back onto the heavy booze, I am finished."

"What bothers you about losing your independence?"

"It is all I have!"

"Can't we reach some kind of agreement?"

"How? I can only eat in one place, eat what is on the table and sleep in one place, at one time. My entire life has always been on some kind of roller coaster, and not the stable life you are used to. I've tried to be settled and controlled and it isn't me. I am used to being where I want to be, not where someone expects me to be. You are used to someone who is reliable, and that isn't me. I am the 'wild card joker' in the pack. I like you Antona, but you treat me almost as a slave, to do exactly what I am told to, and that isn't me."

"Stay over tonight, we'll try to change things. I feel safer with you around, and I want you to stay."

"I'll be there tonight, Antona, and we'll see how things work out."

He put the phone down… now he would have to see what happened.

It would change for two weeks probably and then he would head back again to the same… he was sure, but it would give him time to get some work done on the Putney hovel?

It needed re-wiring for a start, but the drains, plumbing and redecorating all needed doing as well, so the time could be used to moral effect when he could raise the money to do the work.

In the meantime, he needed to let Val move into where he was leaving.

Val often wondered why she always seemed to get the rainy shifts, often wearing nothing but a shift.

Her real bosses had wanted her to work on Marcel; who was now pissed off after his wife had found out, and he was transferred but all it did was to have a more senior canny guy brought in and so it improved the staff and highlighted her to the CIA which her bosses hadn't wanted. It finished the attempt at entrapment and there was no blackmail avenue left to MI6 to use on a CIA asset, after that. They had bollocked it.

DUA also wanted her to stop trying to trap Romel—Gods alive, too many people were trying to make an honest woman of her—it was worrying!

The clothes the team received for surveillance was also worrying.

Cheap rubbish from the charity shop rag collection—after Neville's complaints, they were now getting ex-CIA raincoats designed for the South of America, and probably a tee shirt with 'I work for the CIA on it'.

Neville did actually care about the team, but did not understand their street work as he tried to play it by any book he could find, while they ripped out the pages out—to keep the rain off.

The 'Brits' team, clung together more than ever, to the degree that the budget on mouthwash has ceased to exist as they had to breathe each other's recycled saliva and whatever foods, from salt beef to vegetable curry… too often… while the breath they had coming out was Nuclear War already declared.

Neville had agreed to buy decent stuff to wear, but he'd replaced and moved back to Antona's place which made them wonder why?

If two of the team had to do a sex scene, they did it in thick jumpers and US mail order stuff they had bought for freezing in New York.

The bloody English… always on the cheap unless they were Politicians wasting money!

XXXVII

Huron waited for Boy to get back and dis-entangle himself from Gris, before he commandeered the space in the garden and sat down with the Boy, "Do you ever think of the team, Boy," questioned Huron?

"You know I do, Huron… I miss those guys from Africa as much as you do, and they were DUA's Lunch for what chance they had."

"You know what happened to them, don't you?"

"I know, Huron. They died with Mr Hoo. Irish told me that even if they got out, they were still dead and one of them, probably the Major would hit the bottle and tell everyone, or Benny would try to rob someone, and it would go public. There was no way out for them, no matter what they did?"

"They knew Mr Hoo was going to kill them, Boy, but they enjoyed life again, no matter what happened, and Mr Hoo would die, anyway."

"So they knew Mr Hoo, no matter what he agreed, would kill them, Huron?"

"They knew they would die with Mr Hoo, and they didn't like the idea is more to the point?"

"What happened, and how did they die?"

"They agreed to go under sail like a tourist boat, to get close to the pirates, and that worked while they were using sail, but Mr Hoo went out in a blaze of glory without telling them; he put the foils down, throttle open and raced at the Pirates, despite what they had agreed."

"Mr Hoo killed them?"

"They weren't fools, Boy, and Irish would have been there with Mr Hoo, if he was going to kill them and succeed; shooting him first. Only way out was to play it the way Mr Hoo wanted."

"What really happened, Huron?"

"When they brought us back to Abidjan, my guys told them Mr Hoo was dead buried. There wouldn't be any more hijackings. They could take it *easy* and something in due course would happen if they survived to try and protect them?"

"Roger Turner?"

"Bishop *sorted* him out—the problem was Stephen's son, Mark. The boats in the lagoon would probably keep attacking, but instead of taking the oil, they planned to put explosives on the tankers, and go for extortion as well."

"The stuff from when we hit that site by the National Park when things started exploding, was explosives not ammunition?"

"Yes… we still wanted them taken out, the new English guy dead, and the hijackers stopped dead in their tracks—we decided that one last attack would do that but the guys could survive for everything they had done… yes… they were heroes."

"What happened?"

"My team moved down the coast to monitor anyone coming out of the lagoon or coming down the narrow canal, so we knew what they were doing."

"Who put the plan together?"

"We gave the go-ahead for the original plan but no-one believed, Mr Hoo would just do what he was told—the time for him behaving rationally had long gone, and we knew that, so we told your guys that if Mr Hoo tried to kill them with his Gung-Ho again, they could bail out, and we would put them in the US or where-ever they wanted to go—no problems and no questions asked."

"You gave them a get-out—leaving Mr Hoo to die?"

"When they came in under sail, but before they cleared the isle, Mr Hoo put the foils down, opened up the engines, and when he did, they dived over the side and swam to the isle. My guys picked them up later and took them to Abidjan. We flew them out on US passports, attached to our legation. Mr Hoo went out in a blaze, but the guys didn't—everyone believes they are dead and that is how it stands. Blown apart by Mr Hoo going mad!"

"Are you telling me they're still alive?"

"No-one knows they exist, and it has to stay that way. They are dead if anyone ever finds out they are living. No-one must know, which makes it another problem, because Irish has some knowledge on your current operation. If we use it, we tell the world they are alive, and write their death warrants. They did what was required, and that is we can say all that, but Irish wanted to know what you were doing, and when I told him, he said there is something you should know, and he wants to tell you. I am dialling a number now for you to talk to him."

Huron dialled the number and passed the phone to me… Irish's voice echoed in my ears saying, "You there, Boy?"

"I'm here, Irish. Huron has just told me how you guys got out."

"The Major and Scooter headed back to the Far East, Benny is in Greece and I have a job with the CIA on training. I wanted to talk to you, because there is something you should know from my Ireland days—we actually had a contact in the Security Service who gave information when he could. I knew him from the early days, although we didn't really trust him as he was a Communist and just interested in causing trouble, and we were interested in fighting the British as Irish Nationalists. Heavily involved in the early days. He disappeared, and we heard no more of him until information from the Security Services under some name to protect him started reaching us. It was good medium level information that let us know to a degree of any operations planned against us. We kept his identity a close secret, until one day I saw a photograph of him meeting one of our Security Bosses, and I knew him immediately. Whether he is still a Communist, I don't know—his name I knew—it wasn't important, and I forgot about it until I was chatting to Huron before he left. He was talking about you, Bishop and DUA, and that there were problems with people in the Service, and a guy was helping you guys. I told him I remembered a guy from my early days that was a Communist, and had joined Security, but if I gave the information and he used it, people would know I was alive."

"Is the guy still there, Irish?"

"Yes, Boy, and involved with your operation."

"There is only one man with an Irish name involved in the operation, and that is Thomas Macguire, whom Bishop has known for years."

"That is the guy, Boy—Thomas Macguire… whether he is still a Communist or a member of the Party, I don't know, but he passed us good information during the troubles and fought against the British in the early days, before he disappeared, but if you use me as your source, you are probably sentencing me to death!"

"Why didn't it show up when DUA was recruiting you, Irish? Thomas must have known that you would know him?"

"DUA worked for Defence and Bishop dealt with Thomas, not DUA. DUA discusses nothing with anyone, if he can help it. So Thomas wouldn't have known about me, and probably wouldn't have remembered one guy from years ago in Ireland. He may have gone clean since then, and done nothing, but he was a 'Card-Carrying Communist' and a long-term one."

"Do I tell Huron, Irish?"

"Huron could blow me any time he liked, so it can't do much damage."

I turned to Huron and said, "Huron, the guy he is talking about is Thomas Macguire… says he is a Communist, fought the British in Ireland and then vanished, turning up in Security. Gave them information during the troubles, which makes it sound like he wasn't there in the early days as a Security Agent, but is actually an informant against British interests, and possibly still a Communist."

"It follows to a degree, Boy," said Huron. "We know that he encouraged Simon to put his notes in the filing department, and they were constantly leaked to the Russians. We know he put notes on everything he does in there, as well… Bishop's camera will tell us whether the files are *accessed*, but Bishop *using* him, puts him in a cleft stick, because if he doesn't set it up properly, we know it is him, and if his Masters find out he has betrayed an Agent—that's his life, finished."

"What happens if he tells Eunice?"

"If he tells Eunice, then she will stop looking at the files, if she is doing so—if he tells Deadra then her behaviour will change… he is *hung* if he tells them, *hung* if the camera doesn't work, and *hung* if Deadra and Eunice's behaviour changes, so we leave him be, I think. I'll leave you to talk over old times with Irish."

Huron headed back to the house, leaving Boy talking to Irish, and intercepting Gris, on her way, "Boy is talking to an old friend, Gris. Let him have the call in peace, and then ask him what they discussed… people's *lives* depend on him keeping *quiet*, and you, not repeating it, if he tells you… I'll update DUA and Bishop."

Huron eventually found DUA, and Bishop, and dived straight in, "I can't disclose the source, or he will be dead, if I do, but Thomas Macguire fought the British in Ireland—was an early Communist who passed information during the troubles, to people in Ireland… we have no evidence, apart from the information, which is genuine. We can't use it against Thomas without him possibly finding out the source, although officially the person is dead, and I think you can guess who it is, although I will deny it."

"I think we can guess, Huron—watching Boy on the phone. There are very few people Boy knows that well—the Irish connection says it all. Therefore, Thomas is a communist, a Britain hater and fought against us, before joining Security and leaking information, but with no evidence we can use and no proof he is still doing it…?

"We know his background and the connection to Eunice, but the camera is set up properly, and if he is an Agent, he is prepared to sacrifice others, and we can control him from now on!

That he is using Eunice to pass on his information means that he never needs to take any risks, but what if it isn't Eunice, or maybe Deadra is more than a carrier? This gets more twisted than this Government's policies."

XXXVIII

Huron looked at them for a good while before he spoke…? Words still seemed to rattle around his head as he finally opened his mouth…?

"As it stands DUA, we have as suspects Romel, Ewa, Eunice, Deadra and Thomas, while the incompetents are Lance and Carmella, put in there by Peres, plus Meik as a possible serial killer."

"I know, Huron. It gets more and more like a soap opera every day, and all of them in the same organisation, which is something else, I can't *fathom*. What are the odds on them all being in an old building virtually forgotten about, while everyone else is in the new one? I know it is only a walk up Horseferry Road, but why?"

"I don't think we'll ever know, DUA, but someone organised it and they were well above this crew?"

"What is our plan for Thomas Macguire then Huron?"

"We leave him alone until we have independent evidence we can go on. He could claim that, that was when he was young and he did things but he has left it behind, and apart from warning him, we achieve nothing except to let him know, we know? Until we have evidence on the rest we can't move anyway, and Carmella will protect her team, so we can't even touch Deadra without warning her, Romel and Ewa. We carry on as we were, and stop Gris pursuing Boy for information on this— I have warned her, but she will pay more attention to you than me!"

Deadra was the target now and they had not included Deadra in the original surveillance plans, so Val now had to be within sight of the door, should Deadra and the rain turn up, yet again, and a lousy raincoat she kept complaining about.

DUA said they were going to liven Deadra up, so all anyone could do was wait, but DUA seemed to have a knack for livening people up… it some cases… from the bottom to high up, so something dropped out of either ends?

Deadra heard the phone call, Stockholm—Security being kept out of it, but she couldn't hear anything else, apart from Carmella's loud voice in anger.

That was all the information she had—what the Eggy Project was, she didn't know, but would report it when she found out.

It was Monday, and she normally picked up/put down in filing on certain days, but Wednesday was the only mandatory day, although her handlers preferred she varied the times.

She wrote out the slips, going downstairs to file them and receiving a strange look from Eunice in return, who normally saw her on a Friday, Tuesday and Wednesday.

Darius, back at Coombe Lane, picked up the signal as Deadra put the slips in. Thomas' camera on the opposite side also gave a bird's-eye view of the writing on the slips. He saw the word Stockholm enlarged from the left side of the image.

Some time later as part of his regular checks he moved the image time slowly forward Deadra and 'lo-and-behold', Eunice was opening the file and reading Deadra and Thomas' notes before walking away.

So Eunice was reading information from Thomas and Deadra, but were either moles or just protecting themselves, and why was Thomas still putting the information in there when he knew Eunice was reading it and Darius was sure he did.

Was it that, deep down, Thomas could not believe Eunice was a Traitor or that he knew she was and it didn't matter?

He rang Val to update which meant Val could *stay* out of the *rain*, however his brain had not realised that Val was on a mobile, and went *into* the rain to take the call, and his ears were going to take a while to cool down, after she had got *soaked* again.

He also rang DUA and Bishop to update them and then something crossed his mind.

If the beggars were part of some Network, then in the same way as they used Val to manage everything was someone would be around to watch the beggars who would see Val?

They had been bloody stupid in thinking others would not pull the same tricks as they did, but the glasses' feeds stayed on and transmitting without the team knowing what they saw, which went again, into Langley's machine and never ever came out again.

He picked up the phone and rang Huron, who had taken over now, "Huron. I need time on the machine because I think they have a 'Val', watching the same area as our Team Leader. I need your beast's power because of the speed and number of images!"

"It might be better to send it to Langley, Darius. If you can pipe the feeds into my box, they can go over the fast line and let Langley do the processing with the mega beasts. Probably too much data for my lover."

"I'll do it now, Huron—sooner it gets started, sooner, I get the results."

Darius hooked the feed up. You would need an enormous machine to decode the total data stream, so he wasn't worried.

The smaller machines took the feeds and sorted and routed them into the enormous beast. He checked the setting of the feed and then pumped it through, on its long distance route to find the King Beggar.

On the off-shot, he rang Val, again.

"Yes, Darius, and I *wasn't* just getting dry, and I *love* rain… it saves me taking a *shower*, and I need not *gargle* as it goes into my mouth as well. Can you keep the conversation *short* only I have to move out *into* the rain to get the signal, and the *signal is being affected by my blood pressure going up*!"

"Val, there is a King Beggar out there. It is odds on. I am mapping through your team's vision and sound by person to Langley' to find the face. Those guys have a King Rat. Only thought of it today but you 'Val', have a rival."

"Never thought about it, Darius, but they always have a team and they are even more possessive. They will have two or three but spread around the areas although most beggars in Horseferry Road are in front of the shops… we have given up weekday surveillance on Lance and Carmella now, so I have two sets of people for further involvement, minus the one set we had to throw out—they stay dry while I get wet, which *annoys* me even more."

"Sorry to drag you *out* again."

"*Fine*. I'll go back in the dry, have a coffee and wait while my *knickers dry* off, although I don't expect people will feel I am *excited* apart from the *steam*! At least we have the flat in Marsham Street now, and 3 bedrooms and 2 lovely bathrooms—someone there to do the washing and clean it."

Val did have the chance that night, to be first in the bath to soak, pouring bubble bath to the nth degree, that she looked like a sperm whale *surfacing* with the Listerine, taking the taste of the squid away.

When they interviewed you for Surveillance Teams, she was damn certain they picked nice sunny days, emphasising the carefree life and adventure… not the rain dripping down the back of your neck as you huddled in some thin raincoat, that had already soaked you with the rain while your knickers now ran down your legs, after hours of being washed for the '*nets'* time.

Like the rest, she now kept decent clothes in the flat, and wore her cheap stuff out so it could be ruined—with good replacements, if they didn't keep telling you there wasn't a budget for surveillance—the stuff you wore came from the charity shops before Security bought these rags and issued them as best dress?
They'd followed Eunice all week, and it was not until Sunday to the surprise of the team following from a distance that Eunice met Lance in Richmond Park, when he, his wife and children on their regular Sunday afternoon trip.

Huron, Boy, and DUA finally met up for a face-to-face debriefing.

DUA didn't seem surprised at the information he received whilst Huron stayed deadpan throughout most of the brief meeting, "Lance told me during one conversation that he wouldn't know what was going on if it wasn't for Eunice. It is about a month since we started, so it looks like Eunice meets him once a month for a no records debriefing in Richmond Park, but apart from Deadra and Thomas, anything circulating would be the only other information she would have."

“What about the feeds DUA?”

“Boy had the feeds installed and working since Tuesday to load the enormous machine with, but we still have nothing from it. They couldn’t get it to work, Huron, and now it is working we are still getting nothing out of it. All the feeds are so backlogged, that Marcel is the only guy to get the information out—we have shot ourselves in the foot by moving him to Stockholm, and we still have to shift the feeds to Langley, who take forever to tell us the day of the week, so we got nothing back from the feeds since the beginning of this operation, Huron.”

“What do we have then, DUA?” I asked, “apart from a bunch of CIA incompetents”.

Huron after Boy’s last comment stormed out and Bishop now joined the meeting as we talked about information streams, “All we have is the camera feed from filing. DUA, said Bishop. We know via Larita and Agripina that the Russians know we had surveillance and data processing here, although the CIA will no doubt have got a lot more out of what we have supplied than we have? Romel is the only one we have caught so far, besides Deadra and Thomas putting notes in the files, but Eunice I still feel, does not know she is suspected, and her behaviour should not change as she still has Lance’s confidence and will consider herself safe, so she is probably the one most likely to make a mistake, but Lance mustn’t know about the camera in the filing department.”

“Anything else, Bishop?”

“I’ve had a word with Huron, to get feedback back to us, but he said ‘in so many words’ that the CIA have a major project in the Middle East, and everything else has been downgraded to ‘do when there are free resources’ so they are doing nothing and that is another reason we are getting nothing back on information we pass to them.”

“Since Huron was sitting here and refusing to comment—apart from throwing the CIA bunch out as being a useless, wasteful bunch of time wasters, what do we do?”

“We are now sending out Cliff Kovalik to Stockholm and bringing Marcel back, and hopefully working with Huron, he can get his team back on track on the feeds, since without him, all we seem to get is ‘mañana, mañana’ and nothing else at all from Langley.”

“I know, Bishop. We really are 100% reliant on Val’s team’s surveillance, and even Darius’ ‘King Rat’’s idea has gone nowhere.”

“When is Marcel back?”

“Marcel is back tomorrow.”

Marcel arrived back the following day for an immediate interview with DUA.

“Marcel, we weren’t getting any data from the big machine when you are here, but since you’ve left, we have had a complete shutdown of all information from the machine, while Langley has apparently downgraded our importance to ‘No’, and frozen all data reports. Why?”

"Langley is there for the US, not for you, so you are secondary and these guys are US Citizens, so the US, not your team, matter!"

"So why is the US sabotaging this operation, after they put the hardware and people, including yourself, in—before they sent you to Stockholm?"

"The US is not sabotaging this operation. It has its priorities, and you obviously are not one of them."

"So I can't rely on the CIA, and I am certainly not going to put my people at risk because of CIA games. Clear your people out, Marcel. Take the machine out. All feeds of information are stopped, and I want you and your people off the premises, by tonight!"

"You can't do that!"

"This is a private house… you are a trespasser. It shouldn't take long for Neville to contact his Boss in Scotland Yard—have you out of this house, and the country. Start packing up now and go!"

"I need to talk to my Bosses, in Langley!"

"Talk to who you like, but if you and the equipment, are not off the premises by midnight, my people will cut the cables, break the machinery up, and throw the bits in a recycling dump… you and your stuff gone by midnight—you are useless as it stands—this is a private house, and I am within the law to do this, while the police watch."

Marcel stormed out and into the hardware room where his team were.

"DUA has just told me to get this hardware, and you lot, out by midnight, as you are useless, and he will smash the machine up and dump it in a van if we are not out—what game are you and Langley playing?"

"These Limeys don't tell us what to do. We might take orders from a Yank, but no 'God-damn' Limey tells us what to do!"

"So Langley hasn't frozen the feeds or the data—you've been deliberately holding the data back, as you won't take orders from a Limey! Do you actually know the importance of this operation? I'd better get onto Langley before they find out from someone else… I'm back from Stockholm for what would have been one of the biggest coups in years, over Russia, and my work was stopped, because you want to fight the 'War of Independence' again, you damn *red-neck*.

"What did Huron say when you *told* him?"

"I told him we had machine troubles!"

"So we are all blamed?"

"You like *causing* trouble, don't you, Jonathan? Pack your stuff, you are going now… I'd better find Huron, and the rest of you get those reports moving on the machine, and if you have screwed up this operation, you are back in Langley, minus your jobs, pensions, medical cover and in an army prison which is where this *red neck* is going!"

Marcel went off to find Huron and eventually found him in the second kitchen, "Huron the trouble with the information, was a 'red-neck' ass-hole in my team deciding to fight the war of independence again. There is no problem with Langley, we have the information, but he decided he would not take orders from a 'Limey' only a 'Yank', so he stopped all the feeds. DUA told me he wants us, and the machine off the premises by midnight or his people will break the machine up, and put it in a dump."

"I can understand that. One person coming out of Russia knows the deep mole that has been the primary source of information for years to Russia, although it might be two moles now, and your people by these antics."

"They are just high-spirited."

"They have virtually wiped out the whole project… I'll talk to Langley, and get some priority on these feeds—I'd better talk to DUA, quieten him down before he does do it, and he bloody will—that guys does not muck about and nor does Bishop and he thinks like a freelancer?"

"Fine. I'll start kicking ass again. Who told my wife about myself and Val, Huron? The Surveillance Team doesn't have that access."

"It had to be one of your guys, Marcel, probably the 'Red-neck' as he fancied Val, and she wouldn't touch him. Get rid of him, *now*!"

"He is already packing and on the way."

"Make sure he goes. I want him out now, and in the *cooler*, so he doesn't go running to anyone. On second thoughts… he could blow this project with his temperament. Have our guys come in, Marcel, pick him up and quarantine him—too important to *take* risks. Stay with him until they get here, and I will go see, DUA!"

"Fine. I'll do that now."

Darius was watching the feeds from filing, when Huron found him, "What are those, Darius?"

"Bishop had Thomas put a camera in so we could see who accessed his and Deadra's files—it is Eunice.

"She also met Lance in Richmond Park yesterday, and Boy has now put a feed on her machine, but we can't get the feeds transcribed, co-ordinated… until the monitoring and the screens processing match them up."

"How much have we held you up?"

"From the beginning—Marcel knew what was going on, and he knew we couldn't act without the throughput of his machine—Marcel was holding it up from the beginning… red-neck provided the excuses but Marcel was holding it up? We can capture the password via the keyboard logger, but without the screens linked to it, we can't see what password they used for what or where it was used or what they were accessing. When they are on-line and with multiple applications, we can only guess other passwords, they might use for stuff we don't monitor."

"You still don't know what Eunice is accessing?"

"The biggest problem is where is Eunice getting the information from, and until we get feed reports, we don't have a hope in hell of finding out, or why she would have information of enough use to

Lance, to make meeting him clandestinely in Richmond Park and be of any use. We just don't know; without the feeds, Huron."

"The feeds are being restored as we talk… some guys from my bunch will be here soon to pick up our 'favourite red-neck' – Marcel is monitoring the guy until they arrive."

"We need that feedback on Eunice, Huron. She must have got information that she could pass to Lance, or there would not have been a meeting and we need to know how she is getting it. I can see via the software, the notes left in those files she looks at, are from Thomas and Deadra—there is nothing there, which would interest Lance so where is she getting the information from to pass to him."

They both stood looking at the screens until finally another spluttered into life as the feeds finally started happening and Darius saw Eunice's feedback with Lance's password appearing—the disbelief was palpable to both of them.

Eunice had Lance's password, access and control over anything she wanted. Lance had given a 'Russian Mole', his main *password*. 'It almost makes you want to *weep*', thought Darius as he looked at Huron who stormed off.

Romel now had an email in his in-box with an instruction that meant nothing; apart from a request for a translation course from 'Latvian to Polish', requesting that approval be given to a member of staff, who had requested funding for the Classes and the name of the staff member was Deadra.

Romel considered his coded instructions.

Well, Meik would be outside of the Tate, when Deadra met the beggar and it would be clean, quick and tidy—like all of Meik's work so the instruction was easy to follow.

Romel rang Meik, "be at the Tate to meet Deadra. She is a Russian Agent, and this is an *approved* kill.

Meik, as usual, prepared for his kill; planned the set-up and procedure.

She was a traitor and the killing was approved and he was once again in heaven!

Prilloch received his instructions in the usual fashion, from DUA. 'Someone will try to attack Deadra… kill them if they try' then he considered the rest of the operation.

They had to trap Romel and what better way than for him to plan a murder so they had something they could hang on him?

Prilloch would handle it close with Bishop—long distance—the Boy in close support with Val and her knickers might be dry now but with her cover blown it must be the wind as Bishop had his uses and they included people in MI6 who found themselves facing him and Prilloch in a dark alley. They chose the first who was a Liverpudlian as he knew about dark alleys and thought he was due one if he didn't talk.

Boy's instructions were to have an unobstructed view, working with Val as a pair of tourists.

If DUA was right, Deadra would drop off information to the beggar, and then walk into the Tate, where she would collapse, or failing that be shot, once she left the Tate.

How DUA knew this, Boy didn't know, but DUA was certain that it would happen and they set everyone up for it. They got themselves into position.

DUA said the message had gone to all Agents, and they didn't know them.

Beggars were there as usual, but that was standard.

Val was there with the glasses, scanning from side to side, until she asked Boy to rub her neck, which was the last thing he needed.

It pleased him they didn't do 'crotch guns', otherwise he would need a new holster amongst other things, as he massaged her shoulders and neck, he was getting some hilarious looks from Japanese tourists.

Val leaning back into him made him think… if I have to shoot someone now, it will be through her… which he then quietly mentioned, and she moved aside.

They waited.

Deadra followed her standard Wednesday routine, going down to the filing department and placing some papers in a file.

Then she went to the source file, placing the envelope in the empty folder she was carrying.

Normally she made the drop some three days later, but her instructions this time were to make the drop on Wednesday.

Back at Coombe Lane, Darius watched her via the camera. He had already seen Eunice put the envelope in the file. Now Deadra completed the pickup. She would take her lunchtime stroll to the Tate and drop them off with the beggar.

DUA, courtesy of the cracking of Romel's email system, now knew Romel, Deadra and Eunice's home email systems were linked to the Embassy and that was how they also communicated with each other and with the Embassy—it all came home to roost, once they had the CIA feedback.

Ewa would probably have the same, but there was still no trace of it on her home systems. So whom was Ewa working for?

DUA had come up with the plan to kill Deadra, and they emailed a message from a spoofed Russian mail system to Romel, Deadra and Eunice to set it up and they hadn't the training to check the source and accepted it as an instruction.

Boy's monitoring identified the receipt, but only Romel received the coded kill instruction. Deadra and Eunice had the change of routine instructions, and DUA waited for the attempt to kill Deadra.

This would give DUA concrete evidence to proceed against all of them.

All they had so far against Romel was encoding a message and they couldn't use that as *evidence* in a British Court of Law, as the extraction had been *bordering* on the illegal and *bypassing* surveillance laws, which was something they did not want to raise. This would give DUA a '*conspiring* to murder a Security Operative' charge, which would be a Security Cell for about 30 years and with a very pliable Deadra in custody, believing his own people had tried to kill her; hopefully singing enough to complete the evidence against Eunice…?

There were problems with Eunice as well… Lance by implication had approved her accessing his files and in fact the whole organisation!

They had the link of her taking data, and putting that in a dead letter box for Deadra to pass on, but they had no proof that Deadra had passed it on, or to whom so it was all completely nebulous until they could connect Romel, Deadra and Eunice together with the copied Secret information, the drop, and then they had them or at least a start? A good lawyer would probably have them out in seconds.

DUA hope that Deadra after they attempted to kill would be happy incriminating Romel and Eunice and complete the circle.

Even Lance's authorisation would not cover taking copies security data, and placing them in a dead letter box to aid a foreign power, albeit via a live beggar but they needed the trigger?

It was gut wrenching to have the evidence they needed, but nothing they could use in a British Court of Law under the Human Rights, and Surveillance Acts, which would see a clever QC have everything thrown out, without it even being heard.

Deadra as usual headed down to the Tate—she liked the slow walk down Millbank with the usual faint breeze coming down the Thames.

She had folded the envelope up – now a small thick square with some thick elastic bands around it; making it easy to drop into the beggar's plastic bag, as she leant over him to drop some coins in his bowl as instructed.

She would then go into the Tate like any tourist afterwards and browse around.

Boy and Val were inside the Tate now—Bishop and DUA were watching from the opposite side of the embankment, and would let them when if anything else was happening.

The beggar was in his usual position, back leaning against the pillars, plastic bag alongside him and a small bowl for donations from tourists.

Prilloch was not 'arty farty', and so had wandered off down the side of the Tate, but they would warn him before she arrived.

That left them waiting for Deadra's slow stroll down Millbank, whilst unbeknown to her, she was slowly followed by Meik on the other side—matching her slow steps until she reached the Tate.

Meik already had it planned and she would move into the entrance of the Tate as just another tourist overcome by a heavy day, knocking their head against a wall as she collapsed. His trusty little piece of metal wrapped in cling foil was already nestling in his pocket, with his hand caressing it, like an old friend.

DUA and Bishop watching from Millbank suddenly heard DUA said, "that's Meik! What the hell is he doing there and Deadra's on the opposite side of the road? Why is Meik following Deadra? Get onto Prilloch to cut him off."

"Can't do it, DUA. He and Boy are the only cover, and if we pull Prilloch off and they kill her, our '*bollocks*' are in the mangle for *setting* it up!"

"Well, we said no action until after the drop, so providing Prilloch and Boy are on station and we have Val with those funny glasses recording everything, we should be OK."

"I will let Prilloch know Meik is in the area, just to be sure."

"Can you get a clear shot at anyone past the pillars, and heading into the door, Bishop?"

"Any shot in front of the pillars will go straight into the Tate, DUA—I can only aim for the steps and courtyard.

"That means any attack will be behind the columns, if they know about us? We need Boy, Val and Prilloch behind the pillars!"

"I'm onto them now, DUA. Boy and Val are leaving the Tate; Prilloch is making his way back, and should be there before Deadra and Meik."

"Good. Meik being here worries me. He was in Europe, according to what he told Prilloch."

"Deadra's still mirrored by Meik—Boy and Val are just coming outside, Val is moving to the front so she has the beggar and anyone else in the approach, on record. Boy is staying behind the pillars by the door. At least he has unarmed and armed training from West Africa—according to Huron, he learnt a lot from Mr Hoo."

"He may need it, Bishop. We don't know who, or what they will use on Deadra!"

Prilloch had wandered a bit further than he really meant to on his stroll and was still a suitable distance away when Bishop contacted him. He was now breaking into a sprint, to get back in time and would probably only just make it, as he aimed for Atterbury Street, running parallel to the Tate.

Meik had sped up over the last ¼ mile to arrive *first* behind the columns, at the front entrance to the Tate, and he could now see Deadra *slowly* making her way up the steps to the beggar.

He positioned himself to the left of the door facing from Millbank so he could see if anything went into the beggar's bag, before he dealt with Deadra.

As Deadra arrived, she open her handbag to get some change out, and as she dropped coins, he saw her flick something into the bag as well, and that was it.

He moved across to the door, smiling at her, and stopping to let her pass as he followed her in.

Boy following close behind saw Prilloch come running around the corner, and heard him shout, "Meik," whose hand was already leaving his pocket with something in it.

Deadra turned, and saw Meik's face as he brought up the metal cosh, then saw the brief flash of silver leave Prilloch's hand, going into the side of Meik's neck, as Prilloch threw his knife at a full run, into Meik without even thinking.

Boy immediately turned to the beggar who was now facing Val and a weapon he hadn't known Val was carrying was also facing him. The gun, once again, was a steady H&K pointing at the beggar, as Val showed another side to her character.

Boy flashed some ID that no-one would read, and said, "Security," whilst Neville jumped out of a police car and ran up the steps to where Meik lay. They had parked the police car around the corner and the code sign from Bishop was enough to move it around the corner to the Tate.

Prilloch stood there in a state of shock. He had just killed his best friend without thinking; to save Deadra.

Boy was ready to shoot, but Prilloch had not given him the chance and Neville now had the body covered, with other police cars arriving, and that would include Owley's bunch' who were now taking Deadra and the beggar into custody.

The complete scene seemed to be frozen around them, while everyone else was moving.

Val scanned the area, so anyone around would have their image taken and looked up to see DUA and Bishop arriving from over the bridge on a motorbike and with a complete disregard for road regulations road up the Tate steps.

DUA knew of the relationship between Prilloch and Meik, and now just stood there hugging Prilloch.

Bishop with his usual complete lack of emotion, told Boy and Val to come back with him to Security, and as they walked back in what was for a change, decent weather for once he said, "Who do you work for, Val?"

"SIS, Bishop."

"Might have guessed. Every other Agency seems to be on the team and Marcel was too easy. You told his wife, didn't you when he wouldn't be turned?"

"Marcel has his uses!"

"So do you apparently!"

"We needed Marcel's skills, Val, and you deliberately screwed it up for office politics with the SIS."

"You don't run operations abroad without us, Bishop."

"This has all been in the UK, and you don't have authority in the UK, Val. The overseas stuff was false and never meant to happen. You endangered a major project for Inter-service rivalry—you help to screw up the data feeds we needed to catch these people out, by flirting with the Red-neck, and ditching him. The main Security Committees OK'd these activities a while ago under wraps and your bosses should have some interesting conversations in the next few days.

"Very few people knew that without this evidence the Politicians weren't prepared to touch it, and wanted our heads for breaking UK laws if we failed, and we have broken a fair number of them, believe me.

"The CIA Head of Station briefed them, but not the SIS, as we don't know about your moles, although you fooled us pretty well. Lance and Carmella may not be the only ones to go!"

What happens now, Bishop was a general look and we also looked at each other and who was betraying who?

XXXIX

Finally, Bishop said, "Rough charges, so far, Val. We have evidence of the planned murder, conspiracy to provide classified information, espionage, working for a foreign power, being a traitor; the charges are endless, apart from Ewa."

"What do you have against Ewa?"

"All tenuous. She stayed in on the weekend of the attack… worked with Romel on removing good people from the Agency—all of it classed as incompetence, or nothing we have evidence to prove anything. We can't leave her there, but I don't think there is anything we can try her on."

"Why about Eunice?"

"She won't *see* the light of day and still be *alive*."

"Romel?"

"Romel will be the same charges as Eunice, but it has involved Eunice for over 30 years. They'll charge him with *conspiracy* to murder with Eunice in a secret court—it can never be an open court."

"Deadra?"

"Deadra was basically a courier. After that attempt on her she should sing like a bird."

"What about the Beggars?"

"We wanted the 'King Beggar' and we will be very lucky if we ever find him. We'll roll up the Network, if they haven't already scattered, but we'll catch very few of them."

"Do we leave Thomas alone, or try to bag him?"

"Thomas will *miss* his tea and ginger nuts, but we will try to see he is OK for past observances, because we cannot prove anything against him. Someone with a worse record was Head of Israel for years, and Thomas has three years left for pension. We can't prove anything major, and we won't risk Huron's friends."

"What happens about Lance and Carmella," asked Val, "most of the politics and trouble with SIS started after they came in, and started playing politics. My Bosses want them out!"

"Vance and Carmella are both out. The one we couldn't get is Ewa, but we can't leave her where she is. We only have Boy's opinion that she is an Agent, and she stayed in when Coombe Lane was attacked—no email system on her home computers, either, beyond the obvious… Ewa is out in the wild and she still doesn't understand what the wild means when you are set up?."

"What do you do with her, then?"

"We will take a chance, and lock her away for suspicion, but it won't really hold… we will just have to try until we can get that guy out of Russia, but we can't let her lose—we have nothing else on her and she can't go to trial… nothing on her machine, nothing on data feeds, nothing on phone calls, nothing on anything, but at least we have cleared out this nest of 'rats'."

"What happens to Meik's body?"

"He goes to Gloria Nantucket, and a special Coroner's Court. The effect on DUA and Prilloch will be hard, and I don't know how they will handle that."

"I always wondered about DUA's relationship to Meik?"

"So you know, I will explain some of it. Prilloch is DUA's Son, although Prilloch doesn't know. DUA was in love with Meik's mother, who turned him down, and went off with a close friend of his, who was an animal once he hit the drink. The guy 'got out of his tree' one night and killed both of them. He went back to the camp and DUA realised what had done—DUA half killed him and hung him on the barbed wire fencing so it looked like he had tried to climb back in and left him to die. DUA paid for both Prilloch's and Meik's upbringing after that. Meik was the last thing that reminded DUA of the woman he loved, but DUA knew Meik was an *out-of-control killer*."

They arrived at the Security Services with Special Branch already there and Eunice, Ewa and Romel in separate rooms.

"We'll see Eunice first. No idea what she'll say, but she has been here nearly 30 years, and we don't know when she turned… she was always close to Lance, but he trusted her to give him information as he wasn't bothered and even gave her his password, so he could sit on high and play Politics. She is in here."

"Hello, Eunice. I take it you know what they accuse you of?"

"You are out of your head, Bishop… Lance will finish you."

"Lance is facing JIC at the moment, for giving you his password, and enabling you to pass information to the Russians. We have the evidence on camera of you putting the information into the dead letter box for Deadra to pick up, and before you deny it, Deadra is singing like a bird after Meik tried to kill her—we have a fair idea of your activities with Lance giving you access to everything. That is something you and he won't forget—we have already identified your email system at home and its Russian origins. You can give us information to reduce your sentence, but as it stand, you won't ever see the light of day, and it will be a single cell, in a Security holding prison… yes we still have them, but not illegally anymore."

"You can't prove anything… I know too much for a court to listen to it—all you can do is swap me, if you can prove anything?"

"You are on film, Eunice, so stop denying it. The US could request extradition, so think about that, before you start your threats. No-one will hear you in the US, and you have damaged them, so maybe you start a sentence to keep you here for a few years, and then we extradite but you won't be talking to anybody."

"You can't keep me locked up without a trial."

"Time we spoke to Romel, Eunice, who has added, attempted murder to his crimes."

"I wasn't involved in that!"

"You had the email, changing the routine, as did Deadra. You set it up for Agents to die without authorisation, and that is how we will nail you for the extradited passage to the US, as you could have caused the death of CIA Agents operating in the UK with authority. Sleep well and alone!"

The door closed, and Bishop moved to the next room to talk to Romel, "We cracked your systems, took the software and broke your encoding and decoding system when we started, Romel. Like Eunice you won't be talking to anyone, and the 'conspiracy to murder' charge means locking you away for years and then extradited to the US, so you won't be telling anyone anything."

"You can't prove a thing."

We sent "The message to arrange the murder of Deadra, and you sent Meik to kill her. We also have a record of your earlier activities, and you won't be going back to Latvia or Russia. When you have completed your sentence here, you will be extradited to the US for trial there, and by the time you leave any knowledge you have won't be worth squat, and if you think the Russians would be kind, after you broke their encoding system for us, then you are a fool. If you gave information now, it might be a lighter sentence and no extradition, but somehow I don't think your life is going to be very long, either way."

"That completes those two, now we see Ewa," and Bishop moved to the third room.

"Ewa. You will be aware by now that Romel, Eunice and Deadra are all under arrest, and Vance and Carmella, no longer have positions within the Security Service… you know, you have been very careful and the only marks against you are that when Coombe Lane was attacked, you like Romel stayed in that weekend—with Romel you have been behind a staff retention and retirement programme that has pensioned off good people, and kept the bad and you know there is nothing we can *prove* to a court. We are certain of your links with the Russian Embassy, and you are now being pensioned off whilst we go through Eunice, Deadra and Romel's systems, a complete investigation of everything you have ever touched by Special Branch, who will take you into custody while they investigate as we are fairly certain that over a long period you ran the direct Embassy link. Once again the US has requested your extradition, and we have no reason to deny that request, so you will wing your way in due course to the US for further investigation, as we don't have enough to keep you here or deny their request. The aim was in fact, to keep you and your comrades active until we finished some operations, but we had to move once we realised how far Eunice was embedded and the level of the information she was passing. You will join them in Security's custody in a single cell, kept away from everyone else. If you supply us with information, we can probably make it easier and forgo the extradition, but as it stands you will be taken to a Security Cell, and will stay there, until we have finished other operations and then be extradited to the US."

Bishop looked at her, and there was no change of expression at all.

He opened the door and closed it gently behind them.

Bishop headed back for Coombe Lane.

Boy, Val, DUA and Prilloch were on their way back—Neville has stayed on in London as he needed to talk to Owley, and was on his way to Scotland Yard already.

Neville arrived and made his way up to Owley.

He'd never liked Scotland Yard, but had to see Detective Chief Superintendent Jonathan Owl… his Boss, Mentor and personal arse kicker. He knocked on the door and went in, following the bellow of get your arse in here, Neville.

"My people are telling me that the weapon this guy was carrying, matches the guesstimate of what the serial killer was using, as does his description, what was going on?"

"He worked for Romel, sir. DUA wouldn't touch him. Romel used him. We think killed three people and Deadra would have been the fourth. He was killing for Romel, and the three he killed were leftovers from the Romel/Peres days. No-one would have known about the others and he would have been alive if Prilloch hadn't wandered off, or the Boy would have shot him, which was more likely, but it gave us evidence that should save a few people."

"Yes, I know. Carmella and Lance have already gone—Gloria Nantucket has the body, and forensics will prove whether he killed those other people, I guess. My problem now is with you, Neville. You have proved yourself very well within the activities of this team, and I don't need another Detective Chief Inspector on my team, especially with your very irregular background. I wish the Antona relationship had worked out… it would have made things a lot easier with you in a stable relationship. Security has Special Branch involved, but I want you under my control and working with Security. Someone will take over control of Security as No.1 and No.2, and I have suggested to the powers that you would be a good police liaison officer who has experience of Security Operational issues and is of value to them. You stay answerable to me, but you work with DUA and Bishop as a member of their team, and we will base you at Brixton; try to sort it out with Antona… the problem is you are both obstinate and thin-skinned, and I need you stable, Neville, because if you ever hit the heavy booze again, I won't pick you up from the gutter. Now get out of my office and get some sense!"

Neville headed back to Coombe Lane to find the house like a mausoleum, with Prilloch somewhere out in the grounds, and he took a walk as well, to clear his head.

Gris was trying to console DUA, and said, "Find Prilloch, make sure you create enough noise," and then briefly hugged him.

Neville saw Prilloch but just carried on walking past him. Both always hid emotion, and he didn't know how to approach Prilloch when he thought about it.

Prilloch as a loner would never change, and Meik had been someone they had brought him up with, and the only person he had any rapport with, in any emotional state.

He looked back, as Prilloch looked up at him, and Neville went back—deciding to go for the head on approach and said, "He was a killer, Prilloch. We have to prove it, but he has murdered seven Scots on these streets in the past month. None of them had a chance, and they left families. He was intelligent and we couldn't get him. Romel confirmed that he killed three on his instructions, and Deadra should have been the fourth. If we could have got the forensics from Maastricht, he would have been caught and incarcerated for life in a mental home. You saved not only Deadra, but many other people, if he hadn't been caught. He was your friend, but you probably gave him the kindest exit he could have got. He is dead. It is finished, and people who would have died will live. You can't blame yourself—had you not been there, the Boy would have shot him… he was a dead man walking. You saved us when the attack came here, and you have saved others who would have died. Grieve by all means, but people who are alive owe thanks to you. Don't forget that."

Neville turned his back, and walked to the house until turning around, Neville shouted to Prilloch, "Don't forget to forgive yourself!"

Neville met Huron as he approached, "Just checking, Neville."

"He wouldn't touch me, Huron."

"No, he wouldn't, Neville. DUA is worse, though. Won't talk to anyone. He just stood there according to Bishop, holding Prilloch and crying. Do you know why?"

"Ask Bishop, if you feel lucky!"

"Bishop is with Val at the moment, who didn't realise it blew her cover, and Bishop knew from his contacts it blew her, and kept quiet. Bishop doesn't talk a lot does he—unless it suits him? You are, I understand now, formally seconded to Security until further notice."

"Yes. Owley just told me."

"I heard the latest make-up with Antona moved swiftly to break-up—sorry about that."

"What happens now, Huron?"

"Val as a Team Leader has proved her worth, and we do need the connection with SIS—Marcel is now singing alone, after Val turned him out. Where are you staying Neville?"

"Antona wants me in a spare room, and I can eat in the Bar but I am getting work done on the Putney place, and once that is done. I will probably move back in. Owley wants me working with DUA, and it is permanent now."

"We might still hang around with a team for two weeks and take people out quietly.

"Antona was only in danger from the Romel clearing up, I think! Now I need a bath, and some food, before Valene shuts up shop."

"What happens to Security?"

They have appointed Sir Phillip Norris and Julia Perkins No.1 and No.2—pro-term and that is nothing."

Neville made his way back to Antona's with trepidation dogging every step… he tried to time his arrival, so Antona wasn't around and he could get a shower and head down to the Bar, with Albert usually there as Antona has now put a Snooker table in for him.

Albert knew he wasn't to drink very much at all, which was one reason for him being there, and although the bar covered with a metal coating had no lock and could be opened, but he liked a game of snooker with Albert of a night.

It helped to relax him after his shower and a microwave put in together with a fan and an over/grill attachment so his takeaways could be 'lifelike' was pandering to his low life.

Tonight he came down and found Antona, instead of Albert.

"I had a long conversation with Owley and that included the '*stable relationship, try to sort it out*' plus 'the problem is you are both *obstinate*, thin skinned and I need you *both stable*', Neville, because if you ever hit the heavy booze again, I won't pick you up from the gutter. Now get out and get some sense! Yes, I got both barrels, but I do not have the ability be owned, Antona. Too long on the booze, too long out of bed, too much of myself, and just pouring the drink down to sleep. "I said to the last woman who thought I was worth saving, I am a *collection* of *bad* habits, stewed in 'beer' and carbonated, to pop out at the wrong moment with no thought."

"Yes, I have been getting the phone calls as well, and today I had DUA, and later Prilloch, as if I am some kind of Agony Aunt who needs the second sherry, and if they carry on, I will need it. I thought I could have the same life with you as I had with Roger, with the same routines, and the same timings. I loved Roger even it was a Saturday night only affair and not physical. We had a life for many years, and that was what I understood. I need stability, affection and belief that someone cares for me and yes, I treated you like a dog… 'feed you regularly, not too short a leash and call you in for dinner'. Yes, it was wrong, but I thought that was what you wanted!"

"I didn't know what I wanted, or needed. I had my entire world turned upside down, and I might have cursed Stapleton, but he was a part of life, as was Nat, the plumbing and the pipes. I lived that amidst a drunken haze and the 'shit' jobs they gave me. I had given up on thinking, even though I could think, because no-one was going to pay attention to anything I thought about. It was self-defence with the 'Maginot' line, in the wrong place, and not wide enough. I am feeling at home here, but I can't change a lifetime in a matter of months and 'yes' I do like the car."

"I remember seeing a film once, Neville, in which some character teaches a woman to play pool. Can you *teach* me, Snooker, and *play* with *me* instead of Albert?"

Neville afterwards thought it a strange match, and if Professional they have *thrown* him out of the Professional body, and to investigate himself as a police officer for some of those *moves*, but he still didn't understand how he had *lost*.

He knew at the end he had lost a game, but allowed to win a championship.

The half-house in Putney being refurbished would be sold!

He would know where 'they gilded not only his geld, but where his butter was spread, and his bread baked. There would not be any more 'hiccups'. He would *obey* and not think twice before he did.

The elephants had climbed the mountain with the Rubicon crossed instead of crossing Antona, and he could live with that.

He did not want to face Albert across the cushions for a little while, after Antona, although Albert seemed to have a genuine regard for him and that was something that threw him completely. So many people prepared to trust him, after all the Met had done to him for trying to be honest.

Antona turned over and snuggled into him, murmuring something.

The fundamental problem was she was speaking in womanish, whilst he had difficulty hearing in male.

Boy lay in a similar state, as Gris finally climbed off him once again.

She was taking marriage seriously, and thoughts of having children bestride her husband, who she seemed to keep treating as an exercise machine that never failed, and Boy was dreaming of a broken tool, and no repair facilities.

May arrived—flowers seemed to spring up all over the place. Garden furniture was providing another place for people to sleep, and Prilloch still vanished to *his* garden from time to time— Marcel was often there, on the other side. DUA, to a degree, seemed to adopt Prilloch's habits and was usually out in the garden, or walking through the trees, seeking no-one's company.

Perhaps it was a time to heal for a while.

*** The ***End*** ***

www.ingramcontent.com/pod-product-compliance
Lightning Source LLC
Chambersburg PA
CBHW051518030726
47592CB00006B/2324